WAR PILOT

by

JACK G. SALTER

First published by the author 2007
All rights reserved
ISBN 978-09555169-1-7
Printed and bound in the UK by
Hobbs the Printers Ltd. Brunel Rd
Totton, Hants

This book is sold subject to the conditions that it shall not by way of trade or otherwise be lent, re-sold, hired out or otherwise circulated without the publisher's prior consent in any form of binding or cover than that in which it is published and without a like condition being imposed on the subsequent purchaser.

To:

My late grandparents:

John Gilbert & Florence Amelia Salter

And

James Edward & Emily Jane Boyle

WAR PILOT

THE AUTHOR

Jack Salter was born in 1938 and educated at Hamble School. Following which he trained as an aircraft engineer at the prestigious Air Service Training Ltd based on Hamble airfield. He also learnt to fly during this period.

Much of his early flying was of an unusual nature and is featured in three of his books, Praestet Omnibus Prudentia, Vinegar and Honey and Call of the Wing.

He has two daughters Maria and Zofia who he introduced at an early age to two other passions in his life, piano music and horse riding. Included in his interests is writing which he has practiced throughout his life.

He lives happily in retirement with his South African wife, Lincia, on the edge of the New Forest and continues to pursue his interest in the whole spectrum of aviation.

WAR PILOT

PUBLISHER'S NOTE

Because each of the stories only run to about 80 pages and in order to contain printing costs it was decided to print them under one cover, rather than as separate books. This, in turn, allowed the Publisher to maintain his policy of offering his books at a modest price, available to all.

WAR PILOT

ON THE WINGS OF THE MORNING

A sudden roar, a mighty rushing sound,
A jolt or two, a smoothly sliding rise,
A tumbled blur of disappearing ground,
And then all sense of motion slowly dies,
Quiet and calm the earth slips past below,
As underneath a bridge still water flows.

My turning wing inclines towards the ground,
The ground itself glides up with graceful swing,
And at the plane's far tips twirls slowly round,
Then drops from sight again beneath the wing,
To slip away serenely as before,
A cube sit patterned carpet on the floor.

Jeffery Day

Killed in action 1918

War Pilot

PROLOGUE

War Pilot is a sequel to the author's, A Quest for Flight.

The Herby family is spending its twelfth year in Canada after leaving Hadley in Oxfordshire, England. Samuel Herby has risen to a senior post in the General Govenor's staff and Rebecca, his wife, enjoys the prestige and privileges of living in a stately home, and moving among the social elite that went with her husband's position. Their son, Timothy, is well established in the Royal Northwest Mounted Police.

The war in Europe had started the previous year and news of the casualty figures and death toll begins to filter into Canada from the old country. Newspapers and posters appeal to the consciences and hearts of men, and embrace the call of a mother country to her distant sons in her time of peril.

For some the pull to respond would be stronger than for others. For some it would mean sacrificing a happy and stable life to travel to an uncertain destiny on a continent several thousand miles distant. For many it would mean severing deep and solid friendships, and marriages. For many it would be the end.

Rebecca, in a bid to protect Timothy from the war, claimed it was nothing more than a local skirmish and would be over in a matter of weeks.

Samuel Herby, however, knew that his son was about to arrive at an important crossroads in his life. And because Timothy had inherited the patriotic seeds from previous generations of the family Samuel was confident which road his son would take.

WAR PILOT

ONE

A lone figure on horseback trailing a pack mule emerged from a craggy outcrop and halted at the edge of a ridge. Lieutenant Herby stood in the stirrups, his attention drawn to a dust cloud rolling across the plain stretching out below him.

It was not a horse-drawn wagon or locomotive as he first suspected; it was in fact a flying machine kicking up the dust as it fought to break free from the bonds of earth. He resumed his seat in the saddle, smiling, and consumed by a spate of memories.

In the mind's eye he saw himself crouching on a river bank with his father placing various wooden shapes in the flow of the water and commenting on how the water behaved differently around the contours of the wood. The recollection rekindled his senses. He could see and could smell the freshness of the white calico dressed tight on wooden wing ribs. He caught the tang of the varnish that father brushed on the wing struts. He remembered the stench of the glue they had used on the first kite. He relived the shivering excitement, the inner glow of pride, and the rising feeling of jubilation as the kite divorced him from the earth and carried him aloft. Amongst the steady, spiritual gushing of the air over the wings he heard the rigging wires and the struts creak and groan as they took weight. Then the loud, unsteady clatter of the engine that accompanied his and father's spectacular powered flights. And there quite clearly he saw Marie smiling at him in congratulations of his success.

It reminded him he had not seen her for something like twelve years. They wrote long letters to each other from time to time, and he carried a picture of her in his wallet. He decided, at that very moment, it was time for him to return to the old country, and also time for him to renew his acquaintance with the world of flight.

He moved the horse and mule on and descended to the lowlands to make his way to a gathering of recently erected buildings all wearing a fresh coat of paint. A large sign at the entrance of the netted boundary fence read: Flying Training Corps. A guard in military uniform requested evidence of his identity, and gave him directions for the office of the commanding officer.

Herby noticed the strict military tempo and a sense of urgency as the horse jogged him along between the sidewalks. Groups of personnel passed him by with keen, energetic strides. Smoke poured furiously from a cookhouse chimney. Motor carriages raced by as if there wasn't a moment to lose. Through the open doorway of a hut he spotted a group of men sat before a blackboard and easel. And whilst the activity on the ground moved with a spirit of industry the air above and around the buildings bustled with noise and action. A flying machine took to the air, a short, squat shape with wide wings and a delicately shaped tail. He was interested to see the propeller was situated at the extremity of the nose, and, for certain, the engine ran more evenly than father's powered kite of yesteryears.

A machine floated down in preparation for returning to earth. He could well imagine the sound of the airstreams gushing around the wings and struts, and singing through the rigging. Suddenly he felt a great urge to respond to that strong and familiar call of the air: an eager and urgent desire to get back on the wing.

The tall, smiling figure of the commanding officer greeted him with a handshake, having been warned of his arrival by a guard on a field telephone.

"Come on in." he said. "Guess you could do with some chuck. And a wash and brush up. How long you been in the saddle?"

Herby reined his mount and mule to the veranda rail and followed him into his office. "Two and a half months. I am about to finish my patrol and head back to base."

The officer introduced himself as major Cordell. He directed the law officer to a seat and poured coffee into two mugs and invited him to help himself from a box of cigars. Herby chose instead to fill a pipe with tobacco.

They chatted for a time about the state of the railroads - the Indian reservations - the whereabouts of certain trappers, prospectors and criminals, and the latest news about the war in Europe.

The major said: "By the way are you, by any chance, related to Sam Herby in the Govenor General's office?"

"My father, major."

The major beamed. "If it wasn't for him chasing the government we'd still be charging around on horseback brandishing swords. Thanks to his modern thinking we are learning to fight with airborne chariots. But, tell me, why his interest in flying machines?"

"It's a long and involved story, major, that goes back some fourteen years when we lived in the old country. I helped my father construct two kites, one of which was powered. And after many trials and setbacks we succeeded in achieving powered and sustained flight."

The major leaned across the table eager to hear more. "Was that before the Wrights?"

"Two years before, in fact."

"Then how come it didn't get into the official records?"

Herby said: "I warned you it was a long and involved story, major. You might say it was all tied up with local politics, and a certain individual who was bent on stealing my father's invention and successes and claiming them as his own. As it so happened, the devious individual was killed during a demonstration flight and in the process totally destroyed our kite."

Major Cordell slumped back in his chair. "Well I'll be darned. I've always thought your father was hiding his light under a bushel."

He got up presently to stand before a window that looked out on the flying field. "Guess I got to admit we are fumbling a bit at the moment." he said. But don't get me wrong. The kids are all eager to learn to fly. The only problem is: how will they measure up to the parry and thrust of actual combat?"

Herby said, "The individual can only be the judge of that. You can only teach them to fly, and like anything that requires harmony of mind and limb there will be those who are natural, and those who will be at risk. From my brief experiences of flight I would say a sharp eye, a light touch, and a good reflex are the main requirements of an airman."

The major turned, grinning. "Something tells me you are itching to get aloft again."

"Nothing would give me greater pleasure, major."

"Okay. I'll get you fixed up with some quarters, a scrub, and a meal. Then I'll meet you at number two shed at seven this evening. It'll be in a training machine, not a scout. I guess you know why."

The Wright training machine taxied slowly across the plain that was briefly shadowed by distant hills and the falling orb of the sun. It jolted and lurched on its harshly sprung landing gear, and the two occupants shouted their exchanges above the noise of the engine. A group of students, instructors and mechanics had gathered to watch the proceedings.

"Gee her up there, mountie!" one of them shouted.

"Big White Chief rides again!" another added to their amusement.

The Wright turned and paused. Then it swung into wind. The engine opened out to full revolutions and the machine began to prance along the prairie towards the spectators. Suddenly - it detached itself from the ground and rose slowly and steadily over their heads.

The first attempt at a landing was a little bumpy. The second was better. The third attempt was faultless. And no one was more astonished than the group of observers when after such a short space of time the major parted company with the machine and joined them. He bit the end from a cigar and said: "Watch him closely you guys. He's a natural. He breaths flying like a dragon breaths fire."

Lieutenant Herby felt rather pleased with his performance. The major had barely spoken throughout their time together in the air. Everything had fitted back in to place after what must have been a gap of fourteen years since his last flight. The cagework of the Wright was more refined than father's kite of late, and the airstreams over the wings were less boisterous.

The wings rocked as he turned on the uneven grassland into wind. He flicked the engine switch, and the machine scrambled forward in the frantic sound of its engine, gathering speed and leaping from side to side until the air over the control surfaces became more effective. From a series of leaps and bounds the Wright lifted him into the air. It hesitated. He prompted it with what the major referred to as the control stick, and they rose up over the knot of spectators. He smiled to himself, overwhelmed as he was by a sense of release. He had broken out of the harness of the earth. He had escaped. The earth drifted and tilted beneath the wings as he banked the machine. He glanced over his shoulder to see the trembling rudders leaning toward the horizon. The wing warping that controlled the lateral level felt stiff to what he recalled of father's kites. But in spite of that he was on the wing and being party to it nourished his pride. He looked down between the wing struts at the upturned faces of the spectators on the airstrip. He smiled. They were imprisoned by the trappings of the earth whilst he was free. Free as a bird. From his lofty position he could clearly see snow-capped mountains and a lake to the north. He passed over a range of hills which resembled heaps of smouldering ash spotted with hot coals in the crimson glow of the setting sun. It all combined to make him feel supremely happy and satisfied with his reborn skill of traversing the heights.

War Pilot

For a good twenty minutes he flew around over the flying field, enjoying to the full the Wright's response to his touch on the controls - the playful antics of the airstreams on his exposed face - the sheer and unlimited freedom of it all.

After a time major Cordell grew concerned. He had requested the mountie to carry out one circuit of the field and return to earth: a decision based on the limited fuel remaining in the machine. The flying corps was already under attack by opposing political figures. And each time there was an accident, costly damage to a machine, and the death of its airman, it invariably put up another black mark against the senior officers of the Corps.

What the major feared would happen - happened. The motor of the Wright misfired several times and spluttered into silence. He closed his eyes; he was certain the Mountie would not know how to handle it. The nose would stay up. The machine would lose flying speed. The wings would stall, and the Wright would drop like a stone to its inevitable fate. An interminable silence seized the spectators. Then somebody said, "I guess he's not so dumb after all."

The major opened his eyes to see the Wright gliding silently downwind. It looked safe enough but he would not be happy until it got back on the ground in one piece.

Herby banked and swung the Wright into wind and headed for the airstrip. His actual experience with an ailing engine back in the distant Hadley flying days had not dimmed from his memory. He remembered to keep the nose down to maintain flying speed and to balance the weight of the dead engine. The boundary of the airstrip came close too soon, and he was too high. He put the Wright through a series of zigzags to get rid of the surplus height and to prolong his approach. Scrubland passed beneath his feet followed by the boundary fencing. He eased the lever back - checked it - held it. The Wright flew level a few feet above the ground, and as the air murmuring over the wings fell to a whisper he pulled the stick back. They dropped firmly and safely back to earth.

What normally took him two weeks to reach his headquarters, he accomplished in a week. He rode almost night and day, swapping the horse for the mule every ten miles. Both mounts were almost on their knees when he handed them over to the grooms. He suggested they be rested for at least a couple of weeks. And he asked the horse doctor to give them a look over.

He spent a day completing and filing a full report of his patrol. On the following morning he collected his furlough pass, and boarded the first available locomotive for Prince George.

"You have arrived at an interesting time, Timothy." his mother embraced him in greeting. "A delegation has arrived from Britain to brief us on the latest developments of the war in Europe. From what I gather the Hun is on the run. I suspect it will all be over in a matter of weeks." She slipped an arm through his and led him proudly through the high hall of their home showing him off to the servants: as was her ritual each time he came home on leave.

She stopped him at the foot of the stairs and said, "Go up and change for dinner. We'll discuss more of the war later."

He made his way up the long, winding wood-paneled staircase treading on deep-piled carpet that came soft and gentle underfoot compared to his urgent, tiresome journey of recent days.

He bathed. And dressed before the window of his room. The blue sky beyond the window reminded him of his recent flight. Tapping noises on the door of the room interrupted and heralded the appearance of his father who greeted him enthusiastically with a handshake.

"How are you m'boy?"

"Fine, father. How is everything here?"

"Nothing exciting to report. Except for a bunch of oldies who have arrived from England to escape the pressures of the war in Europe."

Timothy laughed, " Mother tells me they are here to bring us up to date, and to reassure us the war will be over in a matter of weeks. From what she says the Hun is on the run."

Father said, "Between you and me the war is going so badly the Governor General has received an urgent request for men and arms. However, forget all that. I'm more interested to know what you've been up to."

"I've been aloft, father."

"On the wing?"

"Yes, father. On the wing."

His father's eyes blazed with interest. "Was this at Calgary?"

"Yes. And major Cornell claims they would still be riding horses and wielding swords had you not campaigned to get the government to provide funds for the flying machines."

His father sighed. "It was a hard battle but worth it. The old country will need everything it can get its hands on to fight the war in Europe. By the way did you go aloft, alone."

"For twenty glorious minutes or more. But I ran short of fuel and the engine failed. A rather stupid mistake."

"But you returned the machine to earth unscathed, I take it."

"Yes. Thanks to your advice and my flying experience all those years ago at Hadley. It all came back so easy father."

Herby senior moved to stand before the window that looked out upon the spacious gardens of the residence. He said: "Every time I look from an upstairs window in this place my mind goes back to the Hadley days. My nostrils fill up with the smell of the glue, the fresh calico, the varnish and the vapour of the spirit we used in the engine. I hear the sound of the airstreams and feel them on my face. I feel the control surfaces talking to me through the levers and the rudder bar. I hear the clattering uncertainty of the engine. And never will I forget that day we eventually won the battle over old man gravity."

Timothy moved to stand beside him and put an arm around his shoulder. "Do you remember, father, the trouble we had in getting the Carlton brothers to produce more power from their engine."

"Yes, I do m' boy. And do you remember your insistence that we should have more wind. And how you discovered from a sycamore blade how we should shape the propeller."

"Great days, father. I confess I have not enjoyed better days since."

"Neither have I m' boy. Neither have I." He consulted his pocket watch, and suggested they head downstairs before mother got on their trail.

Timothy checked him. "Before we go down I think you should know that I intend to volunteer for war service. Can I rely on your support if mother should try and block it?"

His father turned and placed a hand on each of his shoulders. "You, have long been a man, Timothy. Something, somewhere has been calling out to you for a long time. It's time you answered the call."

They went down and mother introduced him to each member of the delegation before they went through for dinner. And it was during dinner Timothy informed a guest of his intentions to sail to England and join the flying corps. He was told quite bluntly there was very little future in such a pursuit; the average life of an airman in France could be measured in weeks.

The evening wore on, dull, slow, uninteresting. And the fact it did not go totally flat was a credit to mother's flair and imagination. But, eventually, she too was overwhelmed by the tired and bored expressions, and the conversation of the guests. She announced it would be an appropriate time to retire for the night.

Timothy had barely retreated to his bedroom when she entered and leant her weight against the closed door. "Is it true you are returning to Britain with the intention of volunteering for war service, Timothy."

"Yes. It is mother."

She faced him defiantly; "I will not allow my son's body to be added to the growing masses of dead on the battlefields of France."

He laughed. "You have always maintained it is nothing but a skirmish, mother."

She softened her tone and moved to him. "Why this sudden decision my son? Why is it so urgent?"

He said: " You know full well I have a duty to go and help the old country in her time of need. What is more I want to get back into the air."

She stiffened. "You are actually saying you want to return to Hadley and to all those people who took your father's livelihood from him, and forced him to leave the estate."

"You exaggerate, mother. You know there were very personal reasons, involving you, why father decided we should take up a new life in Canada."

"Good Heavens!" she threw her hands up in mock despair. "After all I've done for you - you seek to hurt me in such a manner!"

Her tears came in a rush. But he knew they were symptoms of anger rather than distress. She suddenly turned and hastened for the door. He raced her to it and blocked it with a foot. "Think very carefully before you decide to put obstacles in my way, mother. It may have regrettable consequences."

He allowed her to force the door open and escape.

Four rooms away along the landing Samuel Herby lay in bed, hands behind his head, smiling up at the ceiling. He could well imagine what happened after Rebecca told him of her intended confrontation with their son. She moved into the room visibly angered and distressed, and changed into her nightdress.

"You know it was only a matter of time my dear," he said.

She turned to him tears trickling down her cheeks. "He is so stubborn and inconsiderate, Samuel. He fails to understand that we, as his parents, have a duty to discourage him from being led away by the glamorous propaganda of war."

"Once and for all time you must accept our son is well into his years of manhood. Has it never occurred to you that his life in the police service has been equally at risk? Particularly when out on patrol. I can assure you he is better prepared to go to war than many others." He drew himself to a sitting position on the bed and pulled her gently against him. Her beautiful jet-black hair fell loose about her elegant long neck and the slope of her shoulders. Her eyes reflected her battle against defeat. Her body trembled emotionally as it tried to control her anguish.

"You should feel honoured to think he has inherited much of your determination and stubbornness." he told her.

After a pause for reflection she turned to him, the faint trace of a smile creeping onto her lips. She said hoarsely, "Samuel Herby! I do declare that you are in league with our son."

"Not entirely, Mrs Herby. But was it not for my age I might be going with him."

" It is mutiny!"

" Not at all. A matter of doing one's duty."

She laid herself down beside him and said: "I take it you will not attempt to challenge Timothy's decision to go off to war?"

"It is not necessary, my dear. He is quite capable of making the decision himself."

She reached up and pulled him onto her and eyed him with a yearning, reminiscent of many moons ago in the passionate youth of their marriage.

"You mutineers give me little choice," she said. "Kindly extinguish the lamp."

War Pilot

TWO

Dear father and mother,

The passage by sea never seemed to end and, at times; I yearned for the wings of the odd Albatross that passed us by.

I spent most of the time studying the flight of gulls that accompanied us across the ocean. My desire to get on the wing again grew stronger by the day.

On my arrival in England I presented myself to the War Office and after a period of indoctrination into the ways of the Royal Flying Corps I was dispatched to Gosport, in Hampshire, for my flying training.

Gosport is a charming little place situated near the coast and when flying a few hundred feet above the aerodrome, on a clear day, Portsmouth, Southampton and the Isle of Wight are clearly visible.

I think my fellow pupils regard me as something of a lone wolf because I do not join in much with the social side of life but prefer to spend my free time in the sheds picking the brains of the troops who maintain the flying machines. What is more I'm quite a bit older than the average airman under training.

Father will be interested to know the first machine I flew was a Farman pusher, which is so much like the powered kite we built and flew from Hadley. I have not told anyone here about those days for I fear nobody would believe it and it might draw unwarranted scorn and ridicule upon the family name.

Perhaps in years to come when aviation is more developed an enthusiast in aviation history may discover the truth.

My instructor, lieutenant Blancthorp seemingly impressed with my progress, passed me on early to the more advanced machines. The Farman and Bleriot monoplane has been training airmen for some time, but the Nieuport and Pup are newcomers to the scene. They respond briskly to the controls and are capable of a speed in excess of CENSORED.

Engines of French design are very much in evidence with the rotary Gnome and Rhone being the most popular. The rotary description comes from the fact the radial bank of engine cylinders revolves around the crankshaft. The power of the Gnome is controlled by a device which either gives full power or nothing at all whilst the Rhone has a more refined switch that cuts the ignition to one or more cylinders and reduces the engine revolutions from 1250 to 900. It certainly makes for better handling of the machine.

These engines use castor oil for lubrication and for some reason or another it discharges itself as a fine spray from the engine and blights the cockpit. I use a muffler over my mouth to avoid inhaling it. A lot of airmen who do not protect themselves wonder why they pay excessive visits to the latrines. Higher authority claim they are suffering with their nerves not from an excess of laxatives.

At the time of writing I have logged twenty hours in the air. The advanced machines, generally referred to as Scouts, are single seaters and therefore the more advanced evolutions in the air must be self-taught. An instructor gives a verbal lesson on the ground. Then the pupil is detailed to go aloft and told to put the lesson into practice.

I climbed my machine to a good height so that I had a margin of time and space if anything untoward happened. But I was blessed with good luck and discovered with great delight what fun it is to go looping and rolling the machine in the unlimited freedom of the sky.

I have literally taught myself how to enter and recover from a spin because instructors go out of their way to avoid what they consider to be an intricate and dangerous manouvre that has killed more airmen than those killed in combat. I did it by sitting in a machine and rehearsing the movements of the controls just as father did in the Hadley days before he attempted something new.

In actual practice I found the spin to be misleading in that the earth did not revolve madly as many suggested it would. Instead it came up in a lazy spiraling motion that could be described as hypnotic. And it is this, which I think could be disastrous for the airman because in a state of hypnosis one could easily overlook the rapid loss of height and have insufficient to recover.

And father the mysterious 'drop' you talked about at Hadley all those years ago is no longer a mystery. It is known in the flying corps as the 'stall'. You were quite right in thinking it occurs at a certain angle of inclination of the wings that causes the air to flow irregularly over the top surface of the wing which, in turn, creates a loss of lift, and the machine falls out of the sky. It is however possible to recover the machine providing there is adequate height.

Stalling without power at the engine, or at low revs, is not exactly hair-raising. There is an eerie silence as the nose is raised to bring the wings up to the critical angle. (This is known as the angle of attack) When the total loss of lift occurs the nose of the Nieuport drops away positively. Then it is a case of moving the stick forward (not lever, father) and increasing the revs to encourage the machine to dive and reclaim the clean and steady airstreams over the wings in order to make a clean recovery back to level flight.

Stalling the machine with high revs or full power is a completely different kettle of fish and, in some quarters, is said to have contributed to a number of unexplained fatal accidents. With this in mind I climbed several thousand feet more before I experimented.

The nose went up at a steep angle with the engine at full power. It reached a point where it felt as if we were hanging there in space on the propeller. We lacked total movement and at one stage I thought we would slip earthwards tail first. It reminded me vividly of Grandfather Willy's journal which recorded him and the wing slipping backwards into the oak tree.

I eased the stick back a bit more and without warning, without explanation the Nieuport rolled uncontrollably. I, immediately, switched to low revs. A pause. Then wham! The nose dropped with the rapidity of an excessively heavy hammer. Phew! Never have I been tilted so suddenly, and dropped with such violence. I can tell you, father, I was quite breathless. And, yet, I was equally curious as to the causes.

War Pilot

On the next two attempts I was rewarded with similar violent results but recovery was possible once the nose went down and we gained speed.

During my fourth and final attempt I managed to summon the courage not to switch to low revs. The machine rolled to the inverted and stayed their causing utter chaos. My map departed the cockpit and I hung precariously on my lap strap. For a time I felt helpless and bit of a fool I must confess.

I eventually recovered by switching to low revs and centralizing the stick and rudder bar. After a short delay the nose dropped away pulling us through from the inverted to diving flight from which we made a full recovery.

And now, after a spate of written and practical tests by an instructor they say I am a qualified airman. Snapshots of our passing out parade and the presentation of our winged brevet are enclosed and of which I trust both of you will approve.

Personally I do not think an airman's training ever ends. There will always be something new to discover and learn on the subject of flight. No two flights are the same. The change in the weather can readily affect a machine's engine performance, and its control. On occasions the air is as smooth as riding on velvet. At other times it is like being tossed about as a cork on an ocean. The challenges are endless, and never without their share of excitement and intrigue.

Orders received today indicate I shall depart from Gosport within two weeks. I suspect we shall be going into battle. But prior to our departure I have been granted leave, and permission to fly a Nieuport to Hadley to visit our old friends.

In closing I apologise to mother for writing so much about flying.

Farewell for now, and much love to you both.

Timothy

Samuel Herby refolded the leaves of paper and slid the letter back into its envelope, smiling. He looked again at the snapshots in turn. From one an orderly group of young men looked out proudly displaying the coveted winged brevet on the left breast of their uniform tunics.

Another picture showed Timothy standing before the propeller and cowled engine of a machine. Another viewed him seated in a Sopwith Pup, wearing his helmet and goggles.

Samuel sniffed at the air to counter a growing lump in his throat. He felt so deeply proud of his son. He had followed the family tradition of taking to the air. He had rallied to the call of his mother country in time of war. He had proved that Grandfather Willy's attempts to fly with a flimsy wing had not been in vain.

He crossed his office and stood before a window, and as he looked skyward his tears of joy, for what Timothy had achieved, flowed freely and unashamedly.

Presently he went to the outer office, collected his hat, and told his secretary he was taking the rest of the day off; he would be at home if he were needed.

She watched him go down to the courtyard and crank his Ford motor carriage into life. He climbed aboard, set the gas and gears, and drove away with his head held high. Not in a long while had she seen him look so pleased, and embraced by so much happiness.

"It is most unusual for you to arrive home so early, Samuel." Rebecca remarked as she served tea on the verandah.

"There are occasions when it is justified, my dear. Today is such an occasion." he produced Timothy's letter and passed it to her.

Her eyes widened as she fumbled excitedly with the leaves of paper. "Timothy?" she cast him a sideways glance.

He nodded.

Despite the letter being mainly about flying she read it through twice, and spent a number of minutes smiling proudly at the snapshots. She said quietly, "I only hope he is aware of the fact that the articles of war only provide for death and destruction as a motive to remain supreme."

Samuel drew thoughtfully on his pipe and looked out across the long rolling lawns bordered by gravel paths and a mixture of trees and shrubs. He said: "There will many aspects of the war which will not be to our son's liking, Rebecca, because by nature and inclination the Herbys are pioneers, not warriors. Two generations in the family lost members who pioneered sea travel in unproven ships. And if my father, Willy, was involved in any kind of war, it was a war against the need for knowledge, and a great desire to traverse the heights with the ease and skill of a bird. He died in an attempt to add another dimension of life to mankind.

Be assured, my dear, Timothy has as much as your determination to survive, as he has of his late grandfather's, and my desire, to take to the wing."

Rebecca moved around the table and held his head to her breasts. Their son's departure had drawn them very close in recent weeks. She said: "When Timothy announced he was leaving us to join the flying corps I wept in the face of his desertion, rather than his reasons for doing so. Everything about our life in Hadley all those years ago came tumbling back, our separation, the painful gossip about you and Claire Hadley and the dreadful manner, in which you were cheated out of becoming the first to achieve sustained, powered manned flight."

He took her hand and looked up at her. "You and I made an agreement to put that all behind us when we came to Canada, did we not?"

"Yes, we did, Samuel. But Timothy's departure also made me realize how much I have neglected you over the years. You have every right to disown me as a cold and ambitious woman."

He rose from the chair, smiling. " Perhaps we should pen a letter to Timothy. Then take an early night for you to make amends."

She slipped an arm through his. "Samuel Herby. You drive a hard bargain." she declared. "But I love you dearly."

Timothy banked the Nieuport over Oxford and began to follow the railway line leading to Compton, and on to Hadley. He peered again at the compass heading to check it was the correct railway line. It was.

He grinned as he looked around the nose at a rustic band marking the western horizon, an indication of the ageing day. Beneath the wings areas of copse and woodland were ablaze with the reds, the golds and browns of autumn. He knew of no other season that provided such colour and dignity in its farewell. The chilled air made him think of log fires at the hearth, and the smell of newly-baked scones dressed with jam and cream, and the taste of hot sweet tea. The Nieuport rose and fell occasionally. But with the combined help of its inherent stability, and his instinctive touch on the controls, it regained its composure.

In the lowering temperature and fading daylight the twin shapes of Hadley and Pritchards hill materialized from a veil of mist and wavered between the wings and rigging wires. He spotted the railway halt added during his years in Canada, and which Lady Hadley warned him about when he arranged his visit by telephone. He noted a large building to the west of the village. He saw his old cottage home perched on the hill. The memories began to gather.

He flew around over the estate for a time to establish the direction of the wind, and to select a suitable area of open space on which to land the Nieuport . He eventually chose the paddock behind the cottage; the land behind the manor would have been more convenient but he judged the stretch would be inadequate for a take-off. He switched the engine to low revs and turned in. The scene had not changed in fourteen years. The same string of hawthorn bushes lined the boundary closest to the cottage. The same unruly blackberry marked the distant boundary. The same two oaks stood in rustling conversation in the corner of the paddock. He was a shade too low. He blipped the switch a couple of times - the engine roared correspondingly and checked his descent. Then judging it to be just right he switched to low revs and they floated clear of the hawthorn, touched down, and were quickly arrested by the long unkempt grass.

He picketed the Nieuport down in the shadows of the oak trees, and covered the cockpit with an oilskin cape he'd brought for the purpose. He walked slowly across the paddock carrying a small attache case, bathed in memories of the life he had spent here as a boy. More significantly the day they lost the first kite to the devastating fire - and the momentous and richly fulfilling day when father eventually triumphed over old man gravity. What a day that had been!

Next, his flight with Marie Sawyer as his passenger came to mind. The engine had packed up on him but by the grace of God, and a little bit of skill on his part, they had returned to earth unscathed.

He reached the extended stable in which he and father had constructed the kites. He spotted the stand they used to test the engine and propeller they fitted to Fanshaw's kite. The passing years and neglect, had reduced it to a red, rusty spiderwork of metal. The sight of it brought to mind the occasions when the noisy, lusty engine, bellowing to the world, spun the canvas paddles into shreds.

He stole a look through a window of his old cottage home pleasantly surprised to find nothing had changed. A rocking chair attended each side of the small hearth, and in the middle of the room the same table and three chairs. On the far side a dresser, and around the walls the homely brass oil lamps. It looked as if nothing had been disturbed since they went to Canada.

He moved to stand on the lip of Hadley hill, and relived his early gliding flights - the breathless excitement of careering down the hill to obtain the necessary speed to get the kite on the wing. He remembered the awesome drop of eight hundred feet that separated him from the earth when he launched into the void. And how much depended on him keeping his nerve and listening to the warning sounds of the airstreams around the wings and their changing note around the struts and through the rigging.

The scene from the hilltop also reminded him of the day father stood alone on the summit for the last time before they journeyed to Southampton to board the ship for Canada. And neither had he forgotten mother's lament that father would remain unknown for his feat of being the first to prove that manned and sustainable flight was possible. She had certainly proved to be correct; men on another continent were accredited with the honour a few years later.

He stepped onto the path that wound down to the manor and the village. The same narrow path on which he and father, with the aid of the horses, had hauled the kite back up to the cottage following their pioneering, gliding flights from the brow of Hadley hill. The hauling was hot and heavy work. But the thrill and excitement of the flights compensated for it. As he strolled down the hill he heard the ghosts of the horses snorting and grappling with the bit in their efforts to tow the kite. He felt the spirits of the dogs, Sniffy and Jeppy, walking to heel and occasionally reaching up to touch him with their cool, velvety snouts. Fourteen or, was it, fifteen years separated him from those childhood days here in Hadley. And yet it seemed it only happened yesterday.

Lady Hadley watched his striding figure come into view from the drawing room of the manor. The sight of him stirred up a variety of feelings. He was the splitting image of his father: medium height, compactly built and composed in his movement. He sported a neatly trimmed moustache and wore his uniform peaked cap smartly set. His polished leather-belted tunic carried the drooping wings of his aviator's brevet, and sandy coloured breeches were tucked in brown leather boots. And like his father he wore his uniform with pride.

She moved to the hallway and alerted the loitering servants. They listened to the sound of footsteps crunching on the gravel drive. Then stop as the visitor mounted the stone steps leading to the hall entrance door. Lady Hadley waited for him to press the button of the doorbell, and signalled to Partridge to answer the door.

As the large door swung open they chorused: "Welcome back to Hadley, Timothy!"

He stood chatting to them in turn for a few minutes before lady Hadley greeted him warmly and suggested Partridge show him to his room, and provide water for him to bathe following his long flight.

Within an hour he was sat talking to her privately over afternoon tea, and before a large cheery log fire. She spoke for a time about the many changes that had taken place in the village, much of which he had already learnt from Marie in her letters.

"What did Marie tell you about the Squire?" she said.

"She said he died shortly after we left Hadley."

"Did she tell you the manner in which he died?"

"In his sleep, if I remember correctly."

"That's what we announced officially. The truth is Timothy he took his own life. He went missing and, after a few days, Marie's father and Benson the farm manager found him hanging from a tree up in Hadley wood. A most ghastly affair. I trust you will keep it to yourself. I just thought you and your father should know the truth." She paused before she added, "And now let me bring you up to date with the rest of the village gossip,"

The factory, to the west of the village, that had produced motor carriages prior to the war now manufactured aeroplanes for the war effort and employed womenfolk in the absence of the men folk who had gone to war. Some eighty percent of the male population of the village and estate had enlisted or been called to arms. All of his school friends of old had gone, some leaving a wife and children.

Mr Pook and Mr Cutler who had contributed so much to father's motorised kite had passed on at ripe old ages

He asked her if she could add to what Marie had written about the mysterious disappearance of the Carlton brothers.

"It was all very strange, Timothy," she said. "They were offered a considerable sum of money for their engine designs and the tooling. But evidently the money never materialised. The engines and tools disappeared overnight as did the unscrupulous individuals who tricked the brothers. The Carltons sold their home and factory buildings and left the area shortly afterwards never to be seen again. No doubt highly embarrassed by what had happened."

His mind flashed back. He saw the inseparable brothers dressed in the leather coats, and caps, attending and tinkering with the engine they had provided for father's kite. He saw them rushing him away from the engine that went berserk and caused a fire that consumed the kite. On a happier note he recalled the occasion of his fourteenth birthday when they performed like the American Indians and did a war dance and made whooping sounds at the same time. Later they sat before the hearth of the cottage and passed the pipe of peace around.

How often these two great engineers had come to mind during his subsequent visits to the Indian Reservations in Canada.

"By the way." Lady Hadley changed the topic. "I think you should know Marie has left Hadley. Her father joined the flying corps and trained as an observer. He was killed six weeks after joining his squadron. Marie never gave herself a chance to grieve his loss. She promptly joined the VADS, and after a period of training was shipped to France."

Time had passed so swiftly; he had been so engrossed with the flying at Gosport he confessed that he had not written to Marie to notify her of his arrival in England. He had received his last letter from her some six months past in Canada.

Tapping sounds on the drawing room door preceded the sudden appearance of a young woman who swept into the room. "Mother…" she stopped short on noticing him. She had blue eyes and golden hair of her mother but the shape of the face came from the Herby line, as did the mouth, which could readily express warmth or determination.

Lady Hadley said: "Samantha. May I introduce you to Timothy Herby."

Samantha moved to him. He stood and took her hand in greeting. "How do you do, Samantha."

"Very well, Timothy. Thank you." she smiled and discreetly inspected him from head to toe. She stood back a couple of paces. "Do not tell me. Let me guess. I would suggest you are a war pilot."

He grinned at her. "Not quite. I have as yet to get my first taste of battle."

She brought father's mode of speech very close when she said: "Methinks you will be very gallant, and considerate to the plight of your opponents."

Lady Hadley intervened. "You may talk to Timothy later. Kindly go to Alice and ask her to serve fresh tea, my dear."

In her absence lady Hadley said; "You appear to remember Samantha well."

"I do indeed."

"But she was a mere infant when your parents took you to Canada."

Timothy grinned sympathetically at her. "I remember quite clearly the scene in the nursery that day when my mother challenged you and the squire as to who was the father of Samantha."

Lady Hadley looked down at her clasped hands. "Yes." she said quietly. "It must have looked and sounded quite sordid and improper to one as young as yourself."

"However." he said rallying to her embarrassment. " I would like you to know that I have come to regard what you did for father as most charitable and generous at a time when he was in most need of it."

She leant towards his chair and in a low voice said: "Samantha is under the impression that she is the daughter of the late squire. I intend to reveal the truth to her prior to her coming-out ball. Meanwhile I trust you will not say anything to her that she might construe as otherwise."

"My word is my bond."

She smiled appreciatively at him. "A true Herby. A true chip off the old block."

Before dinner, at Lady Hadley's suggestion, he walked Samantha in the grounds of the manor. He pointed up to the towering shape of Hadley hill and explained how he and father launched the manned kite from the summit, and glided the eight hundred feet to land in the paddock on which they were now standing. He told her about his father's first flight at night and how a local newspaper ridiculed him. He told her what fun they had as children at the annual village fete, and during the annual outing to the seaside. The distant pounding beat of hooves broke into the conversation and drew their attention to a horse and rider as it broke cover of nearby woodland and cantered towards them. Samantha told him it was Molly Langdon exercising a mount belonging to the manor. It was of the hunter breed, reached sixteen hands, and typical of its purpose in life it had a good turn of speed. He heard the grappling of the bit, and the straining of the leathers, as Mollie reined it in and drew to a halt before them. His attention was immediately drawn to the fullness of her breasts thrusting from the whiteness of her sweater, and the firm, shapely allure of her legs and thighs clad tightly by riding breeches. She defied all convention that said a lady should wear a riding skirt and ride sidesaddle. She aroused him as powerfully as she did all those years ago in the haymaking days of their youth.

She said brightly, "Hello, Timothy."

He reached up and took her extended hand. "Greetings, Mollie." Her eyes snared him, deep, intense, desirous, hypnotic, commanding.

"From the wings upon your chest." she said. "I see you are still pursuing the mysteries of the air."

He laughed, "A little less mysterious than when father and I built and flew the kites from here all those years past."

She said, "How long are you staying in Hadley?"

"Three days, possibly four."

She drew her hand from his grasp and goaded the horse on. "I hope we get a chance to talk over old times before you leave." she called out over a shoulder as she retreated.

When she was out of earshot Samantha said: "Her parents died of tuberculosis and her bothers and sisters were placed in an orphanage. Mother adopted Mollie because she felt she could make something of the girl and groom her to our level of society. I have doubts, however, if Mollie will ever lose totally the background of her parents. She will succeed in life because she has stunning looks and at all the social functions here the men are drawn to her like moths around a candle flame."

Twelve guests came to dinner at the manor that evening. He was introduced to the two industrialists who owned the factory west of the village. He met the manager of the small banking house that had been set-up in his absence. He chatted for quite a time with Doctor Markham and his wife who enjoyed reminiscing about the old days and his and father's aerial exploits. They claimed the estate and village had never been quite the same after the pioneering airmen went to live abroad.

WAR PILOT

He met Marie's mother just before they went in to dine. She tried to put a brave face on the loss of her husband, and the absence of her daughter, but her gaunt, haggard looks suggested the grief and sorrow was continuing to knock the stuffing out of her. The experience had aged her by ten years.

He sat next to her at dinner and she seemed reluctant to engage in conversation. Which was just as well because he was conscious of somebody monitoring every move he made. He glanced at each face in turn, around the table, until an emerald necklace hanging around a slender neck, and which dipped into the partially exposed cleavage of a white dinner gown, arrested his attention. He raised his eyes slowly and came face to face with Mollie Langdon who greeted him with a tantalising smile

Wherever he went after dinner and with whomever he conversed he sensed she was keeping an eye on him, and was close enough to overhear his conversation.

She joined him and Samantha and Lady Hadley to bid farewell to the guests at the end of the evening, and afterwards they mustered in the drawing room for a nightcap of whiskey before retiring for the night.

He was sat in bed writing a letter to his parents when gentle tapping noises on the door intruded on the silence of the night. He opened the door to be confronted by the figure of Mollie trying to disguise herself in a long hooded cloak.

He drew her in and quietly closed, and locked, the door. He lifted the hood back from her face and her long straw-coloured hair tumbled down on to her shoulders. They stood embracing each other, muted, indifferent.

Molly stirred and unfastened the neck clasp of her cloak. The weight of the material dragged it to the floor. She stood before him dressed in a black, lace-trimmed nightdress that did little to hide the pink buds topping the blown roundness of her breasts. His hands moved on the trim contours of her waistline and around the curves of her thighs. An air of urgency and expectancy charged the air. A fuse, controlling their thoughts and feelings, ticked slowly toward the inevitable moment of detonation. Her nightdress slipped to the floor. They collapsed on the bed, lips searching eagerly for contact, and burning like hot coals. Craving desires clamoured for release, for fulfillment. Their incessant calling to each other rose to a crescendo. Their frenzied bodies fused and blended into one. Mollie gasped, panted and cried out uncontrollably as he pounded her vigorously with his body. Moments later she let out a long whimpering cry when he delivered, and she hungrily accepted, three powerful salvoes of his seed. A raging torrent took them over the brink and they plunged into a river of divine madness. They were conscious of a freedom previously unknown to them. They floated in a fast-flowing ocean that carried them effortlessly to an unknown shore.

The experience haunted him two days later during the return flight to Gosport. He felt totally relaxed, refreshed and at peace with the world. A frame of mind that contrasted sharply to the uneasy scene unfolding around the trembling engine cowling and before the gentle swaying motion of the wings. Aerial galleons released and unfurled large white billowing sails of cloud that filled the sky and threatened to overwhelm him and the machine.

He climbed the Nieuport up and around the cloud in an attempt to avoid becoming entangled in the shrouds. He managed it with only feet to spare. Presently he looked to the rear. The sails of cloud had merged and viewed the world with the confrontation of a cliff face.

He fixed his position over Newbury and flew on, occasionally pitching and rolling to the unpredictable invisible motions of the air. The earth slowly disappeared beneath a vast blanket of cloud. He kept above it for a time, feeling totally divorced and separated from the earth. This was the true essence of flight in his opinion - complete solitude - out of sight of all things mortal. And if danger posed a threat there were only the Gods to turn to. He debated on what he could expect to find when he went down through the cloud to check his position. He drew a deep breath and took the plunge.

The interior of the cloud enveloped him in an intense steamy grey which blotted out all visual references and only gave him enough light to read the instruments. Everything got very damp to the touch He worked hard to keep the balance indicator in the centre, and the airspeed steady. The Nieuport registered its unease to his unsteady movements of the stick. A heavy shower of rain greeted him as he broke out the bottom of the cloud and almost drowned the sound of the engine. His surroundings brightened for him to discover his map was sodden, as was he. He decided to go to earth to dry out and find out where he was. He spotted a suitable field, turned in, blipped the engine a couple of times to clear a clump of trees, and a line of hedgerows, and floated down to greet the earth in a rumble of wood and drum-tight fabric, and the stuttering note of the engine.

He was on the verge of congratulating his good fortune at getting into the field safely when the Nieuport halted abruptly and tipped onto its nose. It threw him forward and he lay crouched over the windscreen, looking, foolishly, at the buckled engine cover and the jagged stumps of the propeller.

"Don't take it to heart, old boy." the major said when he eventually arrived back at Gosport. "You're not the first. And neither do I expect the last. I suggest you go up to the sheds and get fixed up with another machine. We're off to war tomorrow!"

THREE

The orderly officer yawned. It was time to carry out the final inspection of his night duty and he was pleased. He dressed in a trench coat, wound a long woolen scarf around his neck, and donned his cap. A stinging brittleness of the frosty air awakened him sharply as he moved from the shelter of the hut. His eyes watered and he gasped at the ferocity of the chilled air He hurriedly drew the collar of his coat up around his ears, and masked his mouth and nose with the scarf.

As he made his rounds under a starlit sky, and a chink of yellow light came to view in the east, the aerodrome came to life slowly. The cooks and batmen rose first. Followed within the hour by the troops who took breakfast before they reported to the hangars and prepared the machines for the day's work. By the time he arrived back at the hut and handed over to the orderly dog of the day the batmen were rousing the flying officers in their charge, a number of which tumbled from their beds nursing a sore head inflicted by roistering in the mess the night before. Others moved with a sense of duty. The remainder, not detailed for the morning job, attempted to regain the peace and oblivion their working fellows had disturbed.

Herby strolled to breakfast with James, Cochran, Lentell and McFarlen who shared his hutted quarters, and who had replaced four pilots taken in the cause of the war during the last month. He had not told the newcomers their beds had changed hands four times in the three months he had been operational with the squadron. He walked at a distance as they eagerly discussed the number of Huns they intended to bag that day; he was more concerned with the prospects of good flying weather. A growing band of golden light in the east showed wispy fibres of cloud in the higher regions of the sky. This, in conjunction with the clarity of the remaining stars and the hard frost, augured well, in his opinion, for the morning's flying.

James and Lentell continued their discussion over breakfast and invited others to join in. He listened absently. He did not condemn them for their enthusiasm. Neither did he want to be accused of damping their sense of cut and thrust; they would learn soon enough.

It was not for him to express the view that aerial fighting was not a respectable way of earning a living. It was not for him to remind them that they were involved in the taking of human life which, in times of peace, would be regarded as murder, and be punishable by law.

He finished his toast, drained his mug of tea and walked alone to the hangars wrestling, as he did each day, with a conflict of thought that tore him between his duty to his country, and the principles he used to regulate his own life.

Major Bramley kept his briefing simple. They were on the offensive and, if need be, they'd go over the lines to the other side and bring down as many Huns as they could.

Herby settled in the cockpit of the Nieuport, set the mixture and ignition, pulled the stick right back and alerted the figure standing before the propeller. The Nieuport rocked as the propeller was pulled through six revolutions.

"Contact!"

"Contact!" he called back.

The figure pulled briskly on the propeller. It jerked over and stopped.

"Off, sir."

"Off!"

The propeller was pulled to a more convenient position

"Contact!"

"Contact!"

On the third attempt the engine burst into life and set up a continuous quiver through the machine. And whilst the engine warmed Herby checked the controls, secured the chinstrap of his helmet, adjusted his goggles and arranged his map. The stillness of the dawn quickly scattered in the unsynchronised beat of the stirring rotary engines. Winged shapes began to emerge from the shadows and make their way to the southern boundary.

Herby waved the chocks away, saluted the troops, and got under way using the blip switch to hasten or check the Nieuport's momentum on the harsh virgin-white, frost- encrusted surface of the airfield. He caught up with Bradley and followed him as he turned to head up wind. He drew his goggles down, raised his muffler to protect his face and waited. Bramley looked over his shoulder to check they were ready - raised his hand - then dropped it. They switched to maximum revs. The engines roared. And they set off in formation lurching and jolting on the frozen earth.

Bramley's machine clambered into the air first. Herby prompted his Nieuport with stick and followed him. Out to his left Sangster, the third member of the flight, pitched, rolled and yawed his machine to keep station in the formation. They had met the first important objective of the day; they had got into the air safely.

The passage of the earth beneath the wings slowed as they rose higher. Fields, hedgerows, rivers and roads came into focus. Movement was barely perceptible. The rising sunlight filled the cockpits, but did little for the penetrating cold they all felt.

They crossed the lines to draw the Huns. Almost immediately the major rocked his wings as a signal he had picked up the scent, and banked westwards to go in pursuit. Herby hesitated. He recalled the sight of an eagle flying gracefully near the summit of a mountain during one of his patrols in Canada. And how he had lost sight of it in the blinding glare of the sun. Quite by accident he raised a hand to shield his eyes and the tip of his thumb happened to rest on the disc of the sun blanking out the dazzle and enabling him to see the eagle again.

He placed a thumb tip against the rising sun and sure enough he spotted three Tripes diving in his direction. He threw the Nieuport around, passed underneath and got astern of the Huns. He quickly decided on a tactic as they shot over the top of him and went in pursuit of the major and young Sangster. He swung back round and dived the Nieuport at speed. He doubted if it had ever flown so fast. Then he soared up in a climb designed to cut a path between the Huns and their quarry.

The plan was partially successful. The Hun leader carried on but his wingmen broke off to engage Herby who took evasive action by pulling into a loop. He switched to low revs when he got over the top and the opposite horizon came to view. A Hun came up on his right, as he dived, cart wheeled and came haring back down on his tail. The other Hun, possibly a novice, levelled off at the top of his climb and remained there out of harm's way.

Herby glanced at his pitot; he was going down at a fair old lick. The wing wires made a high-pitched piercing din, the wing fabric strained at the stitching and the propeller screamed hysterically. A large unseen hand pressed him heavily into the seat as he heaved steadily on the stick to recover from the dive. The following Hun passed him by, still diving, and disappeared amongst the mass of the earth's surface.

The other Hun suddenly appeared and got on his tail. Herby heaved the Nieuport into a steep turn followed by the Hun. He felt the accelerations of the turn forcing his head on to his chest; it was an effort to look through the windscreen. In the commotion he heard the chatter of the Tripe's gun. He allowed the Hun to get settled on his tail before he eased the pull on the stick and reversed bank. The Nieuport rolled admirably in the opposite direction and before the Hun could comprehend what had happened the British machine was on his tail. The confused Hun stumbled out of the turn, losing valuable time. Time for Herby to bring the Tripe to the rings of the aldis and trigger his stammering gun.

Within seconds the Tripe was trailing a corkscrew trail of smoke. It paused, fell over, and descended from the combat mortally wounded.

Small black clouds began to scar the air around the Nieuport. Herby was in no doubt that the earthbound guns of the Hun were out to gain retribution for the one he had downed. He dodged between the bursts and climbed the Nieuport toward a number of glinting, winged shapes engaged in battle. He noticed beneath the wings that plant and tree life was conspicuous by their absence. Upturned earth, gashed and trenched, and dotted with craters had replaced the chequered fields of peacetime. Nothing - absolutely nothing was sacred in the wave of the war machine.

Sangster was missing when he reached the fight. The major had got himself and three pursuing Huns in a steep turn in the hope of out-turning his foe. Where the extra Huns had come from was a mystery to Herby. He latched onto what he thought to be the last Hun in the circle, brought it to the sight and let rip whilst he juggled with the control stick and rudder bar. The Hun slipped out of the turn and fled earthwards. He kept his finger poised on the trigger, tightened the radius of the turn, and forced his eye to the aldis against the mounting forces of the turn. A fine spray of castor oil seeped through the scarf over his face. The stick juddered in the light grip of his hand. He had to be quick or the Nieuport would stall. The Hun loomed large in the sight. It was never his intention to kill the Hun airmen; he only wanted to maim the machines and disqualify them for battle.

But this Hun was on edge. He threw his Tripe about wildly to thwart the Newport's attack. Herby gave him a short burst. The jinking helmeted head in the other cockpit came to the sight for the fraction of a second, and in the blink of an eyelid the enemy pilot was fatally wounded. He leapt up in the cockpit and slumped back with his arms draped over the sides of the cockpit. The machine rolled over and went down in a breathless spin that would only be halted by the solidness of the earth's surface

The third Hun, having seen his two comrades dispatched so efficiently, spun away in retreat.

Herby escorted the major and his ragged machine through an angry barrage of ground fire back to their side of the lines. His ears continued to pop and give him moments of discomfort: the effects from the diving and zooming of the battle. He felt weary from the constant pressure changes imposed from the steep, tight turns and reversals. His neck ached from the continuous movement of his head in order to be vigilant. From take-off to landing an aerial battle was never-ending.

There was always a chance some battle damage may go unnoticed, and would only reveal itself on landing. He had seen Ferguson dig a wing in on landing due to unknown combat damage to his wing rigging. And he'd also seen Rogers collapse on the earth in a heap after a Hun punctured one of his tyres and severed a wheel strut, which Rogers had not been aware of.

He followed the major back to earth. But did not relax until his rotary engine clattered into silence and the propeller juddered to a halt. He was sat massaging his neck when the major appeared by the side of the cockpit clutching his helmet and goggles. "Did you see what happened to Sangster?" he said.

"I've no idea major. I was too busy engaging three Tripes who came out of the sun."

"Huns! Out of the sun! Did you bag any?"

Herby eased up from the cockpit and jumped to the ground. "One overtook me in a dive. I think he left it too late for the pullout. I shot down one of his friends. Then I got involved in your scrap and downed another."

The major put an arm around his shoulder and led him toward the flight hut. "How about us taking one and a half machines a piece where the scores are concerned."

Herby said: "You can take credit for the lot as far as I am concerned. But I would suggest you check the blind spot of the sun in future before haring off to do battle

The major pulled his arm away, muttered something scornfully, and stomped away to join his flight leaders.

Herby secured himself a mug of tea and lighted his pipe. He stood before a window in the hut watching his machine being refuelled and his gun magazines being replenished.

He was on the ground for half an hour when he was detailed to lead a flight of machines aloft and go to help open up a retreat for a group of encircled British troops.

Too late! By the time they arrived over the scene the Huns had disappeared leaving a trail of carnage. Machine guns and rifles lay sinking in the mud surrounded by the figures of spread-eagled, lifeless men the airmen had been detailed to rescue.

They headed back home, lamenting the failure of their mercy mission, and grieving the loss of warriors unknown. What was life? He thought. What was death? A blessing or a reward? And what was the purpose of this infernal war?

He was released for lunch and told to report for the evening job. The menu for lunch: Bangers and mash. Followed by rice pudding. Eaten amongst pockets of chatter which were tolerated numbly by those who preferred to sit and eat alone. More missing faces. Yet more friends swallowed up by the fiendish appetite of the war.

He spent the afternoon stretched out on his bed and managed to sleep for a spell. He rose after four and washed and shaved. He wondered if there was any news of Sangster. Sangster the young, innocent, barely out of school, who had tasted so precious little of life. Educated, no doubt, at great expense to his parents as so many of his class were. There would be no return on their investment that was for sure.

He strolled up to the flight hut in the cool evening sunlight, enjoying his remaining moments of peace before he was forced to put on a heavy coat of responsibility. He inhaled the freshness of the air. He clung to his dwindling freedom. He simply enjoyed the pleasure of being alive.

It all quickly dissipated in the roar of the rotary engine at full revs and the Nieuport carried him to the heights with two other machines as company. They patrolled for two hours and saw nothing that constituted the threat of an enemy. Maybe the war had moved elsewhere, he thought. Or ended, perhaps. A vain hope indeed!

The sun had set by the time they got back over the aerodrome. Dusk: it was neither light nor dark. And without definition it created illusions that posed as unwelcome bait for an unsuspecting victim. An airman flying close to the ground in such conditions could easily misjudge and think he was closer to the ground than he actually was.

Noton had only been with the squadron for a fortnight. It was his fifth flight on operations. He only had a total of twenty hours on his logbook. He was happy and relieved to be flying home untouched by the enemy. He looked forward to dinner in the mess, and talking shop with his friends over a couple of noggins of ale.

He levelled off too high over the aerodrome boundary. His machine hung in the air till it ran out of flying speed. Then it stalled and slumped uncontrollably to earth, ripping the undercarriage off, smashing the propeller, and sending his face at full tilt into the buffer strip.

In the gathering darkness troops lifted his unconscious body from the cockpit whilst others took his stricken machine away.

Steak and kidney pie was on the menu for dinner. Herby topped it up with a portion of bread and butter pudding. After which he wandered up to the hangars to present his weekly bottle of beer and packet of cigarettes to each of the troops in appreciation for their care of his machine. He got back to the hut just after nine to discover he had it to himself. He brought his diary up to date, and wrote a letter home. By ten thirty he was sound asleep.

There was a bit of a noise when the others came in after a rowdy evening in the mess. But it was short-lived, and he slipped back into oblivion.

WAR PILOT

FOUR

He felt cold, hollow, and absolutely wretched. He had destroyed his twelfth Hun; his fifth to go down like a flaming funeral pyre. The sight of the Hun pilot leaping from the burning torch without a chance of escaping the death that waited for him ten thousand feet below, lodged permanently in the memory.

He turned in for the aerodrome, switched to low revs, and attempted to find some justification for his murderous employment in the air. In essence he could find no justification for it at all. The Nieuport floated over the wind indicator - he levelled her so that her wheels were all but kissing the grass, and the nose blocked his view forward as he eased the stick back a fraction more. The gushing airstreams over the wings, and along the fuselage, fell to a whisper, to a murmur indicating the moment had come for the machine to relinquish its soul to the laws of gravity.

After reporting in he went into a corner with a mug of tea. He got his pipe burning and watched the other pilots dribble in and report to the adjutant who chalked their claims on a blackboard.

Riley claimed a Hun destroyed. Travers claimed another plus a probable. Knight confirmed he had seen Mcfarlen shot down. And Hodges said he saw James go down as a flamer. The major insisted he'd destroyed a brace of Huns, and added, without a trace off emotion, that the two novices he'd led out had perished in the scrap.

Herby drew on his pipe and speculated on how the relatives of the novice pilots would take the news. To be killed after only a fortnight in battle was difficult enough for any caring parent to swallow. He remembered only too well what it had been like during his early days with the squadron. It had been more of a fight to survive rather than a fight to destroy the enemy. There was so much to learn in such a short space of time. Getting accustomed to flying the machine and firing the gun at the same time. Getting used to navigating over strange territory. Anticipating the unpredictable bursts of the shells from the ground. Recognising the difference between allied and enemy machines. For many airmen the first couple of weeks were exhausting. For a great number – it was painful. And for the majority, it was totally overwhelming.

The survivors rarely escaped totally from their battles. Many, as he was, were haunted by memories of maimed machines and airmen, both friend and foe, tumbling helplessly out of control. Or by a mixture of fabric dressed tight on wooden framing, and flesh upon bone, engulfed by a tongue of flame that roared like a furnace as it swept earthwards . It was difficult to comprehend that amongst the melting, dripping spectacle of fire there once existed a wholesome structure of man and machine, both of which had been alive and eager to grace the heights for which both Creator and designer had intended. He drained his mug of tea, slipped quietly out of the hut and walked back to his quarters to wash and change. The major said he had earned three days off on account he had flown every day for the last month, and often made three flights a day.

By mid afternoon he was sitting with Michelle on a riverbank beneath an overhanging willow that looked upon the gentle gliding flow of a river. The warmth, the stillness and the enchanting song of an unseen bird did much to disassociate his thoughts from the acerbity of the war.

They had met when her mother invited a number of officers from the aerodrome to their home for a wholesome meal, an unrationed supply of good wine, and entertainment in the form of a singsong around a piano played by Michelle. And as the evening wore on so the wine flowed more freely, and certain individuals put social graces aside and let their hair down. Peters danced with a girl in an embrace that some described as indecent. Grant, shattered by a narrow escape earlier in the day when his machine turned over on landing and burst into flames, explored a girl with an intimacy normally reserved for a more private venue. Meaklejohn staggered around trying to dominate the conversation with his annoying, loud, slurred highland brogue.

Herby escaped into the large garden of the house. He lit his pipe, seated himself on a wooden bench and took to gazing at the stars. He drew a sense of orderliness from the permanency of the constellations. He thought of his parents. He dwelt for a time on his life in Canada. He thought of the families of the German airmen he had wounded and killed.

"May I join you?" Michelle materialised from the dim light of the garden.

"But of course."

She sat beside him in the rustle of her silk dress. He caught the fragrance of her perfume and compared it to the castor oil and doped fabric which normally lined his nostrils from dawn to dusk, and, often, followed him to bed.

They spoke about themselves and their families for a good hour. He told her about his parents and his life in Canada. She told him about a father who died tragically in a motor accident before the war, and a brother who was fighting for the French army. The pilot enjoyed the gentleness and dignity of her French accent. It injected him with a measure of sanity that the war was constantly trying to rob from him.

When they returned to the house Meaklejohn was out to the world and Michelle's mother was attempting to revive him and encourage him to take a special potion she had prepared. She said that if they could get it past the Scot's stubborn lips it would sober him up and give him enough mobility to get back to the tender for the return to the aerodrome. They had four hours in which to straighten themselves out for the dawn patrol.

For Herby it was the beginning of several visits to the house. Winter gave way to spring. Michelle's companionship served as a welcome diversion to his warring activities, and a welcome escape from the younger men in his hut whose lives revolved around flying, fighting and heavy drinking. Alone with her he felt human and untarnished by the war. The melodious, balmy compositions she played expertly on the piano sprung him free of his responsibilities at the aerodrome, and set his thoughts adrift from the acrimonious fetters of the war. It was in the music room of her home that they first embraced, and kissed.

As they sat before the river he speculated, as he often did, on the slimness of her waist, the roundness of her thighs, and the curves of her legs all of which she kept out of sight beneath the long dresses she wore. A bird came to a slender branch of the willow overhead and peered enquiringly down at them for a moment before slipping low across to the opposite bank of the river

Michelle stirred. She discarded her wide-brimmed hat and loosened the tie at the throat of her dress. He watched in disbelief as she went through the process of removing all her clothing. "I feel the need to bathe, Timothy." she announced.

He lingered awhile on the sight of her white, subtle, delightfully curved form shadowed by the willows and flecked by traces of sunlight, as she stepped lightly down the bank into the river. Then, conscious of his own flaring desires, he stripped off and joined her.

The occasion marked the beginning of an intensely passionate intimate relationship that, within 12 weeks, was brought to an abrupt end by the unpredictability of the war.

At short notice the squadron got orders to move. Without permission, and barely time to do it, he crept out of the aerodrome and to her home to break the news.

"When?" she said anxiously.

"Within hours. Before dawn in fact."

She eased away from him and held him with troubled eyes. "It can't be, Timothy. I am carrying your child."

Somewhat taken aback by the revelation he stood looking at her in stunned silence.

"Have you nothing to say." she said brusquely.

"What more can I say?"

"You might ask your superiors for special leave to allow us to marry. It would also avoid our child being born a bastard."

"We are at war, Michelle. Your request is unreasonable in the circumstances."

"That's it!" she cried. "You have no intention of making me your wife. Why don't you have the courage to admit to it!"

"I mean it is impossible at this moment in time."

"Get out!" she shouted. "Go back to your English girls where you belong. No wonder the Huns find you such charming fellows to fight."

He gripped her by the arms. "Condemn me if you must, my dear. But I forbid you to cast a slur on my countrymen as a whole. Many are those who have been slaughtered in this dastardly war without a blemish on their character."

She made to utter another outburst. Changed her mind. Wrenched herself from his hold, and hurried to an adjacent room and slammed the door shut.

Her mother who had been drawn by Michelle's raised voice, and had overheard the conversation, came to him. "I do not condemn you, Timothy. Had it not been you, it might easily have been someone else, such is the tragedy of war. Go in peace from this house. I'll care for Michelle and the child."

It was cold. Very cold. The Nieuport clambered and fell about in the air with the floundering gait of an inebriate. The rotary engine coughed and gasped as might a victim struck down with a consumptive disease. He suddenly noticed an unusually heavy layer of ice had accumulated on the leading edges of the wings, and cocooned the struts and wires with a similar crust. So preoccupied with thoughts of Michelle and the ugly circumstances in which they had parted he had ventured unknowingly into heights that were quite unsuitable for the Nieuport. He made to move the stick to discover it was jammed. He exerted more force. It refused to budge. His concern changed to alarm when he looked to the rear to see the tailplane and elevator imprisoned by a formation of ice. He tried to move the stick again. It stubbornly refused to move a centimetre in any direction. The gasping engine spluttered into silence. His surroundings became eerily quiet and still. The symptoms were all there for the Nieuport to desert the wing and plunge, or spin, to earth.

Without the use of the stick he would be powerless to check it. Much as he feared the Nieuport pitched forward and headed earthwards. The controls might unthaw when they sank into warmer air. But would he have sufficient height to get the machine fully organised. It was a huge gamble.

He was on the verge of accepting there was nothing he could do but sit and wait for the inevitable when he saw a face looking at him through the windscreen. Rather strangely the face reminded him of Grandfather Willy's journal in which his grandfather had written that he could balance his solitary wing by altering the posture of his body.

He released his lap strap, stood on the seat and leaned forward with the idea it would make the Nieuport nose heavy and coax it into a dive, which, in theory, should unstall the wings. The earth looked up at him with a crazed expression. He clung on to the top centre section of wing with his life.

Without warning the machine banked to the right and he was mercifully deposited back in his seat when, in fact, the movement should have ejected him from the cockpit. He was equally fortunate the Nieuport did not flick into a spin. He stood on the seat again. This time the left wings dropped and he just managed to slip back inside the cockpit, wedge his elbows against the inside of the cockpit, and trap his knees under the instrument panel, before the machine reached the inverted position and stalled.

He was convinced now that he was doomed. The machine stayed upside down and seemed in no hurry to extricate itself from its predicament. He was acutely aware of a prolonged and deadly silence, and a profound helplessness.

Quite unexpectedly the machine stirred and pointed its nose earthwards. The altimeter indicated they were less than five thousand feet from the ground. He tried to move the stick. It defied him yet again. They were going down too fast. He gingerly hauled himself up and around to crouch over the rear of the cockpit.

The machine eased out of the dive, reared up, rolled over and dived vertically. He turned and fell back in his seat in the nick of time.

An unseen hand pulled the Nieuport out of the dive and he sat there holding his breath as it glided calmly across the lines to friendly territory. If ever he had hung onto life by a thread he was doing so at this very moment. His and Michelle's problems were diminished to nothing more significant than a solitary star in the vast expanse of a galaxy.

Two thousand feet below the earth leered up at him, taunting him with thoughts of his tragic destiny. He made one more desperate attempt to move the stick. But it was to no avail. At about a thousand feet the nose pitched down sharply. He sensed a giant hand reaching up for him. He scrambled from the seat and threw himself over the spine behind the cockpit. The machine ignored him and swept toward the ground. And as he clung on he saw his grandfather again looking, and grinning, at him out of the chaos and confusion of his dwindling remaining moments of life. At the same time an irresistible force wrenched him from the Nieuport and sent him tumbling into space. The impact, when it came, sucked his breath from him. He remembered nothing more.

He gradually grew conscious of being immersed in water, and that he was coughing urgently to prevent it getting to his lungs. His head broke free of the water and his senses were sharpened by the view of dazzling sunlight in a sparkling blue sky. He was filled with a relief and jubilation that compared only to one who had been spared. In celebration he struck out for the shore of the lake that, miraculously, had formed the plan for his salvation.

The stricken Albatross broke away from the line of sight through the Aldis and went down streaming smoke. A flickering flame of fire started somewhere near the centre section and quickly became a spreading sheet of flame. Herby cringed. He did not have to be reminded of the Hun pilot's dilemma. He either stayed with the machine to be roasted to death, or jumped clear of the inferno and survived for precious seconds, as he fell through space, before the impact with the earth thumped the life out of him. Perhaps during that death fall there would be a spate of memories, possibly of a father - a mother - a sister - a brother - a wife - a lady friend - a child.

He flew the Nieuport back to the aerodrome deeply unhappy, as he had been for many weeks, at the number of Hun airmen who had died an incinerated death at his hands. It seemed inconceivable to him as to why two men, who shared a calling for flight, should seek to destroy each other in the pursuit of such.

The squadron claimed six Huns that day and the mess that evening reverberated to the sound of a wild celebration. Nobody appeared to care about Carter, Morgan and Phillips who had perished in the course of the day's combat. He made his way across the aerodrome to an orchard on the boundary. He sat beneath an apple tree, stuffed tobacco into his pipe and lighted it, and listened to the uneasiness of the night. Overhead the stars remained in place whilst spasmodic flashes appeared on the horizon and the ground and air shook and tumbled with the distant conversation of the heavy guns. There was no escape.

His mind latched on to numerous incidents that had come to his attention during the day. The faces that sat in for breakfast and did not return from the dawn patrol. The ones who went out after lunch and did not come back. And those who failed to return from the evening job. A mechanic who suffered a serious injury when he was swinging a propeller. A machine that leapt over the chocks and smashed into a Crossley tender. The tragic discovery of a fellow flying officer who hanged himself after receiving a letter from his wife, in which she said, she had fallen for the affections of another man

In an attempt to escape the dismal reflections he dwelt for a time on the memories of his patrols in Canada. Days when he was surrounded by pine-scented forests, rambling rivers, waterfalls, and when he cooked meat on an open fire on a cold night and in the shadows of majestic snow-capped mountains. It did a little to placate his uneasiness and goad him to go back to the hut past the mess that pounded to a rowdy sing-song and distinctive notes of an out-of-tune piano.

He wrote to his parents: After reading your letter I lay on my bed, eyes closed, thinking of happier times. Thank you both for the prompting. And as Christmas approaches I can't help thinking how the war makes a mockery of the forthcoming event we celebrate each year. (The birth)

War Pilot

There is little I can add to my previous letters. We are in action daily, and far removed from the peaceful, absorbing days of our flying training. Days when we flew in serene, untroubled skies and a lazy and unblemished countryside unfurled beneath the wings. Days when a natural joy and laughter filled the soul.

Alas, no more. Everything, nowadays, is meant to be done with a destructive sense of purpose, which the younger men, charged with the restlessness and recklessness of youth, may find appealing. For certain it holds no attraction for me.

Equally there are others whose features and attributes are not compatible with the violence of war. Their long, fine fingers, a sharp eye, a keen ear belong to a practicing musician, artist, or poet. And in this sphere of their life they excel as is demonstrated by their paintings and poetry exhibited on the mess walls or the music they provide by the gifted touch with bow on the strings of a violin or the delicate fingering on the keys of a piano.

They show great courage by fighting a losing battle against the bacteria of war that destroys all that they have lived, and striven for in their pursuit to further the cultural progress of mankind. They know that war alienates them from what they stand for in the world and yet they fight for King and country and succumb to death as bravely as a flower succumbs to the devastation of a frost. War deprives the world of such rare talent.

Harris, Rogers and Riddlestone will possibly remain unknown to the art world because their works are based on construction and are not included in the focus of the war, which is based on destruction. Harris with twelve great poems to his credit and each of them a gem. Rogers, the artist, describes in his pictures the futility of war and warns those who consider it to be a glamorous and honourable pastime. Last, but not least, Riddlestone, a musician, who, after a day in combat, could lend an air of calming sanity to the atmosphere of the mess with his piano recitals.

By contrast there are those who relish the pace and action of the hostilities: the Hun-getters, the fighters, the aces. But who am I to condemn them. Who knows? They may have been chosen by the Power above all power to rid the earth of its present irregularities and imperfections in the form of dictatorships and usurping authorities.

In closing I apologise to you both if you think I am biased toward introspection. Apportion the blame, if you must, to the folly of this war.

By Christmas day the squadron strength was down to four consisting of the major, the adjutant, Barlow and himself. The photographic cells of the brain contain an album of crumpled and burnt-out skeleton wrecks of aircraft - the gruesome task of retrieving human remains - the awkward letters to bereaved relatives - and the incessant train of military funerals.

Death was not new to him. He had come across it frequently during his long patrols in Canada. He had seen bear kill bear. He had seen Caribou brought down by a starving pack of wolves. He had seen a trapper gamble on the thickness of ice sheeting a lake and fall through never to rise again.

In each instant there had been naturalness about it: man and beast battling against the elements. But there was nothing natural and logical about his victims of aerial combat, who mainly died violently as roasting, screaming torches consumed by the demonic wrath of fire.

He was promoted to the rank of captain when the major received orders to rebuild the squadron. He was assigned to the task of familiarising the newcomers with the local geography from the air and the general nature of the work. He concentrated the text of his briefings on skilful flying. Flying that would not necessarily make then into aces at shooting down scores of the enemy; he left that to their individual instincts. His aim was to keep them out of trouble long enough to get to know their machines really well before launching into the affray of battle.

He led them up and around towering cumulus clouds and took them amongst the folds and gullies to throw their machines around in mock combat and to work some cunning into their flying practices.

He also introduced them to some scenes of the sky their limited flying experience had denied them. He led them aloft to witness the colourful splendour of a day breaking. Few, if any, would ever forget that first take-off in the shreds of night. That magical ascent into the spreading flame of the rising sun which, as they rose higher, burst like a balloon and sent out long golden rays that devoured the black emptiness of the night and gave birth to a new day.

They followed him up in the lingering daylight to watch the sun go down. About them the azure sky faded to a steely blue - to a rustic colour. And in a final blaze of glory to a distinct crimson that painted the machines they flew. Thus another day in their lives was about to end whilst another night stood poised to begin. He constantly warned them about being caught in the sun by the Hun, and showed them how best they could avoid it by his method of putting a thumb tip on the disc of the sun.

Major Bramley looked on with interest and amusement. At last he had got Herby where he wanted him - a flight leader. He was well aware of Herby's dislike of killing German airmen. There were many more like him. Officers and gentlemen who liked to think they were above such barbarism. But in reality a war could not be fought without it. It was one of the perils in the life and occupation of a war pilot.

Ironically Herby had all the qualities of a scout pilot. He was very much a loner, an individual. He flew an aeroplane as though he'd been born into it. And he was an excellent shot, which may have been carried over from his experience as a law officer in Canada.

The quality of the flying of the pilots coming from the training establishments was not good. The expediency of their training, and some the victims of inexperienced instructors, being the main causes.

Floyd had been taught in England to avoid spinning at all costs. Merrydew had never sampled inverted flight. Herby patiently taught them how to overcome these shortcomings. As a result Floyd subsequently spun his way out of an embarrassing encounter with a Hun, and Merrydew got his first Hun after coming out of loop following his escape from the clutches of another.

There was a marked improvement in the efficiency and moral of the squadron. The score of Huns destroyed increased steadily whilst the squadron lost none of its pilots.

Herby did not take it for granted. He had seen many a meek and mild combatant grow violent and aggressive after downing a couple of the enemy. Their successes bred arrogance and over-confidence. Their lives normally ended abruptly and violently. Equally he had seen strong, capable fighters wilt under the relentless daily battles in the air. There were also a number of cultured individuals who found it all too much, and quietly disappeared without trace.

The days matured into weeks - into months. The score for the number of

Huns destroyed, for the revived squadron, stood at 36 for the loss of 2 squadron pilots. Ridges got lost. Landed to find his way, and was promptly made a prisoner of war. Hopkins was last spotted venturing into a spreading cumulus - never to be seen again.

A grave shortage began to add to the threat of the Hun A shortage of spare parts for the machines, a shortage of decent food, and a shortage of simple pleasures such as toilet paper and writing pads.

Any manner of machinery needed fuel and maintenance to sustain it in working order. The war machine was no exception.

WAR PILOT

FIVE

The earth rotated around the nose, and flicked and jerked against the struts and wing wires. His third flight in a Camel and he was in trouble. Serious trouble.

He had gone into the spin inadvertently whilst trying to shake off three marauding Huns. One came down in a frontal attack. Another sneaked up on him from the rear. The third came from underneath and ripped the fabric of the bottom of the fuselage to shreds.

Split-second judgement and his sharp reflexes decided he should bank to the left to evade his attackers. The Camel had an inherent dislike of turning to the left. It waited until the wings had reached sixty degrees of bank and without warning wrested control from him and rolled over and down into a spin.

His first two attempts to recover it from the spin, using opposite rudder and forward movement of the stick failed to halt the rotation. He switched engine to low revs and tried twice more. Again without success. He eased the pressure on the rudder bar. Then kicked it over hard. The Camel refused to answer. The spiralling trenches, shell craters, and the sprawling barbwire came up at a startling speed. He could hear the exchanges of rifle and machine guns waging a battle on the earth below. His body froze at the imminent impact. Death was staring him in the face, a ghoulish expression marked with hollow sockets where once eyes had been, and the bridge of the nose devoid of flesh and nostrils, and shrunken gums, which no longer accommodated teeth. And as quickly as it confronted him it disappeared and was replaced by a vision of a young smiling face aged by the presence of a dark bushy moustache. He recalled he had seen that face before when he had been driven into a corner, convinced that all hope had been lost. It vanished as strangely as it had appeared, and he was certain the face belonged to the late grandfather Willy.

An unseen force moved his hand upon the stick. He pushed it fully forward - paused - pulled it fully back -paused - pushed it fully forward - paused - pulled it fully back and maintained the sequence with a foot pressed hard against the rubber bar. Then he was urged to switch the engine to high revs as he moved the stick forward - and to low revs when he pulled the stick back.

The movement was slight and almost imperceptible at first. Then the pitching up and down motion of the nose grew pronounced. Features of the earth were so close they were on the verge of spinning into confusion. It was, he imagined, like diving into a whirlpool. The Camel stopped spinning; he centralised the rudder bar and began easing the stick back. A massive hand reached up for him- a shadow.

War Pilot

He hauled the stick back and closed his eyes. The machine lurched heavily and he heard a sharp cracking sound as the undercarriage was swiped off. His head hit the buffer strip temporarily blinding and dazing him. Silence. It seemed he was being lifted upwards at speed. He thrust the stick forward to avoid a premature stall. Through his returning sight he had a blurred view of the war-savaged terrain slipping up to claim him. He braced himself. The earth greeted the Camel with a thunderous hollow thud and he suffered a long lurching uncomfortable journey before the machine slewed to a halt beyond a line of trenches. A shrill whistling noise passed close overhead. A brief silence. And the air split in two with the violence of the explosion. Two hundred yards ahead of him the earth erupted. Another shell came over and struck ground barely a hundred yards distant. Its proximity prompted him to leave the cockpit with great haste and dive into the nearest trench.

He thought at first it was deserted. Then he heard troops shouting and the sound of a chattering machine gun interspersed with volleys of rifle fire. He squatted down and lit his pipe. The burning tobacco had a particularly good taste about it. Perhaps more so after his recent dilemma in the air and the subsequent chaotic return to earth. God! He looked skyward. It was grand to be alive.

He vowed he would never go into battle again with so little experience on a machine. On the other hand, it occurred to him, he might not have escaped his attackers had the Camel not spun. And equally he might not have survived had grandfather Willy not intervened and prompted him how to recover from the spin, and only just in the nick off time.

"You all right, sir." the voice came from a face peering at him from a turning in the trench.

He looked disbelievingly at the eyes regarding him from the shadows of a tin helmet. His thoughts flew back in time to his school days in Hadley before his parents took him to Canada.

The soldier approached him, his boots squelching in the mud. He said: "It's Timmy Herby, ain't it. Sorry sir," he'd suddenly spotted the pilot's rank. "I mean captain Herby."

"Harry Griggs! How are you Harry?"

Harry took his outstretched in greeting. "A bit muddy as you can see Timmy. But surviving."

He smiled at the irony of Harry's remark. Soggy mud and clay surrounded them like a plague. The mischievous, undeterred Harry had not changed since their school days. Harry the prankster who placed tintacks on the seats of their schoolteachers and amused his chums when the unsuspecting victims rose swiftly and painfully from their seats with cries of rage and pain.

Yet here he was in squalid conditions, close to death, and able to retain his humour in the face of a prank being played on him by the folly of two governments wrangling over the supremacy for power. He paid scant attention to the train of exploding shells. He was more content to talk about the many changes that had come to Hadley. He did not welcome the factory built on the edge of the village. It was noisy and smelly and he was determined that the five children he reared would never work there. He wanted them to have healthy outdoor occupations like farm workers. "Ever since I joined the army," he said. " I've been thinking more and more about taking the family overseas after the war."

They crouched and waited as a shell shrieked very close over the trench and came to earth with a resounding, crashing explosion that rocked the mud beneath their feet. During the ensuing lull the pilot said: "How would you like me to recommend you and the family to Canada, Harry. There are plenty of opportunities for that type of work."

Harry grinned broadly, "Do you mean that, Timmy?"

"I'll write to my father and tell him of your wishes."

Harry rubbed his hands jubilantly. "Blimey. That'll give the missus and kids something to think about when I write home."

A sergeant major confronted them as he came round the turning in the trench. "And what do we have here." he said brusquely.

The pilot said cheerfully, "Not a mutiny, sergeant major. Simply two friends who grew up in the same village, and who have not met for fifteen years. Now, perhaps, you would oblige and help me get in touch with my squadron."

The sergeant maintained his stern, disciplined stance. "If you would care to follow me, sir."

Herby turned to Harry and took his hand. "It has been fun meeting you, Harry. Be assured I will write to my father as soon as possible. And if I get back to Hadley ahead of you I'll tell them how brave and cheerful you are."

Harry shook his hand. "Thanks Timmy. But don't tell them about the conditions here. They'd only worry."

Harry disappeared three days later during a desperate and frantic attack on the might of the enemy. Of an entire regiment only a handful survived. And the cannons of the Hun smiled agreeably at the tenderness of their fodder.

The sergeant major led the pilot through the maze of trenches and handed him over to a young lieutenant who looked as if he might crumble at any minute under the weight of his responsibilities. "You'll find a dressing station to the rear of us." he said nervously. "They may be able to help you. Failing that you can sit tight here and wait for it to quieten down. But only God knows when that will be."

The pilot thanked, and dismissed, him, and spent time peering over the top of the trench debating on what would be his best route to get to the wood in which the dressing station was hidden. Around him troops manned their weapons whilst others rested or awaited orders. Their uniforms were splattered with mud, their eyes red and sore from lack of sleep. Many smoked a cigarette to calm tattered nerves. Here and there a body lay lifelessly still, killed by a stray fragment of shell.

He scrambled out of the trench and made for the shelter of the wood stumbling and collecting himself from numerous potholes after a passing, low-flying shrieking shell prompted him to lay in the bosom of mother earth for protection on no less than six occasions.

He found as much bedlam at the dressing station as on the battle field he'd just left. Streams of stretcher parties brought the wounded in and the nurses, doctors and surgeons worked feverishly to deal with the growing number of casualties. The senior medical officer looked at him with bloodshot eyes. He said: "Our telephone is out of order. It's difficult to know what to suggest." he placed a hand on his furrowed brow. "Corporal Gledhurst!"

"Sir." A soldier appeared promptly before them.

"Transport captain Herby to HQ, and go sparingly on the petrol. We have precious little left for an emergency."

"Very good, sir."

The journey was particularly interesting for the pilot. It was his first experience of riding on a motorcycle. He likened it to dashing around the countryside with a Nieuport or Camel with a totally exposed cockpit and clipped wings. Corporal Gledhurst demonstrated superb skill in handling the machine. He rode at speed, skirting potholes, leaping over mounds and ruts, and was in complete control at all times.

"You should enlist with the flying corps." Herby smiled , climbing off at the HQ entrance.

I've tried three times, sir. All without success."

Herby gave him his rank, name and squadron number. "Quote that when you next apply, and tell them I am recommending you. I think you'll get through this time."

The corporal drew himself erect. "Thank you, sir. Thank you very, very much." He kicked the foot start and the engine rattled into life.

"Cheerio, sir. And thanks again." He rode off with an expression on his face that told a story of someone who had suddenly come into a fortune.

A French chateau served as an HQ and an officer's mess. The war was not very far away but the building exuded a charm and hospitality of its own. The oak-paneled walls, chandeliers, soft carpeting, and expensive paintings reminded him of his parents' residence in Canada. A slow, elderly officer greeted him courteously and showed him to a telephone for him to contact the aerodrome. Then a Batman was summoned to provide hot water and towels for him to freshen up.

Presently a steward served tea and cakes and Herby and the officer discussed the progress of the war as the daylight faded at the windows, and the distant booming of the guns sounded at longer intervals.

After they had exhausted the subject of the war Herby said, "It may be bit of a shot in the dark. But have you ever come across a VAD by the name of Marie Sawyer in your travels?"

"Marie Sawyer." the old man grinned approvingly at him. "Everybody knows Marie. A wonderful young woman. Lost her father in the flying corps I understand."

"That's right."

A mess steward moved around them lighting the lamps.

"Do you know her well?"

"You might say we grew up together. Then our family moved to Canada. We kept in contact by letter over the years. And when I arrived in England to enlist I discovered she had gone off to war with the VADs. The last time I saw her was several years ago."

The older officer grinned, "You may like to know she is renowned for her fearlessness, dedication and stamina. It's generally said she and a handful of VADs could put many men to shame." He paused to consult his pocket watch. "Now, you must excuse me. I must give instructions for the preparations for dinner. I think I might have a surprise for you later."

Herby sat smoking his pipe. He drew immense comfort from the peace and quiet in the light of the homely oil lamps. He was reflecting on happier times when he was called to the telephone and told by the squadron adjutant to expect a tender to collect him at nine that evening. That was the good news.

The bad news was that Warren, Keats and Frobisher had not returned from the last patrol of the day. He wished more than ever he had insisted on all the squadron pilots getting more experience on the Camel before going into battle. It was a new aeroplane and a sprightly one at that, and had its limitations as had all aeroplanes. And it was the prudent, disciplined airman who acquainted himself fully with these limitations.

He returned to the anteroom and sat mulling over the loss of the airmen. It would not have been so bad had he convinced himself they had just been unlucky in a scrap. But he was inclined to think their lack of experience with the Camel had been their undoing. He thought of the young Keats who looked as if he'd only been out of short trousers for a couple of weeks. He really was not cut out for flying. But fight hard and well he did to prove it could be done. Here was a real hero who would never be decorated or recognised.

Warren was not an aerial warrior either; he was a gambler. He gambled and invariably won. He was to be respected because he claimed that life itself was a gamble from the moment that one was born. It was very probable he was missing and would eventually turn up with his usual exuberance.

Frobrisher was by inclination a musician who could perform on five musical instruments with great skill and artistry and make his performances appeal to both the highbrow and the lesser inclined. He flew his machines well because of the co-ordination of the mind and limbs he practised with his music. He never got involved in political debates. His musical talents would be a sad loss to the mess.

A group of nurses and medical officers entered the mess and made their way to the bar where a colonel told them to order, and told a steward to put it on his account. Without exception they looked tired and haggard and yet they still managed to smile and joke amongst themselves.

Very occasionally in the narrow focus of the war and its depressing effects of death, the daily destruction and the many disappointments, a ray of hope shone through. Herby compared it to the sudden appearance of a bright, fragrant flower in the midst of a barren field. The older officer who had welcomed him to the mess stood chatting to a nurse.

After a time she turned slowly to look in the direction of the pilot. Her face lit up like a beacon in the dim lighting of the mess. He remembered the first time he held her hand when they were very young. He recalled the time he took her aloft in father's kite and very nearly killed her. He thought of the long letters she sent to him in Canada. There had always been something about her, which he could not clearly define. But now as she glided towards him he knew what it was. She radiated warmth, graciousness, poise, strength of gentleness and a natural ability to put people at their ease.

"Timothy - dear Timothy." she said quietly taking his hand. "After all these years we are destined to meet near a scene of battle."

He looked down at her, not knowing what to say. It might have been easier had they been out of sight of her friends.

Ever the diplomat like her charming parents she quickly took stock of his unease and said: "Come - let me introduce you to my friends. We rarely get a chance to meet an aerial warrior face to face."

Following a number of introductions the colonel invited him to go through with them to dinner. A meal that consisted of potatoes, carrots, cabbage and beef, the latter of which some claimed was horsemeat in disguise. If it was, the pilot noticed nobody complained and cleared their platters clean.

Following a dessert of fresh fruit salad the colonel ordered coffee and passed a box of cigars around the table. Then, he invited the pilot to tell them a little about the war in the air.

WAR PILOT

Herby hesitated at first because he felt his destructive duties ran contrary to the principles of their profession namely the saving and preservation of life. He decided to confine his delivery to the flying aspects of his work. He described for them the splendour of a sky at dawn, and at sunset as witnessed from the heights. He explained what it was like to roll and loop a machine in the unlimited freedom of the air. He told them how insignificant he felt when roaming around the towering, filling mass of a cumulus cloud. He described for them the remoteness one felt when the earth was totally hidden from view by a blanket of cloud. How it made him feel part of another world that, in essence, was more spiritual than mortal and how it seemed to cleanse and revitalise him, and make him humbler for the experience.

"Your description of the flying was most interesting, and well received, Timothy. You made a very big impression." Marie complimented him later as they walked in the grounds of the chateau and he waited for the fender to collect him.

They spoke for a considerable time about recent news from home. In a letter from her mother she was told Molly Langdon had given birth to a baby boy. But he did not connect with it.

They exchanged a little of their personal experiences in the war, some of a serious nature, others of a more light-hearted tone. She swung along beside him an arm linked with his and as they made their third circuit of the grounds they lapsed into reminiscing about their childhood in Hadley.

Near the imminent arrival time of his transport and they drew near the entrance of the chateau he stopped her walking, turned to face her, and took her hands in his. "There is something you should know before I leave, Marie. And having heard it you may want to have nothing more to do with me."

She said considerately, "Parted as we have been all these years, Timothy, I like to think you and I have a special friendship created by the bond of our families."

He said, "The point is that since joining the flying corps I have had intimate relations with two ladies. One of which, a French lady, claimed I was the father of her child."

After a brief silence Marie said calmly, "Regrettably it is a common occurrence in war. People get so desperately lonely. Either the woman left at home, or, the soldiers at the front. I hear the most tragic stories from the casualties who come under my care. It is most distressing."

He put his arms around her and hugged her. "Believe me, Marie. It was not my intention to hurt you. You have every right to disown me and send me on my way."

She reached up and cupped his face in her hands. "Is that what you really want, Timothy?"

He said: "As the offended party the ultimate decision must rest with you."

They both spotted the tender pull into the main gates. Marie said quietly, gently, " I want you to go from here, Timothy, with peace of mind and in the knowledge that your confession has not altered my feelings for you. Perhaps at the end of the war fate will allow us to make good all that we have intended for each other."

War Pilot

SIX

He banked the Camel and swung in from astern of the Fokker. It wavered and grew larger in the rings of the Aldis. Suddenly, and uncontrollably, he vomited and his hand froze on the gun mechanism. He could not bring himself to send another Hun down engulfed in flames. Something prompted him to think what gave him the right to destroy the flying machine and its pilot which looked no more offensive than a butterfly, and represented nothing more than gossamer dressed on tenuous membranes - a pulsing, moving, living thing. Who was he to decide he had license to deprive it of the right to live!

He abandoned the attack. But as he did so a shadow swooped down on his left and let rip with its gun. The Hun spurted, and trailed, black blood and like a bird shot on the wing the machine paused in midair, rolled over, and fluttered earthwards to its grisly fate.

In the following weeks the dilemma confronted him each time he went into battle. He could bring a Hun to the sights of his gun. He could grip the gun handle. But he could not bring himself to pull the trigger.

His salvation came in the form of Bradley, the commanding officer, who summoned him to his office. " I see from the records," he said. "You have been scrapping for over eighteen months without a decent break. It's time you got away from it all for a spell. I'll arrange it with the adjutant. Be prepared to get away first thing in the morning."

The moment Herby stepped ashore at Dover he felt a huge weight lift from his shoulders. For the first time in an age the air tasted fresh and cleansed. And he felt absolutely free. The rain shower that greeted him was of no inconvenience. To the north a few rays of sunshine punctured the base of the low cloud and spotlighted the green rolling hills of England.

Was this, in fact, what he and thousands of others were fighting for - the preservation of one's country, and civilisation as a whole. The way he saw it, it was a battle over the ownership of land which, if the truth were known, did not belong to anyone. It was a gift, as was the world, from a Power above all mortal power. It was a gift to all of mankind to share.

He spent his seven days leave in a quiet country inn near Maidstone; he had a great need for solitude. He wrote many overdue letters. He spent a couple of hours each day meandering along the cliff tops of a neighbouring seashore. He sat for periods of time watching the sea birds display the pure artistry of flight in the sea breezes.

War Pilot

Being wintertime the landlady obligingly lighted a fire in the small hearth of his room. He sat for most of the evenings in the flickering firelight, in idle contemplation and reflection. His father had warned him a couple of days before he left Canada that he would reach a point in the war where much of it would not be to his liking because, by nature, the Herby family were pioneers not warring men. Willy Herby had died in his quest for manned flight. Willy's father had perished whilst pioneering the seas in unproven sailing ships. And Timothy's father had admitted having scruples about killing when he served with the colours.

At the end of his leave his dislike of killing as a war pilot had not left him but being away from it all for seven days had given him a chance to rationalise his thoughts and control his emotions. If he had any reservations about how further combat might affect him, he need not have worried.

On his return to France he got immediate orders to leave the scout squadron and report to another aerodrome which hosted a small unit involved in aerial reconnaissance. It meant flying a slow, unarmed DH9 that was very vulnerable to the fury and superior speed of the Hun scouts. This, however, did not deter him. More importantly the new mode of flying operations spared him from the harrowing responsibility of putting his finger to the trigger of a gun. For company he had Fletcher, an observer, who also did the entire camera work.

Fletcher wrote to his wife: At one time fear was my constant companion. It gripped me like a vice, and blinded me to everything else because my mind was constantly focused on death and the repercussions it would have on you and the children.

Not any longer, my dearest; I have teamed up with a remarkable pilot whose quiet confidence and skillful flying has opened up a whole New World for me. I live with great hopes for the future. I think of all the things that I want to do when the war ends. I have so much planned.

Timothy demonstrates occasionally that there is a lighter side to our earnest responsibilities in the war by indulging in a spot of low flying. We speed over the chequered geography, skimming treetops, dodging the rooftops of dwellings, and chasing the contours of the countryside. What fun!

At other times he takes us high to admire the massive white splendour of the clouds. Then he takes me on a joyride through the ravines and chasms, which mark the folds and creases of these billowing monsters. Everything is crackling and sparkling with sunlight. We inhale the blue serene air and, for precious moments, I feel remote from the war. Such tranquillity! Such peace!

The observer smiled as the pilot coaxed the labouring DH9 over the boundary hedgerows of the aerodrome in the clattering sound of its engine, and they climbed to the heights. Within an hour they broke out on top of the pale light of the dawn. The first fingering rays of the rising sun reached them. The struts and wing wires glistened under a fine layer of frost.

They were detailed for a photo-shoot deep inside Hun territory. They would barely have sufficient fuel to complete the flight back to their aerodrome. The military planners claimed the vital and urgent information they needed warranted the risk. The two airmen had been specially chosen for the job.

They crossed the lines unopposed and moved into Hun country. Five miles - ten - fifteen - twenty - thirty… It seemed too good to be true. Perfect flying weather and yet the enemy machines remained earthbound, as did the shells of the artillery. Fletcher got to work loading and reloading the plates in the camera directly they arrived over the grid references, shooting areas of the earth as detailed by his orders.

They completed the work without interruption and after battling with a headwind for two hours they crossed the lines to friendly terrain. Timothy was never one to show his feelings but Fletcher heaved a sigh of relief and permitted himself to be happy and satisfied with the morning's work. He waved enthusiastically to the pilot of a Camel that swept by on a reciprocal heading. Then he grinned when the Camel made a steep turn and prepared to swoop on the DH9's tail. He decided the scout pilot, as was the wont of many, wanted to indulge in a bit of aerial frolicking. And at first he dismissed the staccato of the Camel's gun as a figment of his imagination. But the truth revealed itself when rounds of ammunition punctured the fabric surfaces of the wings and fuselage, and Timothy threw the DH9 about in an attempt to evade their attacker. Fletcher watched in utter disbelief when the Camel veered away, and came back in a second time.

Timothy shouted over his shoulder. "Make certain your harness is tight."

Fletcher obeyed instantly, shocked and confused as he was. It just did not seem conceivable that a dastardly Hun could roam the skies in British camouflage. Neither could he accept the possibility that it might be a novice RFC pilot who lacked proficiency in aircraft recognition. He sank deeper in his seat and squirmed as the Camel spat another succession of rounds at them.

Two missiles found their mark. The first pierced an engine cover and struck a magneto. The engine roared with pain and lapsed into a train of misfiring till the pilot eased its agony by switching it off. The Camel turned away to the right determined to come back at them again. In the silence of the DH 9's engine Timothy shouted: "Hold on tight. We'll spin out of this one."

Fletcher had heard enough unpleasant tales about spinning to make him feel decidedly queasy. He gripped the sides of the cockpit as the nose lifted to a steep angle and everything went very quiet. He felt poised on the precarious edge of a cliff. Suddenly the machine lurched to the left and rolled. For a glancing moment he was sure the soles of his boots faced the sky. Then the DH9 dropped its nose and they went down in the crazy revolutions of the spin. He closed his eyes and held his breath.

He lost count of the number of times they spiralled. He braved an attempt to open his eyes when he decided it had gone on long enough. He stared incredulously at the view down beyond Timothy's head and shoulders. The earth was not spinning madly in a blur as he had been led to believe in conversations with other airmen. It revolved gracefully between the gap of the top and bottom wing, and he was inclined to describe it as graceful rather than vertiginous.

Timothy arrested the spin close to the ground and settled the machine into gliding flight. "We've lost the engine," he shouted. "We'll have to go to earth."

Fletcher nodded. Anything was better than more molesting by the devious Hun. What Timothy had not told him was a bullet had struck him in the thigh, and blood was flowing freely from the wound.

The pilot knew there was a limit to the duration of his strength. He selected a stretch of open ground, got an indication of the wind direction from smoke issuing from a French home, and glided the machine into a position that would give him surplus height which he could side-slip off if need be. He shouted to the observer and pointed to where he intended to alight.

He crossed the stick and rudder bar on deciding they were a little too high on the approach to the selected open ground. The machine sideslipped earthwards without increasing its speed. It was when he judged to have lost sufficient height and he made to uncross the controls he discovered to his dismay he had lost the use of his wounded leg. A wing struck a tree. The ground came up in a rush. He managed to ease the stick back to prevent the machine from going in nose first. Nonetheless they hit the ground hard in a commotion of buckling metal, splintering, cracking wood and slashing fabric. He felt something solid slide back onto his feet and legs and before any great pain had a chance to attack him he was overwhelmed by a gigantic wave of darkness.

It took Fletcher a number of minutes to collect his thoughts after the machine lurched to a halt. He sat tasting the sweetness of the air, and feeling somewhat relieved at finding their chaotic return to earth had spared him from injury. He noticed a solitary white cloud drifting overhead in a blue sky. Somewhere up there in the glare of the sun a lark sang jubilantly to the world. He unfastened his seat belt, reached over to the front cockpit to give Timothy a congratulatory slap on the back, for his skilful flying, when he noticed the oddness of the pilot's drooping head and, presently, a pool of blood gathering on the cockpit floor.

It took him the best part of two hours to summon help and get the pilot on his way to a military hospital for immediate surgery. It took another three hours for transport to come and collect him and the valuable camera and plates.

"You fail to realise we may have lost everything to that scoundrel of a Camel pilot." he complained bitterly to their CO and a visiting colonel from brigade HQ who appeared to be treating the matter rather too lightly in his opinion.

The colonel said: "The point is, Fletcher, you achieved everything we could have wished for…"

But, sir,"

"There are no ifs and buts about the matter, Fletcher. You did your job admirably, and we are awarding you two weeks leave, and recommending that you be decorated for your gallantry."

The observer could not stop the sudden exhaustion of his fraught emotions. Home leave, and a medal, indeed!

His commanding officer said; "War is not a pleasant business and which you must have considered when you applied for flying duties. And had it not been for the splendid airmanship of captain Herby, your pilot, you might have suffered a more tragic fate."

Fletcher decided it would be pointless to continue his tirade against the Camel pilot. They were determined not to discuss the matter. Suddenly the honour attached to his medal and the prospect of home leave was more important.

The colonel said: "Our next priority is to ensure your pilot gets the best of treatment."

"It'll be the first time I've tackled such intricate surgery in this vital area." major Redstone remarked wearily to the gowned and masked figures surrounding him. "And if he is to have anything of a chance we must work with haste."

The operating team had already worked fourteen hours when they made a start on the airman. They toiled for a further two hours cleaning, repairing and stitching the torn tissues. The round of ammunition from the masquerading Camel had penetrated the airman's thigh and made its exit in the region of his groin. It was well past midnight when they finished. The surgeon saw his patient settled in a ward for the night, and ordered his team to get some rest. From the casualty lists they would need to be back on duty in a matter of hours.

Nurse Hogarth normally fell on her bed engulfed by fatigue after a full day in the operating theatre. On this occasion sleep evaded her; her thoughts revolved around the airman and the appalling nature of his injuries. He drew from her a depth of compassion she had never experienced before.

After a sleepless two hours in the stillness and loneliness of the night she could stand it no longer. She put a cloak around her shoulders, returned to the hospital, and sat by his bedside holding his hand, somewhat confused and unable to bring any sense to her reasoning.

Very gradually it began to occur to her she might be having her first real taste of falling in love. For certain no man had had such an impact on her, and aroused her so intensely. She helped feed him till he could help himself. In her off-duty times she pushed him in a wheelchair for long walks in the hospital grounds. She accompanied him when he made his way about on crutches. And after two or three more weeks he used walking sticks. Eventually he moved unaided.

They came before the small lake in the grounds of the hospital. The lake reflected the blue summer sky and its passage of fluffy, white cloud. In recent days major Redstone had said the airman was making remarkable progress and saw no reason why he should not be discharged. The nurse could not argue; there was a grave shortage of beds. But she grew miserable each time she contemplated how she would cope when he was gone. The heat of the sun on her neck, her arms and legs reminded her she was going to miss him very badly. And when he suggested they walk to the glade on the other side of the lake where they would be out of sight, and able to talk in private, she walked beside him feeling as helpless, and willing, as a young bride.

She cried out as he penetrated deeper. But then there followed after each painful spasm a growing satisfaction. Her whole being was consumed by a desire and an overwhelming demand. She embraced him with her arms and legs. She wanted him more than anything she had wanted in her life before. She kissed and caressed him passionately. She wanted to own his entire nakedness. She wanted him to be part of her. Something told her she was going on a new, untried journey. And when he committed her to his seed her world, in the frenzy of her movements, exploded with joy. She lost count of time; she was only conscious of a blissful peace and fulfillment that totally satisfied the hunger of her being.

It passed from her slowly and she descended effortlessly back into the real world. She lay in the aftermath of the experience with a lingering peace of mind. She knew it had changed her; she had given part of herself away that was not reclaimable. And in an odd kind of way she felt deeply proud of what she had done as a service to mankind.

WAR PILOT

SEVEN

The 11th day of November 1918. The blue green sea of the Solent flecked with white horses slipped almost imperceptibly beneath the wings of the Avro. Overhead the pale sun stared down and provided little warmth. Herby whistled quietly to himself; he was entirely content with his present occupation of teaching men to fly. He had spent several glorious months away from the madness and grim reminders of the war.

The Avro lurched in an untidy flow of air that spilt off the land at the coast. Dickinson, the 26th pupil to come under his wing for training, handled it well. The flat grassland of the aerodrome came to view beneath the nose. His pupil correctly adjusted the power and the machine glided earthwards. They passed over a gathering of houses, crossed the boundary, the stick moved a fraction to check the speed and the throttle was closed. They sank a little faster. Then at the right moment his pupil got the Avro flying parallel to the ground. As it ran out of speed the stick came right back and they fell to ground with a slight jolt and the wheels rumbling loudly through the wood skeleton of the wings and fuselage and their drum-tight fabric coverings.

"Take me back to the take-off point." Herby shouted through the Gosport tube that connected the tandem cockpits

"Very good, sir."

The instructor knew that what he was about to do would surprise his pupil. It always did. But there would be little time for the pupil to dwell on it when he realised what he must be about. Another Avro raced past them, tail up, in preparation for taking to the air. Another floated down over the same stretch they had followed minutes previously. Dickinson throttled back and the Avro halted. Herby released his seat strap, clambered out on the wing and above the noise of the chattering engine shouted: "I think it's time you had a go on your own. All right?"

Dickinson shot him a surprised look through his goggles. His lips broke into a grin and he nodded he understood. Herby said: "Do one circuit and landing. Then come back in"

He jumped from the wing and walked clear. He watched his charge turn the Avro into wind and open out to full revs. It surged away in leaps and bounds and rose steadily, carefully in the air. It flew slowly around the circuit, turned over the sea and headed back. Down it came, its wings wavering in the coastal breezes, levelled out, floated quietly past him and landed rather nicely.

He was back in the flight office, and had two mugs of tea ready by the time Dickinson taxied back and reported in.

"Congratulations." Herby handed him a mug of tea.

Dickinson took the mug with trembling, excited hands. "Thank you, sir. Did I do all right?"

"Not bad." Herby grinned at him. "At least you brought yourself and the machine back in one piece. And that is what I'm supposed to teach you."

Dickinson sipped at his tea. He said, "When may I go again?"

"I suggest you have your lunch. Take a rest and ponder on what you might have leant from your solo flight. Then come back just after two."

Dickinson thanked him and went away to a group of fellow pupils who were waiting to offer him their congratulations.

Herby grinned. That was the great thing about flying training. It was all about difficult, uncertain steps in the process of teaching and learning and then, if one persevered, an immense reward and satisfaction for instructor and pupil alike.

Since the kite experiments at Hadley, with his father, and his own flying training days at Gosport, he had not known happier times. He was in no doubt what he intended to do when he returned to Canada after the war. He walked outside the flight office and scanned the sky to the southwest. He had sent another pupil, Swanson, off on a simple navigation flight around the Isle of Wight. He was due back about now. He spotted the small shape of an Avro low on the horizon, heading for the aerodrome. It grew larger, ignored the regulation height of the aerodrome circuit and raced by. On the other side of the aerodrome it zoomed up in a climbing turn to the right that had he pulled a fraction tighter would have flicked the machine into a spin and for certain have killed him. He joined the downwind leg and pulled another tight turn at low airspeed onto the final approach.

Flying affected men in a variety of ways. It taught some personal discipline. It humbled others. But there was a minority who shortly after going solo became so inebriated by their success they threw away the reins of responsibility and their sense of discipline in the bargain. Swanson was one of the latter. He had been heavy-handed and clumsy in the initial stages of his training. He had not shown to be attentive in the classroom work. He was not a natural when it came to flying. So to prove to others he was up to it he tried to put up some classy flying displays which if allowed to continue would ultimately kill him not to mention the loss of a valuable machine.

As Herby waited for him to taxi in he was joined by Benson, chief flying instructor. "I trust you have thought up something to stop him repeating that sort of performance," he said.

"Indeed. Yes indeed."

Benson mumbled something incoherently and retreated.

Herby waited for Swanson to clamber down from the Avro. "Right, master Swanson. Follow me to the sheds."

Swanson trailed behind him in silence, head bowed. He new something was coming but was not certain what to expect.

In the shed where the machines were overhauled and maintained Herby confronted him with Sergeant Boswell.

"Could you explain to this young man, Sergeant Boswell, how long it takes to construct one of these machines?"

Boswell said: "A considerable time. You see it not just a case of making the many parts to strict dimensions. There's all the glueing and fitting together. Then there's all the rigging checks and engine tests to make certain the aeroplane flies as it should."

"So you could say it takes several weeks?"

"More like months, sir."

"And what do you and the men think when some reckless and inconsiderate airman wrecks one of your machines?"

"We feel it's bit of a shame after all the time that's put in to get it into the air in the first place."

"Are you not angry with the incompetent fool who did it!"

The sergeant chuckled, "We'd skin him alive if we had half the chance."

Herby turned to the red-faced Swanson. "Do I take it you have got the message?"

"You have made your point, sir. I apologise." Swanson said humbly and was acutely aware the whole conversation had been overheard and overlooked by fitters and riggers working on a neighbouring machine.

"Thank you very much sergeant Boswell." Herby ended and led Swanson from the hangar.

In fairness he could not have chastised the boy more harshly; in a matter of weeks he would be risking life and limb in battle, daily.

The mess was bubbling with speculation that the war had ended when he went in for lunch. The peace armistice had been signed at eleven that morning according to the rumour. He ate his lunch and ignored it; he'd heard it all before.

He went aloft with Peterson that afternoon and got him to demonstrate he could fly accurate level turns. Then he closed the throttle and told him to practice a forced landing. Acres of trees and bog slipped beneath the wings. A herd of fallow deer broke cover and sped across the terrain in leaps and bounds. A horse and cart laboured along a narrow track. Smoke curled up from the chimney of a forester's cottage. He was pleased to see Peterson not only checked the wind direction in the process of planning his forced landing but he also recognised firm ground, as opposed to a boggy surface, on which to land the machine. He had the makings of a good pilot.

They returned to Gosport in time for the instructor to brief Dickinson and send him off to do an hour's circuits and landings. He grinned knowingly as the young Dickinson strode proudly out to his machine.

He took Swanson up for just under an hour and went through the motions of teaching him a stall-turn, a loop and a roll. He regarded the lesson as something of a treat and a compensation for the humiliation that he had subjected the boy to in front of the troops regarding his bad airmanship. Swanson, however, did not take to the aerobatics with the enthusiasm he had for his low flying over the aerodrome. In the dying afternoon light the earth and sky rose and fell about them to the accompaniment of the rising and fading note of the engine. Herby made sure that each pupil who passed through his hands could perform the manoeuvres competently before they went off to the operational squadrons.

They landed in the last shreds of daylight. He had a short discussion with Swanson about the flight. Then dismissed him, and settled in the instructor's domain to complete his chores for the day: reports on the progress of his pupils, and some notes on what he intended to teach them on their next lesson.

WAR PILOT

Toby Hudson came and sat down beside him, and lighted his pipe. "I hope we are not doing this for nothing, Timothy. It's official, they say. The war ended at eleven this morning."

Herby stared into space. It was difficult to digest in one gulp. It seemed the war was destined to go on forever. He laughed, "I'll believe it, Toby, when I get my marching orders." He turned to Toby. "What do you intend to do?"

"I won't go on flying. That's for sure. I would like to get hold of about five acres and set up a market garden. I've been doing what I want for the past five years. It's only fair I let my wife do something of her choice for a change. She comes from farming people, you know. What do you intend to do?"

"Return to Canada after a spell in my old home near Oxford."

They spent a few minutes on their paperwork before Toby said: "By the way a DH9 arrived whilst you were up this afternoon. And the observer, a fellow named Fletcher, was asking after you."

Herby met Fletcher in the mess at dinner. There was so much excited chatter around them, concerning the ending of the war they found it impossible to hold a decent conversation. At the end of the meal they took a stroll together up on the aerodrome. Overhead a vast array of stars mounted vigil on the night sky. And they both agreed they couldn't remember last when the air tasted and smelt so clean and fresh. Fletcher rambled for a time about their flying exploits in France. He also commented on the absence of the medal ribbon from the pilot's uniform.

"I never wear it," the pilot said. "Because there are far too many gallant and courageous dead men who are much more deserving than me."

"The trouble with you Timothy is that you are too modest and hide your light under a bushel. Many say you could have been a Brigadier, or I should say a, Wing Commander by now if you had pushed harder."

The pilot laughed, "Evidently the same was said of my father when he served with the colours in the African campaigns. You see the Herby family, throughout its history, have shown themselves to be pioneers rather than warriors. My father warned me before I left Canada that the carnage and destruction of war would possibly affect me. A war that is invariably started as a squabble between politicians - not started by the likes of you and me.

In recent months it often crossed my mind what the politicians would do in each country if the man in the street, in each country, refused to take up arms."

Fletcher changed the subject and said: "Did you keep in touch with the hospital after your discharge?"

"Only inasmuch I wrote a letter to express my thanks for all they did for me. And I subsequently answered a questionnaire, sent by Redstone, the surgeon, regarding the success of his surgery on me."

So you never wrote to the nurse you told me about in a letter you wrote when you were recuperating. What was her name?"

"I expect you are referring to nurse Hogarth."

"That's right."

"I asked Redstone to convey my thanks when I returned the questionnaire. Nothing else."

Fletcher stopped walking. "Whether it is of interest to you, or not, Timothy, the story goes that nurse Hogarth was kicked out of the VADs for conceiving a child out of wedlock, and compounded her disgrace by refusing to suggest who the father of the child might be."

In the privacy of the darkness the moments he had shared with Charlotte floated from the pilot's memory. He relived the day when a young radiant flower invited him to engage in intercourse and pierce the tissue that separated her from true womanhood.

He recalled the evening he received news of his pending discharge from the hospital. He went to her quarters under the cover of darkness since regulations forbid such visits.

"I have come to say farewell. My transport leaves at dawn."

Charlotte smiled, "Won't you come in?"

"Do you think it wise?"

She reached for his arm and drew him in. "I don't think anyone will care very much," she said. "They are either too tired or have other pressing matters on their mind."

A cheerful flickering fire heated a kettle of water. An oil lamp cast its light across a table on which a letter had been started. A mature couple, most probably her parents, looked out from a framed photograph nearby.

She showed him to a worn leather chair. "I overheard at dinner that you might be leaving. Are you going home?"

He said: "I am to report to the war office for a medical. The results of which, I suspect, will determine what I do, and where I go next."

She knelt down before his chair and held his hands. Hesitantly and rather self-consciously she said: "Do you despise me for what happened down by the lake?"

He looked sympathetically at her. "Why should I despise you, Charlotte?"

"Because I yielded to you so eagerly."

He got up from the chair and lifted her at the same time in his arms. "I have no regrets. Do you?"

She leant her head against his chest. "My only regret is it has to end." she sighed. "Your fruits went beyond my wildest dreams. What is more I yearn for more."

Fletcher interrupted at this point and said: "No matter how you look at it the girl is in quite a pickle. Abandoned by the VADs, disowned, so I'm told, by her parents, and mother to a bastard child."

Lady Hadley had convened the meeting of the village council to discuss the ending of the war. There was much to be done if the village was to adjust to the renewal and continuity of peacetime conditions. Employment, education and welfare figured largely on the agenda. But what concerned lady Hadley, and what she thought many others had not taken into account, was the great number of men the village had lost to the war. Of two hundred and thirty who went to war the latest figures revealed that only fifty-three had survived.

The meeting progressed slowly. Miss Brighstone, village nurse and midwife, informed the meeting that a number of families were in urgent need of a good, nourishing meal. Others needed clothing but were too proud to ask. Doris Cathaite, who had lost a husband and two sons in the war, was living below the poverty line. Doctor Rainbridge confirmed he had been refused access to her home to check on the welfare of her other five children. The reverend Peach claimed he, too, had been turned away at the door.

"Then you must use force, and consider it as a case of being cruel to be kind to the five neglected children." Lady Hadley told them.

Miss Featherbed, headmistress of the village school, complained she was desperately short of writing materials. Lady Hadley promised to give the matter her immediate attention after the meeting. Then she moved the meeting on to the subject of employment.

The Reverend Peach, who had volunteered to investigate the situation before the meeting, informed the meeting the automobile factory that had changed to aircraft production for the war was very likely to revert back to building automobiles. But he had it on very good authority that the number of employees required would be very limited. He therefore thought the meeting should concentrate the returning warriors on agriculture work on the basis that they could live without automobiles but certainly could not live without food.

The idea was well received. The chair moved the meeting on to any other business. There were no offers so Lady Hadley seized the opportunity she had been waiting for. She paused to collect her thoughts and steel her nerves. Pale rays of afternoon sunlight angled through the French doors and glanced upon the stained and varnished wooden flooring which marked the surrounds of the drawing room carpet.

"The matter I am about to raise," she said. "May strike you all as very controversial and unethical. The truth is we have so few men left in the village to find work for. Our real dilemma is how are we to re-populate the village when so many of our men perished in the war. How, also, are we to satisfy the needs of the womenfolk in their pursuit of marriage and family life when they greatly outnumber the men folk.

We could, of course, allow our young women to venture further afield to find a husband. But with huge numbers of young men killed in the war the prospects for the women would be little different than those facing them here in the village." She paused to prepare herself for the final thrust of her delicately poised proposal.

Doctor Rainbridge said: "I think our young women would fare better amongst friends."

Miss Brighstone said a little scornfully, "It does not answer how we are to replace the young village men we lost in the war."

Lady Hadley said: "I hope all of you will draw comfort from what I am about to propose is that it would only be of a temporary nature. I suggest our returning warriors take it upon themselves to serve as a husband for more than one woman. Possibly serve three or four women. And by so doing it would quickly re-stock the numbers lost to the war."

Six faces looked at her in stunned silence - six accusing expressions - six condemning minds.

Miss Brighstone said: "Our first priority must be on the health of the surviving warriors. Tired, unwell men do not produce healthy children."

"Here - here." acknowledged Horace Thrift, bank manager, and father to three attractive daughters.

"The point is," doctor Rainbridge said. "If we allow our young men and women to get mixed up in this sort of impropriety we could find ourselves behind bars."

Four heads nodded solemnly in agreement.

Lady Hadley motioned to Bessy Hartington who represented the village women's institute. Bessy said slowly, "At the moment there is a general air of gloom and despondency amongst the womenfolk. What with those who have lost a husband or child on the battlefield, and those who have worked long hours in the fields or factory, they are generally at a low ebb. Therefore it is most likely that the comfort of a man, shared as it is suggested, and the thought of bearing a child, would help to give them fresh hopes for the future."

Loud murmurs of dissent filled the room. Lady Hadley wisely detected the strength of the opposition, and made a tactical retreat by drawing the meeting to a close. After the customary tea and biscuits, during which she felt a tension and hostility she had never experienced before, the committee members departed, deep in thought, and certain members shocked to the core.

She collected the dogs and took them through the stable yard to the orchard. She was losing the vitality and inclination of her earlier years. At one time the petty squabbles and differences of opinion with the village committee were of little consequence. But since the war began it irritated and unsettled her. She had come to yearn more and more for the seclusion of a small country cottage and the chance to put a brush and oils to canvas. She had tried too long to run local affairs alone. She had thought it possible when the squire was alive. When he died she realised how loyal and compassionate a husband he had been and, what was more, a valuable and prudent counselor when it came to making important decisions about the estate and the village.

The dogs led her from the orchard into the paddock. She came here often to be alone with her thoughts and to dwell on some precious memories of her past. She heard the spiritual gushing of wind on calico, and the whistling of the wing wires and struts as they cut the air. In the mind's eye she saw a shadow fall to earth. She heard the rumbling of the wheels and the drumming sound of the wings as the kite rolled along the paddock. Samuel Herby smiled down at her, dressed in the hat she had presented to him for his flying experiments. She greatly admired his courage and strength of character, and the manner in which he accepted his achievements with modesty. He had done what no other man had done before. He had proved that manned flight was possible.

She relived the gentleness of his voice. She saw gypsy faces in the light of a campfire. She heard the music of an accordion and fiddle. She tasted country wine. Starlight companions of the night. Then that supreme and unforgettable moment when they made love on the riverbank in the dawning day and their bodies were cleansed by a gathering of fresh, sparkling summer morning dew.

The youth of yesteryears, she sighed. Gone, unreclaimable, unforgotten and secreted in a closet of the mind. Faded as an aged painting, but priceless as a gem. She called the dogs to heel and headed back for the manor. In the yard she found Molly Langdon busy grooming a horse.

"By the way, Molly, Timothy Herby will be arriving in a few days. You might arrange to open, and air, the cottage for him. Tell me if you should need anything."

There was a time when the mention of his name made Molly's heart flutter. Not any more. In recent months Lady Hadley had introduced her to Horace Chase, a country solicitor, twelve years her senior and whose short, podgy looks did not do him justice. Nature had compensated him for his stature by providing him with an abundant handsomeness below his waistline, and a reserve of stamina that would put many a younger man to shame.

Her relationship with Horace had been subject to a lot of gossip in the village. People, who had been her friends and neighbours, in the street where she lived before her parents died, now scorned and shunned her. Some branded her a snob when she moved up to the manor to live. And because there had never been any official announcement about the child she gave birth to, a small vicious group in the village regarded her as a loose woman and branded her as the village mare.

The truth was, she genuinely loved and respected Horace and it hurt her when the village gossips dragged his name through the mud as well. How often she wished she and Horace lived elsewhere. She'd do anything to get away from the wagging tongues. She could not bring herself to tell him of her anxiety; he had come from the city to set up a country law practise and, after five years of struggling, he was beginning to make a success of it.

The matter occupied her thoughts again that evening as she sat before the dressing table mirror combing and brushing her long fair hair. The clanking of his motorised carriage as it turned into the entrance to the manor interrupted the stillness. Her pulse quickened. She hurriedly placed an evening wrap around her shoulders, and moved downstairs.

He kissed her hand in greeting and she patted his hand in appreciation of his gentlemanly gesture. He beamed at her, set the ignition and gear, and she lurched as the carriage jerked forward and got under way.

It took an hour to reach Oxford a journey that did not share the comfort of riding in a saddle or between the shafts of a horse-drawn carriage. Nevertheless Mollie enjoyed the status of the motor carriage. She enjoyed being seen in it with Horace. He told her the next one he purchased would be less noisy and have many refinements. They went to their usual roadhouse: a cosy, intimate establishment that catered exclusively for the wealthy and influential members of society. It was said members of parliament and the royal family frequented the place.

Horace led her to a corner alcove where they could speak freely and without being overheard. Mollie was delighted at the way Horace treated the waitresses. He spoke to them politely and never made them feel inferior. He gave a girl their order and she retreated.

He turned to Mollie and reached across the table and took her hand. "Happy?"

"Very. Thank you, Horace."

He said quietly, "It may come as a big surprise to you, Mollie. But I have made plans to leave Hadley."

Her happiness melted instantly. "You can't do that Horace!" she blurted out. "You said the law practise was picking up." She looked at him horror-stricken. "Or are you leaving because it is something I have said, or done, to embarrass you." She fought hard against a strong temptation to weep. For the first time in her life she had found a man she thought she could rely on. A man, she had convinced herself, she could cheerfully serve for the rest of her days.

Horace smoothed her trembling hand. He said, "Family tradition steered me into the law profession. But ever since I was a small boy I wanted to work on the land. My late parents may turn in their grave when they learn what I intend to do. I have purchased a farm in the west country." he squeezed her hand and beamed at her. "I would like you to become my wife and help me run it."

Her emotions exploded in a mixture of joy and relief.

"Don't you realise, Horace." she trembled. "You'd be taking on more than a farm. You'd be taking on my poor background and my illegitimate son, Peter."

He said gently, "You have never tried to hide anything from me. Mollie, and for which I respect you highly. As far as I am concerned the past is the past. The future looks far more important and exciting. Combine the circumstances in which you were brought up, and the easy life I have led, I think there is a great deal we could teach each other."

Mollie took out a small handkerchief, dabbed at the moisture in her eyes, and blew her nose rather loudly. "I just can't believe it, Horace. It's something I've wanted for a very long time."

"I will not press you for an answer this evening." he said. "Think it over for a couple of days before you make a final decision."

She said: "If I decided not to go with you - would you still go ahead with the farm?"

He said: "That would indicate you are not in love with me. In which case it would be pointless for me to hang around Hadley knowing that I no longer served a purpose in your life."

She smoothed his hand. "I was not trying to hurt you when I asked you that, Horace. I wanted to know how determined you are to take on the farm. You see, if for any reason the farm didn't make good, the village gossips here would blame me for making you leave a successful legal business."

He said boldly: "It will not fail. You and I will make certain of that."

The food was served and they ate in silence. Mollie thought of what the farm would mean to her. It had long been a cherished ambition to live the life of a country lady. She had no wish to hold power or dominate people of lesser rank. She only wanted to dress and behave as a lady should, and for her son to avoid the strife of her own childhood.

Horace knew the labour on the farm would entail him getting his hands soiled, and working longer hours. He would toil, he would sweat he would be in daily contact with the odours of the animals. Above all, each night, he would have the luscious orchard of Mollie to feast upon.

They got back to the manor before midnight. He braked the carriage near the entrance gates for them to exchange their farewell; it avoided having to stop the engine whereas if they stopped near the door entrance it would have meant turning the engine off, because of its noise, and then having to clamber out and re-crank it.

"Thank you for such a lovely evening, Horace. I promise to give you an answer soon."

He gave her an affectionate grip with an arm. "That's why I brought you straight home," he said. "You need a clear head for such important decisions."

Mollie smiled in the darkness; if they had gone to his cottage, which they usually did, it would have taken her three or four days to think straight; Horace was a powerful and comprehensive seducer whose passionate antics appealed to her savage, primitive instincts.

Despite its distance from the manor Lady Hadley heard the carriage stop at the gates. Then pull away a short while later. Motor carriages were incredibly noisy beasts. She visualised Mollie walking up the drive, mounting the steps to the main entrance, letting herself in, treading quietly through the hall, and climbing the stairs to her room. Something told her it was a blissfully happy Mollie.

She reverted back to the papers on the desk before her. The farm accounts confirmed the War Office owed a considerable sum for produce used to feed the troops, and some hundred and eighty three horses the estate had bred for military service. She would instruct Horace Chase to write for the monies owed to her. It would go some way to placate the Bank who was expressing their concern at the volume of finance that she had borrowed.

She put the file aside and inspected another. The railway authority was behind with their dues. She allowed the line to pass through the estate on condition she was paid a levy. The factory built on her land to the west of the village paid her a rent. So looking at it from all angles she was far from being insolvent.

She moved on to the farm production reports. The beef and mutton returns were reasonable. The arable was marginal. The milk yield was down. She made a note to discuss it with Benson, her farm manager.

She had completed the paperwork, rehearsed her conversation with the Bank for the forthcoming meeting and was on the point of retiring for the night when gentle tapping on the study door heralded the presence of Samantha who put her head around the door and said: "Am I intruding, mother?"

"Not at all, my dear. Come along in."

Samantha closed the door and came and stood before her on the other side of the desk. "There is something I'd like to discuss with you, mother, which you may find rather embarrassing."

Claire smiled and invited her to be seated. "Have I not told you since you were a girl that you must feel free to discuss your doubts and anxieties with me. What else is a mother for."

Samantha blinked at her. "This is a very delicate and sensitive matter, mother. It concerns my origins."

Claire had a shrewd idea of what was coming. It was premature perhaps. But typical of fate to take a sudden change of course.

"Whatever it is - is troubling you, young lady. So stop beating about the bush and get it off your mind."

"Well it is like this: Over the years I have overheard several villagers and staff in the manor, remark that I look and behave more like a Herby than a Hadley. And since Timothy visited us tongues have constantly wagged about how alike him and I are. I really don't know what to believe."

Claire smiled sympathetically at her and reached for her hands. "The truth is, my dear, I badly wanted to have a child. But however hard the late squire and I tried it never happened. So the squire, out of his love for me, contracted Samuel Herby, Timothy's father, to give me a child and make my wish come true. We had to be discreet of course to preserve the squire's family name and reputation. But I assure you there was nothing sinister or devious about it." She paused. "You, my dear, are the product of that liaison between me and Samuel Herby. I had planned to tell you prior to your coming-of - age ball."

Samantha faced her in silence, the hint of a smile on her lips, a trace of moisture in her eyes. Claire moved round the desk and embraced her.

"I hope the revelation is not too painful for you. Perhaps tomorrow we should take the pony and trap up on the hills, just the two of us, and I can tell you the whole story."

The moisture became a trickle of tears and Samantha said: "Yes. I would like that very much, mother."

EIGHT

He felt the rocking hand of the Batman on his shoulder. Figures stirred about him in the flickering light of an oil lamp. Sleepy, unwashed faces. Faces pale and pinched by a boisterous evening in the mess. Tired faces aged and lined by living in fear of the unknown. Vacant eyes in sunken sockets. Trembling hands. Gnawed fingernails.

Tread heavily to the flights after a tasteless breakfast feeling hollow, empty. A brief chat with the troops about the fitness of the machine. Contact! The rotary engine provokes the stillness of the dawn. The threshing propeller sends back blasts of icy air, a chilling reminder of the work that lies ahead.

Full power! Man and machine lurch and bound along upon a white, frosted grass till gravity, tired of its fight, releases them to the heights: a murderous swarm let loose.

Shrieking wires in a dive. Pressures on the head and the heaviness of the legs when pulling out of a dive or hauling into a tight turn. A wounded Camel trails torn, ragged fabric. A Fokker rears up streaming smoke, falls over, and goes down in a spin.

He sees a sea of faces of the men he lived and fought with. Numerous have disappeared over the years. He remembers only a few by name. So many have come and gone to the savage hunger of the war machine. Nightfall brings a brief respite from the warring activities of the day. Though reminders of the war are not far away. The blackness of the night is constantly raped by the flashing and booming of the heavy guns, which make the earth tremble and shudder with the nervousness of a volcano threatening to erupt.

A mighty crash awakened him and he found himself looking up at the dark ceiling of the room; it was his third night in the cottage since his discharge from the flying corps. He had not realised just how much the war had affected him.

He moved from the bed and stood before a window of the room. Up before him an invisible jeweler displayed his gems on the dark velvet cushion of the night sky. Instinctively he looked toward the horizon expecting to see the flash, and hear the shriek of the next shell. Instead, in his mind, he heard the familiar chatter of a rotary engine. He caught the vapours of castor oil, doped fabric and the personal odours of sweat-stained fur and leather. His mind released mental photographs of Riddlestone, Rogers, Harrison, James, Cochran - McFarlen, young innocent faces, fresh to the squadron, quickly paled by the rigours of their aerial employment. Withered flowers of youth, consumed by a decay that is as devastating and rampart as blight. A nation's backbone prematurely sapped, weakened and destroyed. The insanity of it all.

> Who killed a Fokker,
> I said the Camel with my gun and trammel,
> I killed a Fokker.

> Rumpty Bumpty had a big fall,
> His wings burnt off till he had none at all,
> Along came a Fokker and plonked down beside him,
> And frightened Mr Camel away.

He washed and dressed, and sat in father's old rocking chair by the hearth, smoking his pipe and with a mug of tea to hand. His thoughts gradually drifted away from the war and he began to think about the private dinner he had had with Lady Hadley the previous evening, and during which she told him of the proposal she had put to the village council, regarding how the community might replace the large numbers of men they had lost in the war.

"I am sure you would participate if you were invited Timothy. Would you not?"

He said: "I would asked to be excused, since I am already guilty of sewing too many indiscriminate seeds."

"But, Timothy," she pleaded. "the village is in urgent need of your type of stock if it is to produce a strong, healthy generation for the future."

He said: "You told me earlier that Molly claims I am the father of her child. There were other women. Two more in fact. A French girl and a nurse from the VADs."

"Timothy Herby!" she declared. "Your mother would have a blue-vinegar fit."

He rested his hands on the arms of the chair and looked her straight in the eye. "I did feel a measure of guilt at one time. Now, however, I draw comfort from the fact my giving of life has compensated, in part, for the lives of the German airmen I took in battle." He paused. "You may like to consider accepting my children and their mothers into the village community as my contribution to your re-stocking programme."

Lady Hadley said: "Can you imagine how Marie's mother would react if I tell her of your connections with these women and children."

He said: "I'm sure she would be no more shocked than if you suggested I share a bed with women other than her daughter. My image in the eyes of the community is not important. The least I can do is try and provide these women and children with some form of security for the future."

Lady Hadley eyed him with a smile. "Well, you can dismiss Molly from your considerations. She is engaged to be married to a wealthy solicitor who has purchased a farm in the west country. They move there within the month. And as for your other lady friends and their offspring you should first ascertain that they would like to live here. And, secondly, what contribution they could make to the community. If they possess certain skills and talents it would help my case when I recommend them to the council."

Heavy rapping of the door knocker of the cottage immediately dispelled his recollections of the dinner and the conversation.

"Good morning, Timothy." Samantha greeted him brightly at the door "Mother suggested we take a brisk morning ride. Then for you to join us at the manor for breakfast."

He changed into boots, cap and sweater, and went with her up on the downs. They raced one another and generally had fun. The fresh air and exercise did much to tame the restlessness of his last three nights. And he got to know her better. It amused him to discover her speech and manners were very reminiscent of father as was her way of handling a horse.

They reined in on the way to the manor to allow the horses to cool. Riding alongside him she looked across and said: "I am pleased mother suggested we ride together, Timothy."

He grinned back at her. "You think she had a reason for doing so?"

"I'm not sure. I've been told you intend to return to Canada, and I would like to talk to you, confidentially, before you depart."

"Go on."

"Due to local gossip I have suspected for many years that I am related to the Herby family. And in recent weeks I prised the truth from my mother. The point is I would like to make contact with my father. Is it possible you could assist me?"

He reined his horse to a halt and she did likewise. "Whatever is done must be done with discretion." he said. "Otherwise it might offend my mother."

"Is she not aware of my existence?"

"Quite to the contrary. It would be like opening up a painful old wound," he said gently.

"I have no desire to hurt anyone, Timothy."

He paused for a moment. "I think it would be prudent of me to inform father of your wishes when I arrive back in Canada. Then he can decide on the next move."

She said: "Would it be possible to take a letter to him from me?"

He nodded. "I'll deliver it to him personally at the Govenor General's office. You may, also, like to include a snapshot of yourself."

They moved the horses on and spoke no more until they arrived at the main entrance to the manor.

Samantha said: "Whatever people say, or think, about the circumstances of my birth I feel a great pride at my links with the Herby family."

He laughed across at her." That being so I'm sure father would be interested to know what you have in mind for the future."

"I decided on that a long time ago." she smiled. "Mother insists, however, I wait until I come of age. I intend to maintain the tradition of the Herby family and take to the air."

Her revelation, and knowing how much it would mean to father, spurred him to get his affairs in order before returning to Canada. He travelled to France to invite Michelle to live in Hadley with their child. He made the crossing of the English channel at night, in stormy conditions, and in a ship that was crammed to capacity, and rife with sea-sickness. The train journey that followed was equally uncomfortable; the railways had not yet recovered from the disarray of war.

His journey was a wasted one. Michelle's mother greeted him warmly and told him her daughter now resided in Sussex with a disabled army officer.

He arrived at the address four days later where he met with a hostile reception. "You have brought nothing but shame to my family." she stormed at him. "Get out of my life you irresponsible dog. And stay out! You are not worthy of being called an officer and gentleman." And in a final wave of fury she slammed the door shut in his face.

He was in London a week later drawing up his papers for the return to Canada with a provision for Marie to accompany him. He was told he would get a sailing date within eight to ten weeks.

After midday he took a cab across the city to the War Office records department to enquire after the whereabouts of Charlotte Hogarth. His inquiry proved difficult at first; rules and regulations forbid such personal information being passed to casual callers.

To add weight to his inquiry he said, "I am requesting this information on behalf of Lady Hadley of Hadley manor."

The clerk disappeared into an adjoining room. Presently a woman officer came to the counter and directed him to a screened cubicle.

"What actually is your interest in nurse Hogarth?" she said sternly.

He said: "Nurse Hogarth cared for me after some intricate surgery. And I never had the chance to thank her."

"With respect you told the clerk you are acting on behalf of Lady Hadley."

"A colleague told me nurse Hogarth had fallen on hard times. I told Lady Hadley, who is a close friend of my family , and she offered help for nurse Hogarth."

The eyes of the woman officer held him critically. "Did your informant also tell you Hogarth was given a dishonorable discharge from the VADs, that she has also been disowned by her parents, and that some cad has literally left her holding the baby. I don't mind telling you I have nothing but respect for the misfortunes of woman, and nothing but contempt for the weaknesses of men."

He waited for her to simmer down and to stop fidgeting irritably with the papers on the desk before her.

He said: "Nurse Hogarth's misfortunes are regrettable. However I do feel her future should have the priority of our time. That is why I am here."

The woman sighed heavily, "The Benevolent fund has done a little to ease her plight. But the poor girl is living in appalling accommodation with her infant, and is very short of some essentials. It puzzles me as to why she is so stubborn and refuses to name the father."

"Could it be that such stubborn qualities helped us win the war." he suggested.

"Perhaps it was." she managed a smile, scribbled an address on a slip of paper and handed it to him. "Be warned it is in a poverty-stricken area of the city."

He took a cab to a main street near the address, and made his way on foot through a number of backstreets and alleyways. The scene was far from that of a nation, which had been victorious in war. Haggard figures sat listlessly on the doorsteps of their drab homes. Inquisitive eyes watched his every move from behind tattered curtains. Two small boys came and begged money from him. It was not surprising why politicians of the socialist brand argued so vehemently with their opposite numbers on the issues of social deprivation and inequality. It was no wonder why certain government officials attempted to sweep it under the carpet and pretend it did not exist. It made for depressing and embarrassing viewing.

He came upon the address amongst a huddle of terraced dwellings. The door opened to a lean, untidy woman who sucked a smouldering cigarette.

"And who might you be?" she said coarsely.

"I'm Timothy Herby. I'm here to visit Miss Hogarth."

The woman looked him up and down. "The lady don't get many visitors. So I'd better go and find out if she wants to see you. What's yer name again?"

He told her and she went inside shutting the door in his face. He stood waiting, conscious of a small group of people who had gathered across the other side of the street.

The woman returned, invited him in, and led him up several stairs and landings. The air reeked of dry, dusty floorboards, unwashed bodies and wet distemper. On some of the landings the wall paper was being pushed from the walls by a profusion of damp.

The woman pointed to a door, "You'll find her in there. But I warn you - don't give her any trouble. She's a good woman whose fallen on hard times."

He waited for her to head back downstairs and hesitated before he tapped the door with his knuckles; he had not forgotten the reception he got from Michelle. He need not have worried.

The warmth and serenity of Charlotte's smile in greeting dissolved any misgivings he had. She received him with open arms and they stood embracing each other for several minutes.

"I have much to answer for after reducing you to these miserable circumstances." he apologised.

She eased away from him, her hands still in his, and beamed up at him. "There is no need to reproach yourself, Timothy. Come - let me take your coat."

She prodded the coal fire into flame, and settled a kettle of water on the heat, and invited him to her bedside where an infant slept peacefully in a cradle. "She is such a good child." Charlotte said. "Always happy and contented."

He said: "She cost you a dishonourable discharge from the VADs. Made your parents disown you. Then reduced you to living in this inferior place."

Charlotte said: "You forget our Saviour was born in a humble stable, Timothy. He came to no harm. Believe me, we have much to be thankful for. We have sufficient food and clothing. We have a roof over our heads. And I have a daughter who is a constant source of joy." She turned to him. "It is of no importance what my nursing superiors think of my behaviour. Or my parents for that matter. As far as I am concerned, my child comes first. It is the first duty of any caring and responsible mother."

Over the tea later he said: "You will not be able stay here for many months. The child's needs will become more demanding as it grows."

She shrugged his suggestion off with a smile. "I will cross that bridge when I come to it," she said. "What is more, Timothy, I want you to understand I do not hold you responsible for what happened. I am as much to blame, and I confess I do not have a single regret." She paused and heaved a sigh. "I saw so much pain, suffering and death as a nurse, I often thought I was doomed to see nothing else. The intimacy I shared with you, and the arrival of our daughter, a wholesome, healthy, lively human-being, kindly rid me of that terrible prospect. Motherhood has given me a new lease of life and I shall be eternally grateful."

He said humbly, "Do you realise that by reciprocating my passion you proved I was capable of producing an offspring after that intricate surgery by

Redstone, the army surgeon."

"So, there you are, "she said cheerfully. "What happened was a blessing in more ways than one."

He said: "It is not, however, an excuse for you to stay on here. I am inviting you to come and live in Hadley where you and the child will be well accommodated and enjoy a standard of living to which you have been accustomed. I should also like to get you and your parents on speaking terms."

She said: "In France you told me you intended to return to Canada when the war came to an end. On that basis, and being an unattached lady, if I did accept your invitation I would insist on working in Hadley to support my child and myself."

He said: "Your experience as a nurse would be of enormous value to the village. What with the poor families, and the warriors returning with their handicaps, I am sure you will be kept busy."

He scribbled the address of the cottage on a slip of paper. "Write to me as soon as it is convenient for you to move. And I will arrange for you to be collected. Now, perhaps, you will furnish me with the address of your parents."

The detached residence stood in the suburbs of Surrey amongst properties owned by a head master, a doctor, a banker and members of the stock exchange. The affluence of the area was a far cry from what Charlotte currently enjoyed. Her mother came to the door challenging him with an expression that blended aloofness with superiority. Behind her a man lingered, stern-faced and whose bristling moustache suggested he could be quick to anger.

"Mr and Mrs Hogarth?"

"Yes." the woman said frostily.

Herby introduced himself and added, "Would it be possible to step inside, and talk to you about your daughter, Charlotte?"

"Are you from the welfare?" Mrs Hogarth demanded.

"No."

"Then, what are you doing here?"

"It is not a subject I would like to discuss on the doorstep of your home."

She edged the man backwards. "You may come in. But be assured we are not really interested in Charlotte. She has let me and her father down very badly."

They did not invite him to be seated or offer to take his hat and coat.

"What is it we should know about our daughter?" the woman said.

"First things first." her husband interrupted. "What actually is your connection with our daughter, Mr Herby?"

The pilot said: "I was seriously injured as a result of a flying accident and Charlotte, amongst others, nursed me back to a full recovery. I think you should know she was very dedicated and very professional in her work."

"But not, by all accounts," Mr Hogarth maintained. "Professional in her personal conduct. She conceived a child out of wedlock, disgraced the VADs and never considered for one moment the scandal and shame it would bring to the family name. As far as I am concerned it was a stupid and unforgivable mistake."

Herby tossed the question casually at him. "Have you ever fought in a war, Mr Hogarth?"

Hogarth recoiled heavily from the challenge of the question. After a very long pause he said hesitantly, "I can't say that I have."

"War, Mr Hogarth, could be described as the ugliest of all evils. It confronts the individual with any number of situations, which do not exist in times of peace. Charlotte was not the only victim of the circumstances in which she became entangled. There were many more like her, fine, young women, as were many fine young men, caught up in a catastrophe not of their making. And until you have personally undergone the experiences you will never understand why the principles and morals of the individual go astray.

I suspect there are many families facing the same dilemma as you and Mrs Hogarth. Therefore you should not feel alone in what I regard as a tragedy rather than a stigma."

Mrs Hogarth said: "I think Mr Herby has given us something to think about, Henry." She led the pilot through the sitting room, showed him to a chair, and invited him to join them for tea and biscuits.

When she went off to make preparations the pilot told her husband some truths about the war. He told him about the charmed life he had led in the air compared to the troops who fought the battle on the ground and lived in trenches knee-deep in mud and water. They were gassed. They lost hundreds of friends in a single day. They were short of food. They suffered a great loneliness at being parted from their families. At all times a stubborn and relentless enemy - the Hun - confronted them.

When Mrs Hogarth returned and served the light refreshment the pilot described the constant train of wounded arriving at the casualty stations and hospitals. Where the surgeons, doctors, orderlies and nurses, like Charlotte, had to contend with horrific wounds under the most trying conditions, forever short of medical supplies and equipment, and suffering from lack of sleep. And yet throughout they remained calm and cheerful, no matter what the odds were.

He drew the couple closer to him, particularly Mrs Hogarth, when he told them of his visit to Charlotte. Mother and baby were doing well. But their accommodation left a lot to be desired, he said. And that Charlotte had chosen Helen as a name for her daughter.

Mrs Hogarth's eyes lit up. "That's my Christian name, Mr Herby." she declared proudly. And to crown the success of his visit she requested the address of Charlotte's abode, before he left.

WAR PILOT

NINE

Long strings of flags and a large, WELCOME HOME banner billowed in the thrust and bite of a bitterly cold wind. A crowd of people huddled together in groups around the railway halt at Hadley. Warriors of a past generation stood poised with their musical instruments.

The last of the villagers to survive military service in the war were expected home on the afternoon train. The train was already twenty minutes late. Lady Hadley instructed her chauffeur to distribute thimbles of cognac amongst the groups, and suggested the band play music to distract the gathering's minds from the increasing grip of the chilled air.

The musicians had performed for several minutes when a ticket clerk came and announced the train was approaching. The village council took their places at the end of a long red carpet. Relatives and friends of the men and women, returning from the war, filed through the small ticket hall and congregated as a mass on the inadequately sized platform. They waited with great excitement and eager anticipation as the seething monster of a train clanked by them and drew the screeching carriages to a halt next to the platform.

Carriage doors swung open against the pressing crowd. Uniformed figures trickled out to fall into the eager arms of a wife - a mother - a father - a sister - a son - a daughter - an aunt - an uncle.

Following this brief reunion the returning warriors were directed to make their exit from the halt and parade along the long red carpet to be greeted at the end by Lady Hadley and the village committee. The band struck up and played a rousing, 'It's a long way to Tipperary'.

Corporal Williams, fifth lancers, came first, followed by troopers Beal, Harper and Winter of the Oxfordshire Yoemanry. Sergeant Daniels, ninth fusiliers, trailed behind on crutches. Robson, fifth horse, hobbled along with a pair of sticks. Private Kitson, medical corps, walked bravely in the absence of his right arm. Prucilla Thrift, VADs, pushed sergeant major Figgins, tank regiment, in an invalid chair; the war had robbed him of both legs. And finally in the rear came Marie Sawyer, VADs, escorting sapper Hutchinson, Royal Engineers, who had lost his sight in both eyes. A great number were not coming home and among them were 'Spindle' Baker, 'Tubby' Cracknel, 'Cryer' Popham and Benjamin Hampton. Spindle and Tubby went down on the Somme offensive. Cryer got killed in the massacre at Ypres. And Benjamin lost his life at sea.

One by one the survivors were greeted and congratulated on their bravery by the village council. And Lady Hadley, with tears in her eyes, said how very proud she was of them all, and what a credit they were to the estate and the village, whilst relatives and friends looked proudly on.

One by one they were ushered into waiting horse-drawn carriages and taken to the manor where Lady Hadley had arranged to wine and dine the whole village in style. There were roasted carcasses of beef, pork and lamb. There were large bowls of steaming vegetables, and potatoes baked in their jackets. Lashings of fresh fruit were brought out of winter storage. Jellies trifles and small mountains of fluffy white cream. There were sweets and chocolates. There were firkins of ale and cider, and large flagons of wine.

And later there was music, dancing and singing

Marie Sawyer was shocked to find how much her mother had changed. The death of her father had been a great blow to her mother. But she should have rallied by now. She seemed so preoccupied and vacant.

"Are you worried about anything mother." she said shortly after they got home from the celebrations at the manor.

"Not really, dear. Although you must admit a lot has happened in our lives, in recent years."

Marie said: "We were not the only ones to suffer. The whole nation has suffered."

Her mother looked at her over the rim of the cup of tea she was drinking. She paused and said: "I am astonished at what the war has done to you. You are wafer thin and enough to warrant the consultation of doctor Markham. Tell me, my dear. What was it really like? The war I mean. You obviously did not tell me everything in your letters."

Marie said thoughtfully, "For certain we were kept busy. And, without a doubt, there never was a dull moment."

"And from what I see you went without sleep and regular meals. Did you not rest at all?"

"Rarely, mother. The wounded were our priority."

Her mother took her hand. "True to the spirit and dedication of your late father. I am sure he would have been very proud of you."

Marie said: "You, too, mother have never shirked from your responsibilities."

Her mother said: "I regret I lost all that when he perished in the war. Try as I might I cannot regain the vitality I had when he was by my side."

"Life must go on, mother. We owe it to father to live, and work on, in his memory."

"That is all very well, my dear. But you must appreciate the years are catching up on me. Everything is such an effort."

Marie placed a consoling arm around her. "You will feel much better when you are convinced the war is over, and the village gets back to how we knew it. I can assure you that more families than ever will want your help and comforting advice. Especially at the moment when so many are without a breadwinner."

Her mother roused herself. "What do you intend to do now the war is over, my dear?"

Marie smiled, "Much depends on what Timothy has in mind."

Her mother said: "Like you he has changed considerably. He looks ten years older than he really is. And I hear he spends most of his time walking alone on the hills."

"Nobody escapes the injuries of the war, mother - just nobody. Flesh and limb may be lucky enough to escape injury. But what is often overlooked, and is very vulnerable, is the mind. It can be emotionally battered and may heal in time, as do most physical injuries. Equally it can be scarred for life and readily affect the health of the victim."

"It has certainly affected Timothy. " her mother remarked. "He was well aware you were returning home today. And what does he do. He flies off to a place called Ower in the West Country. Most selfish and inconsiderate in my opinion."

"Not at all, mother." Marie laughed. "In his letters from Canada Timothy mentioned several times he intended to visit his grandfather's grave if he ever came back to England."

"Is that the one who jumped from a hill top with flimsy apparatus in an attempt to copy the birds. And in so doing killed himself, and left a very young widow and child?"

Marie smiled, "That's the one, Grandfather Willy Herby. And Timothy's visit to the grave may be the tonic he needs to help him recover from his experiences in the war. I wonder," she mused. "I just wonder what he is doing at this moment in time."

The pilot sat alone in the small lounge bar of the Wheatsheaf inn, in Ower, enjoying a jar of real English ale, and a pipeful of burning tobacco. It was a long time since he felt so relaxed and untroubled. All in all it had been a marvelous day.

The flight from Oxford, in the Avro, had been thoroughly enjoyable. He'd felt completely free and answerable to no one. A good-natured farmer had not objected to the sudden appearance of a flying machine on his land, and furthered his benevolence by allowing it to roost there for a number of days whilst its pilot completed his business.

The pilot walked to the small churchyard about two miles down the road and after a search found grandfather Willy's grave in a corner under the shade of a solitary pine tree. The mound was badly overgrown but the inscription on the headstone, although faded by the effects of weather and time, identified the deceased. He spent a quiet and thoughtful hour squatting by the grave. And it was an elderly lady, who trimmed the grass and put fresh flowers on the grave of her late husband nearby, who recommended the Wheatsheaf inn to the airman when he inquired after suitable accommodation in the area.

He was not disappointed. The fat, jolly-faced landlord and his wife received him warmly. They took his bags, sent him off to freshen up, and when he got back to his room they served him a meal of sliced boiled ham, cauliflower and potatoes dressed with cheese sauce. They followed it up with spotted dick pudding in a puddle of syrup. And finalised the meal with cheese and biscuits, and a pot of tea. He relaxed in an easy chair after the food and immediately fell asleep.

He slept solidly for four hours. By which time darkness had replaced daylight at the window of his room. His surroundings were unbelievably quiet. Nothing stirred. He put a comb through his hair, put his pipe and tobacco pouch in a pocket, and went down to the lounge bar.

A yeasty smell of ale, a drift of burning tobacco and a log fire. What more could a man ask for? The landlord came through from the other bar and the pilot ordered another jar of ale.

"Everything to your liking, squire?"

"Yes. Thank you."

The landlord refilled his jar and said: "Tell me if I'm being nosey. But are you down here on a casual or business visit."

The pilot said: "A bit of each you might say. I am very interested in meeting anyone in the village who might have met my grandfather, William Herby."

"Herby?" the landlord frowned. "I don't know any of the regulars here, by that name." He paused. "Except the one who's buried in the churchyard."

"That's him. That's my grandfather."

The landlord grinned. "He's got a queer saying on his headstone, something about being dead, but not destroyed. We get a lot of visitors to the village coming in here for refreshment. And they always talk about that headstone and what the writing means."

The pilot said, "I suppose it means what it says: he is dead but not destroyed because, as you say, people continue to come in here and talk about him and the headstone."

The landlord said: "I didn't think about it like that. Tell me, what was the cause of your grandfather's death?"

"He fell to his death whilst carrying out flying experiments from Brasher hill from what little I know."

The landlord stroked his chin, thoughtfully. "There is one very old boy in the village who may be able to help you," he said. "Albert Huggins is his name. There's not much he doesn't know about the history of Ower. He'll probably be in later for his nightcap. Like me to send him through?"

"I'd be most grateful if you would."

The landlord laughed, "He's a spit and sawdust man by choice. But when I tell him who you are I think he'll come through." he hurried away to attend a spate of orders in the public bar.

An hour before the inn closed the lounge door latch lifted, the heavy oak door creaked ajar and a balding, bright-eyed elderly gentleman put his head around the door. "Mr Herby?"

"Mr Huggins?"

They shook hands in greeting and the pilot pulled up another chair before the hearth, ordered a jar of ale for his guest and offered him a fill of tobacco from his pouch.

"The landlord tells me you may remember my grandfather who is buried in the local churchyard, Mr Huggins."

The old man packed the tobacco in the bowl of his pipe with a thumb. "I think I knew him better than most around here because he wasn't really an Ower man. He lived at a little place down on the coast called Sealake."

"How did you come to meet him?"

"By accident as a matter o' fact. I was about nine years of age at the time and I was out riding m' pony one afternoon when it suddenly stopped dead in its tracks. And no matter how I tried it wouldn't move on. They all get wind-up if they spot something odd. But I couldn't see what it was until I happened to look overhead and see the biggest bird you ever saw, floating down in the shadows of Brasher hill. It didn't fly like an ordinary bird, though. It was a big clumsy creature that looked uncertain of which way it wanted to go. One minute it was soaring like a kite. In the next instant it was diving like a hawk. It came to ground about a quarter mile away. And that's when m' pony started to move on again.

I came across the man and his apparatus in a clearing. He was stood puffing on a pipe. I watched him from the cover of some trees, not wanting to approach him because he looked the sort who didn't want to be troubled. Then he lifted the apparatus, which I could see now was in the shape of a bird wing, and carried it back up the hill, and stopped many times to take a breather. You know - it's eight hundred feet to the top of Brasher's.

I saw him come down again the following Saturday. But this time I followed him to the top of the hill to find out what he got up to. I found out he had the company of a young woman and a child. And because I was young and knew my manners I didn't get too near. I just stood and watched him step in a hole in the middle of the wing. Then he would lift it onto his shoulders and trot off down the hill and launch it into the air.

Back he would come quite some time later. Fiddle with the wing and delicate tailpiece. And off he would go again down the hill and pitch into the air once more. This went on all day. And come evening time he'd pack his small tool box, arrange the wing on a bogey, and with the lady pushing a perambulator beside him they made their way off the hill and walked back to their small cottage at Sealake." He stopped speaking to put a match to his pipe.

Herby enjoyed what he'd heard. "What was my grandfather like in appearance, Mr Huggins."

"He wasn't as tall as you. You've got a lot of his looks about the face. He had a big bushy moustache that made him look a lot older than he actually was. He always came dressed in the same clothes for his flights: polished brown boots and gaiters, brown cord breeches, and in the collar of his tunic he tied a white silk muffler pinned with a gold stud whose head was decorated with the shape of a bird in flight.

He didn't talk a lot to the lady; he was either fussing about with the wing and tail, making adjustments, or he was looking at the behaviour of the weather. I think mainly the wind and from which direction it was blowing. And gauging how strong it was. He spoke to her of course when he came back with damage to the wing and she would set to work with needle and thread to repair a rent or tear. He took full responsibility for making good any damage to the framing of the wing. He didn't come back very often, after a flight, without some damage."

"How long did you actually know him?"

"About six months in all. I went to watch him every Saturday. In the summer a lot of folks, walking the downs, came to watch him. Some were amazed and full of admiration for what he was doing. Others thought he was missing a bit up top. But all in all I think everyone respected his pluck and determination.

When winter came on I got to know him better when he ran into many difficulties with the wing. The strong winds caused him many mishaps. It was during this time that he asked me to help him steady the wing when he trotted down the hill in advance of jumping into the air.

The lady always rewarded me with a bowl of hot broth that she had heated on an open fire. She also gave me big chunks of thick crusty bread. She was a pretty lady, I remember, with pitch-black hair, bright blue eyes and always smiling. She supported your grandfather loyally in everything he did. Not once did I ever hear her complain or use a word in anger. And I can tell you it was bitterly cold up there on the top of Brasher's in the middle of winter. Many was the time I saw her, fingers blue with cold, stitching a repair to the wing."

He took a fill of ale from the jar and looked reflectively into the flames of the hearth. He said: "I won't forget the day your grandfather shook my hand in gratitude of the help I'd given him with the wing. Following which he said: what you are witnessing at this moment in time, young man, is a man struggling to understand the behaviour of the air in the hope he will conquer the mysteries of bird flight. Mark my words, in not many years hence, man will acquire enough knowledge and skill to enable him to span oceans and continents in the mode of flight."

Herby said: "Tell me, Mr Huggins. Do you know what happened to my grandmother after my grandfather fell to his death."

The old man blew a stream of tobacco smoke up at the ceiling. "She stayed on at the cottage for a bit, and I rode there each Saturday to chop wood, run errands and generally help her. Young as I was I got keen on her? In my eyes she was something special.

Then as if losing her husband wasn't enough she lost her father-in-law in a tragic mishap at sea. He was trying out a new type of rigging on a sailing ship. The rig came apart, the ship turned turtle and all hands were lost. He'd been helping your grandmother out, financially, up to the time of his demise. Things got a bit desperate for her. I went to the cottage one Saturday and found her packing and getting ready to move. By all accounts the pastor of Sealake had got her a position and accommodation in a country house near Oxford. She said she had been left without a bean to her name and much as she didn't want to move she had to put the welfare of her son first. She'd been told she would be working for a top-drawer family who would ensure she had a roof over her head and food in her belly, and a few pennies a week in pay.

I found out later, because we wrote to each other, that she had gone into service at the manor, and the squire and his lady accepted her son as if he was one of their children. She admitted the family had helped her out of a crisis by taking her, and her son, on. But she confessed she badly missed her husband and Sealake and the Saturdays they spent up on Brasher hill. Then her letters stopped coming.

I made up a saddle pack and rode to this place Hadley. And when I arrived and asked to see her I was told to go straight back home and mind my own business. I left the estate but in the village I nosed around and got a snippet of information from one old lady. She said your grandmother died suddenly and her body was taken to Ireland for burial." Huggins took a pause to take a fill from his jar of ale, and to pull on his pipe.

Herby said: "Did you find out what my grandmother died of?"

"The old girl said local gossip had it that she fell from the window of an upstairs room."

"Did the old lady suggest what made her fall?

"No. Only that several villagers thought it all a bit fishy."

Herby supped his ale. And put another match to his pipe. "Do you know what became of her son after her death."

"No. I came back here. And didn't bother any more about it."

The landlord came through and announced last orders. Herby treated the old Huggins to another jar in appreciation of all that he had learnt from him. Huggins said: "How long you be staying in the village?"

"Perhaps two or three more days."

"How would you like me to take you up on Brasher hill, and to show you where your grandfather launched his wing apparatus."

War Pilot

"I'd like that very much, Mr Huggins. That would be something very special. Thank you."

"Right. Be outside here tomorrow at eleven of the clock. I'll pick you up in m'pony and trap."

They set off promptly to the agreed time, next morning, warmly dressed, and tucked in a rug for protection from a raw biting wind that increased its harshness as they became more exposed on the heights. The pony had a lot of the Welsh cob in it. It hauled them up the long winding track to the top and never faltered. Huggins drove a stake in the ground and tethered the pony to it. Unsupervised it might have passed its time grazing and accidentally gone over the rim of the hill.

Huggins invited the pilot to accompany him to the brow of the hill where he pointed down in the depths to a solitary oak standing in the corner of a pasture. "That's the tree your grandfather aimed for each time he went down. He ended up in the tree one time and came back in a right mess. He ripped his clothing as well as the covering of the wing."

It was a long time ago, but Herby remembered reading about it in Grandfather Willy's journal. The flight had shown him that when he dropped his feet from the tail stirrups it altered the balance of the wing apparatus.

The pilot said: " Were you here on the day he launched the wing and, for reasons he could not explain, it turned back and careered him into the hill face?"

"Was I." Huggins chortled. "I've never seen people take to their heels so fast. He hit the ground so hard it knocked him out for a few minutes. The wing snapped in half. Your grandmother had to revive him. Then she spent an hour stitching a long rent in the covering, and he, at the same time, rejoined the snapped sections and made a repair by binding the fractures with fishing cord. He still looked a bit pale and shook-up when he finished but he put on a brave face as he made preparations for another launch. He must have hurt a leg because he hobbled when he tried to run down the hill.

Herby looked down in the void before them to the miniature features of Ower some eight hundred feet in the depths. It must have been an awesome drop for Grandfather Willy especially with the flimsy wing and precarious tail stirrups. He thought he and father had walked a tightrope when making their exploratory flights from Hadley. But Grandfather Willy, using and relying on a more fragile knowledge, had exposed himself to a much greater risk.

It may have entertained the spectators, watching a young man in brown boots and gaiters, a moleskin tunic, white muffler and cap, run down the hill with his wing and leap into the air and descend erratically to the lowlands. Others were probably drawn by his courage and pioneering spirit since the unstable nature of his flights left nobody in any doubt that he was gambling with his life. There was also a loneliness about his endeavours. He had his loyal wife always in attendance. He had the admiration and support of the spectators. But the moment he launched from the hillside with the wing he was totally alone and at the mercy of his wit and skill.

Huggins led him to a bare patch of earth. "This is the spot your grandmother laid the fire and heated the broth which she brought in a metal pot. In the summer they brought a picnic basket." He turned and pointed. "See that small white cottage on the coast. That's where they lived. They came here all that way, your grandmother pushing a perambulator, and your grandfather pulling the wing and box of tools along on a bogey. It was a fair old walk. Then they had the long climb up here."

WAR PILOT

The pilot suddenly found himself reeling from a bout of vertigo. It cleared slowly and out of the confusion he was confronted with the face that had confronted him when he was involved with the Nieuport that got imprisoned by ice, and the other occasion when the Camel spun out of control and he ended up in the lake. There were the same brown eyes the same heavy moustache and the same familiar reassuring smile. He was in no doubt it was Grandfather Willy putting in an appearance.

"You feeling all right?" Huggins said. "You went a bit pale and shaky."

The image faded. "Yes. I'm fine. The bracing air up here is very intoxicating."

At that very moment their attention was arrested by a sudden cessation of the wailing wind which was replaced by what the pilot thought to be the gushing sound of a wing cutting air. It came from their right, growing in volume as it approached them. Both of them crouched as it passed overhead. They looked up and perhaps, in their imagination, they saw the spiritual construction of linen sewn tight around spruce wood framing, its knifing thrust on the air falling to a murmur as it went over the brow of the hill and faded into the depths.

Huggins turned to him. "That happens every time I come up here. I've never told anybody about it because they'd only say I'm going potty. I think it has something to with those words on his headstone. He might be dead. But by the visitations, like today, he most certainly is not destroyed."

Herby grinned and nodded.

Bert led him back to the gig. "There isn't anything else for you to see up here. So come back to my place and I'll show you something else that might interest you."

They arrived back down in the village within an hour and he helped Bert take the pony from the shafts, remove the tack, and turn it out. Inside the cottage Bert stirred the range fire into life and put a kettle of water on one of the hot plates to boil. He disappeared into an adjoining room. And presently returned with a sketchbook and handed it to his guest. "I've kept them all these years because they give me many happy memories of that time in my life with your grandfather."

Page after page made up a pictorial story of Grandfather Willy's attempts to fly. A sketch showed him running down the hill with the wing. Another viewed him after he had got into the air, his legs dangling a few feet from the hill face. In another he was well away from the side of the hill with his legs reaching back to the tail stirrups.

Bert had captured with a humorous touch the day Willy came to grief in the oak tree. And the occasion the wing turned back into the hill scattering the bewildered spectators.

Amongst the collection of sketches grandmother Herby smiled out as she attended the fire and pot of broth, and in another she sat repairing a tear in the wing with needle and thread. She was accompanied in each picture by the perambulator.

The final sketch in the book depicted Grandfather Willy's dramatic demise: a crumpled wing, a hunched, lifeless body: a bird at rest after falling foul of the elements. Tears and laughter spent.

"The book is yours." Bert grinned at him.

The pilot said humbly, "Be assured my father would be delighted to see this. But you said it is an important part of your life."

"It was. But I'm on the downward path where my life is concerned, and I don't have family. Anyway its part of your family history and I want you to have it."

As a reward for his hospitality and generosity Herby took the old man aloft for an hour, in the Avro, the following day. They flew out over the coast to take a look at the cottage, came back inland and made a dip and climb salute over the grave in the churchyard. Then climbed over the top of Brasher hill where the pilot closed the throttle and they glided down the trajectory followed by Grandfather Willy, albeit rather more sedately than his pioneering flights. It gave the old Huggins some idea of what it was like for the young birdman, he had helped all those years ago, which, in total ignorance, launched courageously into the unknown and descended erratically to the lowlands - and ultimately to his death.

They passed low over the historic oak tree before they climbed back up and headed back to the pasture.

"The biggest experience in m' lifetime." Huggins beamed at him as the pilot helped him down off the wing. "I've wondered all my life what it must be like. Now I know. And if I go to my grave tomorrow, I'll go as a happy man. I might even meet your grandfather again, and that would be grand."

He passed away peacefully three weeks later.

The first part of Herby's flight back to Oxford passed happily as he navigated blind above an endless blanket of pure white cloud. Divorced from, and totally out of sight of, the ground made him feel he was travelling in another world. The exquisite scenery of azure sky and virgin cloud was complemented by the musical overtures around him. The drum-tight skinning of the wings and fuselage gave a resonant beat to the engine. The airflow plucked shrill fully at the taut flying wires. In unison unseen musicians of the bass and cello worked deep notes from the wing struts. Somewhere amongst it all he thought he heard the trumpets and other members of the wind section. Up before him the sun glittered in the sky like a huge chandelier.

What changed it suddenly he was not sure. It could have been a shadow glancing across the face of the sun, or an unidentified object catching his sight and startling him. He found himself weaving amongst a number of zooming, wheeling, and spinning winged shapes. Black crosses on olive green marked the presence of Hun combatants. Staccato sounds prompted the smell of gun oil and cordite. Vapours of castor oil filled his nostrils. He banked the Avro wildly to avoid a shape that reared up before him enveloped in flames. Death! Destruction! It was the infernal war all over again. He felt chilled and his feet and hands were trembling upon the controls.

He put his head into the slipstream. The unwelcome intrusions to his mind retreated reluctantly, and threatened to return if given half the chance. The experience drained him physically and mentally. He took the Avro down below cloud to get his bearings. The airfield at Oxford came into view in the nick of time; a paralysis was creeping up on him with the intent of seizing control of both his mind and limbs.

He vaguely remembered setting the Avro down and paying for its hire. Thereafter everything passed in a maze. He thought he saw Marie with Lady Hadley's chauffeur and the motor carriage, which he had arranged to collect him by telephone, the previous evening. He recalled nothing of the journey to Hadley.

At some stage somebody said doctor Markham should be summoned. The pilot pleaded feebly that he only wanted to sleep. He was encouraged to sit on a bedside. Gentle hands removed his boots and top clothes, and directed him to lie back. His legs were lifted on to the bed. Sheets and blankets were tucked around him. Silence blissful silence… he was sliding down a tapering corridor of darkness where the waiting arms of oblivion waited in readiness for him.

TEN

He stood poised with the wing on the brow of Brasher hill, his head protruding from an aperture midway of the span, his arms fed through leather loops attached to the under surface of the wing. The miniature features of Ower village peered up at him from the depths. He waited for the boisterous wind to calm a little. He was puzzled.

Back in the summer the wing had flown reasonably well and much as he expected. Now the cold, harsh winter winds caused it to misbehave and play tricks on him. Dangerous tricks.

During a lull in the force of the wind he started to trot down the hill with the wing, knowing that each step he took made it impossible for him to turn back. And was he to lose his nerve it would be the end of his experiments. The lift of the wing suddenly plucked him into the air, away from the face of the hill, and out over the surrounding countryside. He tried to dismiss the discomfort of the loops as they drew tight around his arms and wrenched at his shoulder sockets. And how his old spinal injury plagued him when he arched his body to reach for the tail stirrups with his feet. He remained alert to the traits of the wing. He'd learnt from experience that if he flew into a silence, it was a warning that he and the wing were about to plummet earthwards. He pushed on the stirrups and the tail hinged down and as it did so the air striking the deflected surface pushed the tail up and the wing down. As he descended the air smote his face more keenly and tugged at his clothing. For some glancing moments in time he felt jubilant and free, and filled with a measure of achievement. He drew back on the stirrups and the upward deflection of the tail caused him and the wing to recover from the dive and soar up in a long sweeping curve. But it was short-lived. The wing, as it was prone to do, began to roll and he had no means to control it. Reducing the pressure on the tail stirrups seemed to prevent it becoming worse. Though it was not enough to cure or solve the problem entirely. He invariably put the wing back in a gentle dive.

His studies of bird flight through his telescope left him feeling uncertain as to how they controlled their turning flight. He thought he saw them twist their wings near the tips. He considered they might beat one wing faster than its neighbour to obtain the same result.

He had nothing to control his wing. It continued to tilt as they sank lower. And just as he thought they would fly into the hill the wing tilted more and carried them round in a turn that cleared the hill face by inches. They glided across a river and a patch of woodland. The view of two rabbits hopping across a meadow reminded him he was very low, and the wing continued to carry him around in a turn. His dilemma was: would he get back to earth on flat open ground before the unpredictable wing took him elsewhere. Over a flat stretch near the base of the hill he moved the tail stirrups to offer the wing to the air just as he had noted birds did prior to their return to earth under a canopy of feather. He was not, however, able to copy, and accomplish, it with anywhere near the same amount of skill and precision. As the earth rose up he dropped his feet from the stirrups and the wing was still moving forward when his feet touched ground. He toppled, and collapsed on the ground in an undignified heap.

Breathlessly, wearily, and aching from head to toe he disentangled himself from the wing. It was enough for one day. He'd made seven descents from the hill and had learnt and accomplished precious little.

He carried and dragged the wing back up the often-steep contours of the hill, labouring and sweating from a continuous ache in his spinal region. Which he was forced to endure for another two hours during the journey on foot back to his cottage home? Rosemary trailed behind him, pushing the perambulator, and, knowing of his pain, wishing she could help him. But knowing it was impossible till they got home.

After bathing, feeding and settling the infant Samuel for the night she helped Willy pour heated water from a wood-burning boiler into a tin bath set before the hearth fire. The tension of his pain eased as she bathed him with warm water and massaged him with her soothing hands.

Later she dried him down, had him lie face down on a rug before the fire, and rubbed horse linament into his back and shoulders. The heat of the oil penetrated the thickness of tissue, muscle and the brittleness of bone, bringing a welcome relief that allowed him to think straight on the subject of his flights without the distraction of pain.

They had supper and spoke little; they were not great talkers. He washed and cleared away the cutlery and utensils of the meal telling Rosemary to rest. She touched him with a grateful hand, smiled agreeably and took up her embroidery in an easy chair by the hearth. Presently he sat opposite her watching her with admiration. She was a pretty and intelligent girl, devoted to the family, and extremely tolerant and loyal to his pursuit of manned flight.

When they retired for the night he lavished her with affection and satisfied the deep, intimate cravings of her physical desires by wandering through the body of her orchard, touching and plucking the heaving ripeness of her fruits. He knew when he had served her well and adequately - she lapsed into a sound, fitful sleep.

Thus ensured he slipped quietly from the bedroom, and settled at his desk in the spare room. He lit the oil lamp, opened a large thick journal and with quill and ink to hand he wrote of his flights that day and the observations he had made. He concluded by writing he had made little progress.

He moved his attention to the skeleton of a gull he had retrieved from the seashore, and which he had covered in silk to represent its plumage. He held it before him with full spread wing, set it at various angles, and tried to imagine how it moved its wings to affect a turn. And, what was more, how it got back on an even keel following a disturbance by the unstable vagaries of the air.

It was now six months since he had worked and pondered on the mysteries of the athwartships balance of the wing. His failure to find a solution taunted and frustrated him relentlessly.

As he sat on through the stillness of the night he was prompted to think he should be more adventurous. Perhaps he should dive the wing at speed on the premise it would dominate the air rather than be controlled by it. That, he told himself, was feasible. Though getting proof of it created another problem, the invisibility of the air, itself

He was quite certain that many mysteries of the air, and the barrier against the knowledge of sustained flight, could be resolved if the air was coloured and visible.

He passed a weary hand across his face. Morning, noon and night and in every free moment of his time his thoughts reached out in all directions, yearning, fighting to tear down the curtain that separated him from the knowledge he needed so badly. The light pressure of hands on his shoulders startled him. Rosemary said: "Come Willy, dear. You must rest."

He got up from the chair and embraced her. "Be patient a little longer, my dearest." he said. "Methinks this obsession for flight will not last forever."

She cupped his face in her hands. "I do understand. And I am very proud of you. But you must care more for your health."

In the stillness of the night he whispered enthusiastically, "Shall we walk along the seashore on the morrow? And will you write notes as I make the observations through the telescope?"

She smiled and nodded. "Now you must rest. Daybreak is only two hours away."

He extinguished the lamp and followed her to the other room. And as they embraced each other beneath the bed covers he said: "If only I could solve the lateral balance. Then I would be that much closer to matching the gliding flight of the gulls."

He trotted downhill with the wing. He'd lain awake for most of the night and at the first signs of daylight at the window he had dressed and ignored Rosemary's request for him to wait for her; he was possessed by a consuming desire to get on the wing. He was determined to learn from the flight today and prove or disprove his theories on how flight should be conducted.

A cold, blustery surge of wind snatched him and the wing quickly into the air. He reached back for the stirrup cups with his feet and elevated the tail downward to which, after a slight delay, the wing carried him earthwards at speed. His eyes watered under the attack of the icy flow of air. And knots of turbulence thumped against the wing and caused the tremors to reach his arms. The faster the wing descended the smoother their passage, he thought. And the more stable it also seemed to him.

At last he was confident he had found the key to the lateral balance and, in celebration, he reversed the position of the stirrups. The wing lagged awhile before it changed direction and flew him up in a long graceful climb, poised and balanced whilst the inertia was strong. But as the speed slackened the wing rolled suddenly. Too late! He was powerless to check it. His feet fell from the stirrups. The earth came back into view over his right shoulder. He looked vertically down at the patch worked countryside of the lowlands. The earth glanced beneath his head when the wing rolled him to the inverted before it fell over. He watched helplessly as the earth rose up, spinning briskly. He sensed a hand reaching up for him; he was not afraid. More so he lamented that everything was coming to an end. No more exhilarating launches from the hill and those brief spectacular moments of freedom in the void. No more picnics on the downs with his wife and son. No more of the long nights of the mental challenges, the pondering, the theorising. No more Rosemary. No more Samuel - the impact was imminent. An unseen hand stood poised to hood the flame of his life.

Timothy Herby awoke from the dream with a jolt, dazed, perspiring and shaking - to discover Marie holding his hand and smiling down at him. Other details and features of the room came slowly back into focus.

"What happened?" he said.

"You collapsed when you got out of the aeroplane at Oxford."

"I also had a bad turn on my way back from Ower," he told her. " I came over very tired. I just wanted to curl up and sleep."

Marie smoothed his brow with a hand. "And sleep you did, Timothy, for over sixteen hours. You were sorely tired. You tossed and turned several times. Was it the war?"

"No. I had a most graphic dream in which I went far back in time and into the body of Grandfather Willy. And carried out the flying experiments from Brasher hill with his flimsy wing, forever groping for the skill to conduct stable flight, and ceaselessly clutching at straws where the search for knowledge was concerned."

Marie listened patiently as he enlarged upon the details of the dream. He talked on for over half an hour. And near the end his voice came more slowly and quietly. The deep frown on his forehead melted away. His eyes lost their vacant expression. He relaxed comfortably on the bed.

"Would you care for tea?" she placed a hand on the side of his face.

"Please. I could drink an ocean."

In her absence he lay recalling the events of the dream. Never had a dream been so clearly etched on his mind. And he noticed he was still emotionally touched by it. The images of Grandfather Willy had cause to give him a renewed courage, a revived determination and a rationality to face life's most daunting adversary. From hereon he was confident he could face up to, and triumph over, any lesser enemy of life.

When Marie came back she added a dimension of comfort to the room as she drew the curtains and lit the lamps. He let her serve the tea and get settled.

"Do you remember when we met in France," he said. " And I told you of my indiscretions."

She nodded at him sympathetically.

"Can you recall what you said?"

She said: "Did I not say something like we had a loyalty to each other created by the bond of our families. And we might make up for lost time after the war."

He took her hands in his, "And on reflection do you still feel the same?"

She smiled down at him, "Come, Timothy Herby. What is all this questioning leading to?"

"I'd like us to get married and make up for the lost time you mentioned"

She laid herself on top of him and kissed him fully on the lips. "Without delay, my dearest. Without delay." she whispered breathlessly.

She broke the news to her mother and lady Hadley the following day, during afternoon tea.

"Would it not be prudent to wait a little longer," her mother said. "Timothy is so pale and strained. He is far from the young man we once knew."

Marie said: "You fail to understand mother that but for Timothy's health and stamina he might well have become a raving lunatic, as have many soldiers, sailors and airmen."

Claire Hadley jumped to her defence. She said: "Marie is quite right, Heather. We may have triumphed over the Hun. But the price the nation has had to pay in terms of the colossal loss of life, and human suffering, will go down in the history books as the most expensive in living memory. Marie's experience as a nurse will soon get Timothy back on his feet. And last but not least Marie has been neglected for too many years in her private life. She might just as well have been a nun."

Marie laughed and thanked her for her support. Her mother said: "Perhaps I am getting old and don't understand."

Lady Hadley said cheerfully, "I suggest we look on the bright side and begin preparations for this happy and desirable union. It is a pity that Samuel and Rebecca will not be in attendance. We must ensure a photographer is available."

Rebecca sat on the veranda, in the fading daylight, with an open book before her. She had instructed the servants to start supper when Samuel came home from the Govenor General's office The book failed to hold her; the war in Europe had ended and Timothy was safe. His days as a war pilot were over and she was infinitely happy and relieved. She couldn't wait to see him back home in Canada.

She turned to a sound behind her to find Samuel smiling from the doorframe, holding up the paper leaves of a letter. His teasing expression told her the letter was from their son. She beckoned to him to bring the letter to her and said: "When is he coming home?"

"He makes no mention of it."

She read the letter through quickly which, as always, was mainly about flying. He had evidently recovered from what he described as, minor injuries from a flying accident several weeks past. It irked her that he should be telling her after the event. And he opened up some old wounds by saying he would be sojourning in Hadley when he was discharged from the air force.

Pierre, the butler, interrupted to ask if he should serve supper. They agreed and requested he light the lamps.

During the meal Rebecca said: "Do you think Timothy intends to stay in England, Samuel?"

"What do you think, my dear?"

She said gloomily, " He says in his letter he is making for Hadley after he leaves the military. I have a suspicion he will stay."

Samuel teased her with a grin. "You do, do you?"

She nodded solemnly.

He said: "In the diplomatic bag today there was Timothy's application to return to Canada."

Rebecca stirred excitedly. "We must prepare his room. And you must have a word with the police commissioner to get Timothy his old job back."

He reached across the table and lightly gripped her wrist, "Restrain yourself, Rebecca. Our son is not returning alone. He has applied to bring Marie Sawyer with him."

The revelation both hurt and disappointed her. She had made plans for her son and for her son alone, long before the war ended.

Samuel watched her slump in the chair and go very quiet. Throughout their marriage the relationship had moved through a succession of sail and anchor situations. Rebecca would get carried away by the sailing enthusiasm of her emotions which, more often than not, were triggered by an impulse and lacked any consideration of the consequences. And often it was necessary for him to step in and drop the anchor to prevent her making a fool of herself.

Nothing more was said till Pierre came and removed the dessert bowls, and served coffee and cheese and biscuits.

Rebecca said: "Will the ending of the war affect the situation in the Govenor General's office?"

He lit his pipe. "Morrison hinted today that there was bound to be a number of changes. He suggested some of us oldies may have to stand down to make way for the younger men returning to civilian life from the military. And for certain, he said, the finances of each department will be put under review."

Rebecca sat erect on her chair. "Are you saying we could lose this house, and all the other privileges we enjoy?"

"It is a possibility, my dear."

"But Samuel." she protested. "What is to become of us?" She moved outside and stood with her hands resting on the veranda rail as she looked out into the darkness.

He said: "We move to Calgary." He joined her at the veranda.

"Calgary!"

"Yes, Calgary, Rebecca. Bill Cornell is resigning his commission in the military, and plans to buy up a number of redundant machines and start up a civilian flying school. He has invited me to be his partner in the venture."

"Where will we live?" she demanded.

"There are several log cabins available in the area."

"No." she sniffed indignantly. "I will not accept that. It would be a step backwards to no running water and earth closets."

He moved to stand behind her and gently rested his hands on her shoulders, "For many years, my dear, we have lived a life to suit your wishes. Now I think it is only fair we pursue something of my choice. That is: spending what working years I have left helping teach young men and women to fly."

She turned to face him, took his hands, and looked up at him. "I know you consider it selfish of me, Samuel, not to want to give up the good life we have enjoyed here. But to go and live in a log cabin would surely draw the scorn of our friends and acquaintances in the office. It would be most humiliating."

He kissed her gently on the brow. "Many of our friends and others will be in the same boat as us. They too will have to accept drastic changes to their style of living. And make sacrifices like us.

"Those days are over for me." she sighed. "I am tired and losing the vitality of my earlier years."

He said: "You forget Timothy and Marie. They will need help to get on their feet. It will be good to have young people around, after all the oldies we've been mixing with for the last few years."

She played with the collar of his shirt. "How will Timothy figure in your plans?"

"Unless he has any plans of his own he is welcome to join Bill and me. According to his recent letter he has been a flying instructor for several months. That would be a valuable asset to our venture."

"Oh. I don't know what to say, Samuel. It's all too much for me."

"Look," he said. "When we set sail from England all those years ago, did you have any idea what lay ahead of us?"

"I was much younger then, Samuel.

"You've still got the spirit of a young filly."

She leant heavily against him. "I wish I had."

He said: "I think you know you were responsible for my steady promotion in my work appointments through your influence on the Govenor General's wife and senior staff. That is why you will be equally important in the aviation venture. Your social skills will be needed to get us government contracts. There will be much for you to plan and organise." He ran a hand through her hair. His other hand fondled her gently about the breast. She touched him about the loins. "Samuel Herby!" she quietly protested. "You are leading me astray."

Timothy sat posing, in uniform, before an easel and canvas upon which Lady Hadley worked with brush and oils. She suggested the painting would be a gift from her to his parents.

"Did you enjoy your visit to Ower?" she said.

"Most interesting. I gathered quite a lot more information on the history of my family. But there was also something of a mystery. And from what I gather your family was implicated. I think you may be able to clarify a couple of points for me."

She said: "You must understand, Timothy, I was not yet of this world when your grandfather died so tragically."

"It's not my grandfather. It's my grandmother."

"Surely your father has told you about your grandparents."

"He has told me a great deal about Grandfather Willy. Of grandmother he has told me nothing. And my mother claimed she died before she ever met her. I think father has remained reticent because of the discovery I made in Ower."

Lady Hadley moved into full view from behind the easel and canvas. She said nervously, "And what did you discover in Ower?"

"That my grandmother fell from a window, here in the manor. And her body was removed to Ireland for burial."

She moved back behind the canvas and easel. "What else is there to know, Timothy."

"I would be interested to know what prompted her to fall from the window."

After a long pause she said: "What I am about to tell you is based on what the squire's mother told me several years ago. Much of which is now vague in my memory. You grandmother came here through a link between the pastors of Ower and Hadley. Evidently your grandmother was destitute. The squire's parents took pity on her and invited her to Hadley, with her child, to be employed as a chambermaid. By all accounts she was a quiet and reliable worker.

She had been at the manor for six months when the tragedy occurred. The gardener found her body in the grounds, beneath the window of her budoir dressed in her night attire. It was suspected your grandmother ended her own life. And to keep the Hadley family free of scandal the church arranged for her body to be transported to Ireland for burial."

She carried on painting for a long spell. He waited patiently.

At last she said: "A number of weeks after the incident the manor was presented with another death. Daniel Crowfoot, a coachman employed by the manor, was found hanging by his neck in the woods on the estate."

He said slowly, "Was there a connection with my grandmother?"

After another long pause she said: "From what I recall of the conversation with the squire's mother I think some were of the opinion that there was. That Crowfoot attempted to have his way with your grandmother, and that she tried to escape his attention by escaping through the window. But top-drawer families considered such events as ill for the reputation of the family name. I think the doctor rushed through another suicide verdict, hastily arranged a funeral, and within weeks it was all forgotten. Or so the manor hoped it would."

"What happened to my father when grandmother's body went to Ireland?"

"He must have told you the manor took him into its care."

"He never told me a lot."

"Well the squire, Richard Hadley, and his lady fostered your father. They rather hoped to send him to a prestigious school, and buy him a commission with the colours. He convinced them, however, he was not a scholar, and he felt that military men should start from the very bottom where rank was concerned and learn to take orders before they were privileged to give orders

From what I was told the squire was not well pleased. Though it was said he admired your father for being a man of principle.

As you know, your father served as a regular soldier for five years and accounted well for himself, particularly in the African campaigns. He led a party of officers to safety after they lost their nerve during a tense battle. On another occasion he led a daring rescue to save the lives of a dozen soldiers who were staked and about to be beheaded."

Timothy said: "Oddly enough, he never told me. Mother did and she always lamented his refusal to accept the medals for his gallantry."

Lady Haley said: "It went against him of course. As did his view that the authorities should be trying to make peace with the natives instead of trying to wipe them out.

He came back to Hadley after his soldiering. He settled for doing odd jobs around the estate. Then he met your mother who was teaching at Hadley school. They married. I think you know the rest." She paused in her work and put her head round the side of the canvas. "Now - are you satisfied, Timothy?"

"To some extent, yes. At least some of the mysteries have been solved. But it puzzles me why the generations of my family, honest and hard working on the face of it, should end their lives so tragically. It just doesn't seem fair."

She came fully into view holding her palette and brushes. " I have long thought that life itself is a mystery and is equally mysterious in the manner it touches us and determines our individual destinies. We like to think we are in control of our lives. But I personally think it is mapped out from the day we are born. Very often a trial turns out to be a blessing in disguise. That too I have discovered."

Her words continued to surface in his thoughts weeks later as he stood at the ship's rail with Marie and waved to the quayside below at the gathering from Hadley who had come to see them off. Claire Hadley was quite right; life did act in a mysterious way and had an uncanny knack of sorting things out for the best.

Mollie Langdon had gone off happily with Horace Chase to start a new life in farming. Charlotte had written to tell him she had been reunited with her parents. And the grief-stricken family of Harry Griggs received news that he was a prisoner of war - not killed as they had been led to believe by the confused administration of the chaotic war.

As the ship began to ease from the quayside he was reminded that it was almost eighteen years to the day when he set sail for Canada with his parents. The ship gave a long blast on its siren. The quay slipped further astern. He remembered they had departed on a morning tide under a heavy grey sky, and it was raining. Today they were departing on an evening tide. He and Marie waved their final farewells to their friends receding into the distance. A fierce, crimson sunset painted the whole world a delicate pink. A gull glided noiselessly toward them, wings outstretched and stilled. It rose up in a long graceful curve; cart wheeled, and went diving back to the stern of the ship.

In mid channel Marie faced him and took his hands. "A penny for your thoughts, Mr Herby."

He smiled at her. "For your information, Mrs. Herby, I keep asking myself: why is it men choose to engage in the shackles of war when they could be fighting to preserve the freedom and joy of peace."

****

PART TWO

AIR DUEL

Air Duel

PROLOGUE

Air Duel is a sequel to War Pilot.

When Timothy Herby returned to Canada after the First World War he vowed he would never take part in aerial combat ever again. He settled in Canada as a flying instructor helping his father and Bill Cornell run a small flying school that did well for a number of years, and during which time Marie gave birth to their son, Paul.

When the flying business went through something of a depression in the late 20s, early 30s, he embarked on flying the mails across the wide ranges of the country and, combined with his old connections with the police service, he did a bit of intelligence work for the government.

In his often long absences from home Marie thrived on raising their son and trying to inspire him to ultimately become a concert pianist, whilst grandfather Samuel Herby lived in the hope his grandson would take to the wing like previous generations in the family.

But Paul was not inclined towards music or flying for that matter. He revelled in the out-door life, travelling the outback for months on end sharing his life with the backwoodsmen, the trappers, the prospectors and the Indians, who taught him how to negotiate storms, floods, avalanches, blizzards and how to survive in makeshift shelters and how to hunt for his food. They also taught him how to protect himself from extremes of heat and cold. And his eagerness to learn won him many friends and admirers. He grew into a tall, handsome young man. The shortcomings in his academic pursuits disappointed Grandmother Rebecca Herby. But she adored him nonetheless.

In 1936 rumours that Germany was engaged in a big build-up of military armaments reached Canada. A pocketful of critics argued that Hitler and his cronies were not doing it for fun. They went as far to say that, he was spoiling for another war.

Timothy Herby was inclined to agree. His vow not to get involved in aerial combat again had not left him. But something deep within him suggested he should go back to the old country and offer his services in her time of need.

At the age of 51 he arrived in England with his family and after installing Marie and Paul at the manor with Lady Hadley, he went and volunteered his services to the Royal Air Force. And whilst he undertook a number of refresher courses, and enjoyed a series of promotions, in the process, Marie enlisted Lady Hadley's help to encourage Paul to get at the keyboard of a piano.

He was having none of it. Without so much as a hint or warning he followed in his father's footsteps and joined the air force. In the early part of 1940 he graduated as a flying officer. He was 20 years of age.

Air Duel

ONE

The 1940 air offensive against Britain had receded and reliable intelligence sources suggested the Germans had diverted their wrath and resources to another front. The Royal Air Force busied itself reorganising, and deploying, pilots and ground crews to other urgent theatres of the war.

"What do you suggest we do with Herby?" the wing commander said, sliding a ruler beneath another name on the list before him.

Squadron leader Cromer looked at flight lieutenant Bagshaw. "What do you think, Roger?"

Bagshaw stirred. "Personally, I think he would be better suited to army co-op. Or coastal, perhaps.

The wing commander frowned heavily at him. "On what grounds!" He had enjoyed a successful career as a barrister before the war.

Cromer said: " Herby has some odd ideas about aerial combat, sir. He is of the opinion that it is only necessary to shoot enemy aircraft down, and that every precaution should be taken to avoid killing the pilot. I think you must agree, sir, that had we all fought along those lines our total score would have been significantly less."

The wing commander said: "Be that as it may I see he has been credited with 12 enemy aircraft destroyed, plus 3 probables. According to his ground crew he has never taken a bullet in battle. So, all in all, this would indicate to me that he is both a careful and clinical scrapper."

Bagshaw said: "Have you read the report, sir, in which he claims the Germans are shooting each other down."

"That's irrelevant!" the senior officer snapped.

Cromer and Bagshaw recoiled in their chairs; it was obvious the wing commander would not be trifled by station tittle-tattle. A Merlin engine roared into life outside the hut. They waited for it to taxi away. For a time the wing commander studied a number of options on a separate piece of paper.

At last he said: "I see a number of pilots are required for a P. R. unit near Oxford. You say Herby is a good pilot who is loathed to kill fellow airmen. So what could be a better choice." He scribbled a note against Herby's name. And slid the ruler beneath the next name on the list.

Flying officer Herby stood with his engine fitter on wooden staging arranged around the naked engine of the Spitfire he flew. "You think it is more likely to be the gauge than the thermostat?" he said.

"I dunno rightly, sir. The flight sergeant, he says we was to do it by starting with the easiest bits first."

In the cockpit of the machine an instrument fitter whistled merrily as he went through the motions of removing the radiator temperature gauge.

The engine fitter continued with a routine look around the engine, peering into dark and awkward corners with the aid of a mirror and battery-powered torch. He paused occasionally to wipe away residues of grease and oil. "How's your car, sir? After we fitted the new gasket."

"Bang on, thanks. I can actually get up hills in third, for the first time ever. I think you got it done in the nick of time. I have a hunch I shall be on the move from Biggin, shortly."

"What's the chances of us going with you?

The pilot said: "It all depends on what the top brass have in mind for us."

"It's a big shame." the fitter moaned. "All of us lads have been right proud and happy to work for you."

Herby grinned self-consciously. "Be in no doubt I owe all of you a great deal. Your dedication to looking after my aeroplane not only contributed to my success in battle but also kept me alive."

The figure in the cockpit clambered out, clutching the gauge, and headed for the stores whistling merrily as ever. A N.A.F.F.I. van pulled up before the open doors of the hangar. A queue quickly formed.

The pilot said: "Do you think you'll have the problem sorted out by the time I get back from lunch?"

"We'll do our best, sir.

"Thank you Mr Simkins. I'm sure you will."

The engine fitter paused in his work to watch him clamber down from the staging and stride out of the hangar. Flying officer Herby was always eager to learn more about the mechanics of his aeroplane. And he was always polite and friendly. A real gent he was.

On the other side of the aerodrome the pilot went to his living quarters and opened a window. He stood inhaling the fresh air traced with the warmth of late summer and the cool advent of autumn. The scene before the window was one of great peace and tranquillity: sharp contrast to that in recent weeks when the aerodrome was bombed several times and the roar of Merlin engines, and the scurrying flight of Spitfires and Hurricanes had dominated the lives of everyone from dawn to dusk.

As he looked skywards he was reminded of the many battles he had fought up there in the blue yonder surrounded by the crackling and ferocious roar of the Merlin to his touch on the throttle. And he battled physically with the lurking, unseen hand of gravity that thrust him into his seat or braced him against the seat harness during the relentless wheeling and turning to attack a quarry, or to outwit the pursuit of another. The excited chatter over the radio, the clatter of guns, the aching neck, and the straining eyes. It had been a hectic time and he had thrived on his weekly visits to the roadhouse.

He moved from the window and made his way to the mess for lunch where life was getting back to normal. Gone were the soiled and creased uniforms, the pale, unshaven faces, the nervous chitchat and the bubbling anticipation of a call to the dispersal or air raid shelter. Around him members of the mess talked rationally over a civilized meal served by smiling WAAF waitresses.

He went back to the hangar after lunch to find his Spitfire squatting outside. Evidently the ground crew had found nothing wrong with the cooling system. They had fitted a new gauge and suggested he take the machine on a short air test.

He went aloft for half an hour. Enjoyed a session of aerobatics and ended the flight by diving at maximum speed, pulling out on the approach to the roadhouse then putting the Spitfire into a neat flowing roll over the top of the building just before he joined the circuit at Biggin and landed.

He'd come across the roadhouse of an evening after a feverish day in battle. They'd been scrambled six times and he had scored his ninth victory that day: a good clean shoot in which the enemy machine went down in a corkscrew of smoke and its German airman had parachuted to safety. That had put a nice ending to the contest.

He smiled agreeably as he drove the small open-top sports car through the country lanes and breathed good wholesome fresh air; a welcome change to the oxygen he'd been gulping for most of the day. He spotted a number of cars parked by the roadhouse and decided its popularity warranted a visit. A decision he was not to regret.

The young woman who waited on his table smiled so brightly and made him feel so welcome he made a point of returning there once a week thereafter.

He made his customary visit that evening to find that apart from two couples he had the place to himself. He had grown attached to the atmosphere of the quaint old building with its whitewashed walls and thatched roof, and the impression it might tumble down at any moment. It had been converted to a roadside restaurant to attract officers from the surrounding fighter aerodromes: a prudent and perceptive idea of the middle-aged lady proprietor who ran it with the aid of a niece and local labour.

Heavy oak beams supported the ceilings, horse brass festooned the walls, and each of the small round dining tables hosted a lace tablecloth, a vase of flowers and polished silver cutlery.

He had barely sat down when the young woman appeared and hurried to his table, awarding him her usual sparkling smile in greeting. "What would you care for this evening?" she said.

He cast his eye down the menu. Then looked up at her drawn, as he always was, to her long brown hair, hazel coloured eyes, and the colour flooding into her cheeks.

"As it might be my last visit, I'll treat myself to steak and chips." he grinned at her.

She scribbled the order on a small pad and said: "With your usual raw chopped onion, I take it?"

"Your memory never fails you."

She went off smiling.

The window by his table looked out on a garden in which a shed needed a coat of paint, and a patch of lawn that would benefit from a shower of rain. Further back hens pecked at earth in the confines of a run. He found his eyes straying skywards, and his mind was back in the cockpit of his aerial dogfights till the young woman returned and interrupted his thoughts.

"Did you say this might be your last visit?" she said shyly.

Her interest moved him. He said: "Many are already in receipt of their marching orders. I see no reason why I should be excluded."

She looked uneasily around the room. Made an attempt to speak. But the words failed to materialize. And she hurried away in defeat.

He ate in silence, curious to know what she had wanted to say, and regretting he might leave Biggin without ever knowing. A major disappointment because she had assumed a growing importance in his thoughts and feelings over the weeks.

He finished eating as a party of fellow officers came in laughing and joking amongst themselves. He acknowledged them with a nod, paid the bill to the old lady at the kiosk by the exit, and moved into the car park.

He was getting into the car when a door on the back of the roadhouse opened and the young woman hurried to him. She made an obscure apology, pressed a small folded piece of paper in his hand, and retreated in haste. The door shut and had it not been for the piece of paper in his hand the swiftness of her visit might have left him feeling her presence had only been a figment of the imagination.

In the rapidly fading daylight he read the note in the car. She requested he telephone her when it was convenient. He made the call later from the mess and when he thought the roadhouse had closed down for the night.

"Oh, hello," she said nervously. "I don't really know where to begin."

"Perhaps we should begin by introducing each other." he suggested. "I'm Paul Herby."

"Melanie." she said diffidently. "Melanie Taylor." She hesitated for a time before she added: "When you said it might be your last visit, Paul, I don't know what came over me. I just could not imagine you not coming to the roadhouse each week. I suddenly realized I was going to miss you." She paused. "I know I'm not saying this very well. And you'll probably think I'm rather silly."

"Not at all. I regard it as a compliment."

The conversation seemed to dry up at this point. He seized the initiative and said: "May I come and see you."

"When?"

"Now."

There was a long pause

He said boldly, "Would you like to see me?"

"Of course but…"

"I'll be there in ten minutes."

There was nothing like the romance of a night sky strewn with stars, he decided as he drove back through the country lanes. He could not quite remember when he last had leave, and he felt justified in taking a late night for a change. He switched the engine off as he approached the roadhouse and coasted quietly into the yard at the rear.

Melanie came and greeted him the darkness and led him inside to the living quarters. The local girls had gone home and her aunt had retired for the night. They settled in a cozily furnished sitting room, and Melanie had changed from her black working dress and white pinafore and hat into a pale blue blouse and royal blue skirt. She regarded him with that devastating, sparkling smile.

As she served him tea and cakes she said gently, "Is there any reason why you should not stay on up at the aerodrome. I mean there will still be aeroplanes flying from the aerodrome, won't there? Or has there been any kind of trouble?"

He looked at her curiously. "Trouble. What kind of trouble?"

"I overheard some officers, the other day, talking about one of the pilots up at the aerodrome as being something of a crank. From what I could gather the person, in question, dislikes killing German airmen and he has also reported the Germans firing at each other."

He grinned at her. "It would appear I have become the subject of air force and local gossip."

Melanie moved to the edge of her chair and colour raged to her cheeks. She said nervously. "Are you the one they were talking about, Paul?"

He nodded.

She put her hands over her face. "How embarrassing. I am so sorry. It's none of my business. Really, it's not."

He removed her hands slowly and smiled assurance at her. "Since you have heard their side of the story I think it only fair you know my point of view. Yes - I do try to avoid killing German airmen. I like to think we share a common bond in wanting to fly, and are only implicated in this war by the folly of dictators and war-hungry politicians. Wars are not started by the likes of you and me, Melanie. Hence the reason I only take it upon myself to destroy the weapons of war."

She took his hands. "Please accept my sincere apologies, Paul. I had no right to pry into matters that don't concern me."

He took her off the subject by requesting more cake, and tea.

Presently they were sat at ease talking about their families and where they had lived and grown up. And Melanie grew quite excited when he told her about his youth in Canada amongst the huge lakes and towering mountains. His travels across the Great Plains and his encounters with timber wolves, big grizzly bears, the Indians on the reservations and the many other great characters who populated the great outdoors of the country.

It was well past midnight, and he noticed she was beginning to tire, when he suggested he leave. He stood, took her hands in his and said: "I would very much like to put our friendship on a permanent basis, Melanie."

She blinked up at him. "I'm sorry, Paul. But it's not possible. You see I am engaged to be married."

AIR DUEL

TWO

Across the English Channel on a French coastal aerodrome occupied by the Luftwaffe oberleutant Engel Staffel was also the subject of conjecture and speculation by certain elements of the Reich. Tall, fair-haired, blue eyes and possessed of the typical Germanic arrogance; he had risen up through the youth movement to eventually achieve his ambition to become a fighter pilot for the Motherland.

On leaving the sheltered world of his training, however, and graduating onto the harsh reality of operational flying he was soon disillusioned by the conduct of many of his fellow officers who were more intent on achieving personal goals and accolades with total disregard for the successes of the Motherland.

It ran contrary to all he'd been taught during his indoctrination in the youth movement, and it angered him deeply. But he kept quiet and bided his time.

At the end of the 1940 offensive against Britain he had six Hurricanes and two Spitfires on his score card - and three Messerschmitts.

Of the latter Heindecker was the first to fall to his guns. Heindecker, his flight commander, a glory seeker who attached more importance to the number of enemy aircraft he destroyed than the number of wing men who were killed protecting his tail. When Staffel joined the flight Heindecker often found himself unprotected in battle because Staffel had engaged himself in a separate fight.

He warned Staffel it was not to be. And Staffel argued in turn that there was no point in his leader making a kill if he lost a wingman in the process. His teachings in aerial combat stipulated that the object was to inflict as much damage on the enemy whilst ensuring the minimum losses on one's own side.

Heindecker accused him of insubordination and threatened to have him relegated to a ground job. Staffel took exception to being threatened.

During a heated fight with a mixed bag of Hurricanes and Spitfires he got his Messerschmitt into Heindecker's blind spot, sighted his guns on his fuel tank, and let rip. The end was both fierce and swift. Heindecker and his machine were ripped apart and the remains quickly melted in the intense heat of the explosion.

Dinstard, his next victim, also went totally against the doctrines of the youth movement, which constantly reiterated that Germany would only remain supreme through the joint efforts and allegiance of its people. Individualists like Dinstard would only retard and delay the Motherland's progress toward world domination. They must be removed.

AIR DUEL

And Staffel did just that during the disarray of another battle with the British. He made the attack head on and concentrated his sight on Dinstard's cockpit canopy. He only made the one pass; he noticed a pursuing Spitfire had taken an interest in his own tail. One solitary round of cannon fire was all that was needed to discontinue Dinstard's life. .

Truber was the son of an SS officer who had been involved in the campaign against Poland. The boy revelled in telling other officers about the distasteful activities pursued by his father, particularly the harassment and execution of the Jewry.

Staffel regarded such talk as a smear on the Motherland and it sickened him to think he was fighting alongside such perverted advocates of human misery and degradation. It was a blight that must be removed if Germany was to gain any measure of respect from the world when victory was secured.

He swooped on Truber, swerving away for a bit, then banked the Messerschmitt to come around and find Truber's machine moving from the left to the right. He closed the range, allowed for deflection, and thumbed the gun button. The devastating rounds of ammunition converged and raked the other Messerschmitt from nose to tail. Truber slumped forward and his machine slowly nosed over and went down in an ever-increasing dive from which it never recovered.

Staffel did not suffer any scruples; he had rightfully removed another potential threat to the reputation of the German nation, in his opinion.

It did not occur to him that the British had witnessed two of his deeds. A Hurricane pilot saw him dispose of Heindecker. A Spitfire pilot witnessed his dispatch of Dinstard. The reports got into the British newspapers. And a German agent operating in England felt copies of the newspapers were worthy of being smuggled into Germany, to the High Command in Berlin.

The High Command's first reaction was to treat it as nothing more than a wave of propaganda designed to undermine the morale of the Luftwaffe. The SS, however, suspicious and wary of infiltrators of the Luftwaffe, decided the matter should be investigated.

A staff car arrived at the aerodrome and Staffel was ordered to report to the aerodrome commandant. He appeared immaculately dressed, erect, confident, his boots polished to perfection. He drew to a halt with a smart salute and an accompanying click of the heels. "Herr commandant!"

Kressler, his commanding officer, did not reply immediately. He gave him a chance to weight up the gathering of surly SS dressed in their familiar long black leather coats, and black, wide-brimmed gangster style hats. Their organisation did little to enhance German culture, Staffel thought. But it had to be accepted they had done much towards the Fuhrer's rise to power, without which the nation would still be in a state of decline.

Kressler was an aristocrat whose interest outside of flying revolved around his love of classical music and the theatre. He was considered by many to lack the ruthless instincts of a predator where aerial combat was concerned. But nobody could dispute his unquestionable loyalty to all those under his command. Many of the younger pilots looked upon him as a father figure.

Normally he kept his conversation with his pilots on Christian name terms. On this occasion, for obvious reasons, he kept to a more formal tone.

He said: "Whether it is true or otherwise, Staffel, it has been reported to High Command that our airmen are shooting each other down. Naturally we are keeping an open mind, knowing as we do the value of propaganda it can serve for the enemy. But I think you would agree, from your experience in the youth movement, that it is necessary to investigate the matter, in the interests of the Motherland's security."

Staffel did not flinch. His training had taught him to deal with any number of crises. His only dilemma was his lack of trust in the SS who presented a formidable barrier between him and High Command; they were given license to act on the spot without prior consultation.

Kressler said; "The point is, Staffel, the number on your machine, is clearly quoted in the reports. Have you ever bore a grudge against a fellow officer?"

Staffle felt five pairs of eyes focus on him.

He said: "Naturally, Herr commandant, we all have our differences from time to time."

"And?"

"I am merely quoting a statement of fact."

A member of the SS said: "To your knowledge did another pilot use your machine? Possibly during a time you took a rest."

"I never took a rest." Staffel told him. "We were warned it would be a concentrated offensive and there would be no rest until we achieved the objective."

Another of the SS said: "We understand you attended a rally at Wembley, near London, in 1936. What was the purpose of your visit?"

Staffel said: "Since you know I attended the rally I would have thought your intelligence network would have known the details of my visit. I compiled a full report for my unit captain in the youth movement."

The most hostile member of the interrogating party moved forward. "I gain the impression you are treating this matter rather too lightly, Staffel. You should remind yourself that you are in a very tight spot. The evidence is weighed heavily against you."

Staffel said forcibly, "And I object to your attempts to mount an attack on my honour and integrity."

The commandant intervened. "Did you by accident, or otherwise, destroy any of your fellow airman?"

Staffel drew himself erect and looked directly into the eyes of the interrogating party. "I prefer to leave that to your discretion, Herr commandant, knowing as you do of my allegiance to the youth movement, the Luftwaffe and the German party as a whole."

The room went very still. An SS member whispered, at length, in Kressler's ear. Then Kressler looked up. "You may go, Staffel. But you are forbidden to leave the aerodrome until further notice. I trust you will respect my wishes without the need to enforce your confinement by military regulations."

"You have my word, Herr commandant." He saluted, snapped his heels together, and made his exit.

Back at the dispersal hut, he loosened the collar of his tunic, and changed his boots for shoes. He stood for a time looking at the scene through a window where a number of machines were undergoing servicing by mechanics bared to the waist in the warm sunlight. A disarray of chairs outside the hut accommodated pilots who slept, read or wrote letters, or simply lounged and listened to music and song from a gramophone, lured as most of them were by the soft, husky voice of the female vocalist.

Air Duel

The sudden lull in the offensive had taken most of them by surprise; and rumour was rife. The hierarchy claimed the enemy had succumbed and the land and naval forces would conclude the invasion. Another source suggested the resources were being switched to form new fronts in Russia and North Africa. This was supported by a number of pilots who had received orders to proceed to fresh assignments. A number of the younger officers dared to suggest the war planners at High Command had contracted a complaint commonly known as "cold feet".

Staffel put it all to one side. He tried to speculate on his future following the recent meeting with the SS. If they were in any doubt they could reduce him to the ranks and, or, demote him to flying a desk. Extreme humiliation!

Worse still, if they were to judge him guilty, they could take him away to be shot at dawn: a quick, painless experience if somewhat premature at his time of life.

Unter dispersed his thoughts, as he appeared, trudging along, head hung low, and giving the general impression he was carrying the world on his shoulders.

"What's the latest, Unter? You look as if you are about to be decorated with the Iron Cross."

Unter paused before the window; hands thrust deep in his trouser pockets. He looked utterly miserable and dejected. "You can smile, Staffel. I suspect you have not been earmarked for the Russian campaign."

Staffel laughed. "What's so bad about it. You'll still be flying."

"Yes, " Unter grumbled. "Flying donkey droppers."

"Mmmm…I see what you mean. Care to join me in a glass of good vintage French wine to drown your sorrows?"

Unter accepted and moved into the hut.

Staffel handed him the wine and said: "Don't despair fellow airman - your very best health - and let's hope you'll soon be back on fighters."

They drank to it. Not once but followed it with a second and third glass of wine.

Unter said: "Have you received fresh orders yet?"

"No."

I hear the SS interviewed you earlier. What's on their minds?"

"Nothing special. They were only making routine inquiries. By the way are you going on leave before going up to the front?"

Unter's miserable expression returned. "They've given me three days. Take the travelling time out of it and I have a solitary day of freedom."

Staffel took a card from his wallet and handed it to Unter. "Instead of going home, go to the address on the card. It'll save you a lot of travelling. Tell her I sent you and I guarantee she will ensure all of your needs are met."

Unter turned the card over in his hand. "You know I am opposed to such women, Staffel."

"Ursula is special, Unter. She has the connections with the best of our young women. It will be an experience, you'll never forget, I promise you."

Their conversation was interrupted by the sudden and noisy arrival of a motorcycle. Presently the corporal rider appeared in the open doorway of the hut.

"Oberleutnant Staffel! The adjutant wants to see you immediately."

Staffel quickly changed back into his boots, secured the collar of his tunic and donned his cap.

"Who knows, Unter." he shouted as he clambered onto the pillion seat of the motorcycle. "We might be in Russia together."

Air Duel

The adjutant looked him over critically as he halted and saluted before his desk. He was a non-flying type who bent his energies to rigid discipline when it was required of him.

"Here are your orders, Staffel. You have been given the benefit of the doubt on this occasion. But be assured you won't be so fortunate the next time it happens."

AIR DUEL

THREE

Before and beneath the gently swaying nose of the Spitfire the Southern Counties began to disappear under a solid mass of cloud. The pilot grew conscious of being cut off from the ground, of being isolated, of being reduced to a mere speck in the universe. At the same time he was wary of being pounced on by an enemy aircraft using the blind spot under his tail. He rolled the Spitfire onto its back, as he did at regular intervals, to deter any shadowing aircraft.

He was on the verge of completing his thirteenth sortie since his posting to the Photograph Reconnaissance Unit in the heart of the Oxfordshire countryside. The officers' quarters and mess were accommodated in a large rambling country house requisitioned by the air force. The food was good. Everybody went about his or her duties, cheerfully, quietly, and efficiently. Hadley manor lay 15 miles to the north. And he continued to enjoy the privilege of flying a Spitfire.

The type of flying was quite different to the parry and thrust of the fighting from Biggin. His current flights were of much longer duration, and took him deep inside enemy territory, and in the absence of any armament in his machine he was more vulnerable to the wrath of the enemy; a PR Spitfire carried cameras in place of guns.

Until recently life on, and emanating from, the unit had swung along smoothly and without incident. The Jerries threw up flak and shells occasionally but it got nowhere near the height at which the Spitfires operated. The gunfire got a bit closer when they reduced height for the photo-shoot. But it always seemed to be more of a nuisance than a threat to life. Then a week ago a nasty accident. For the take-off and landings a tarmacadam strip of road, camouflaged by an avenue of trees, running through the estate of the country house served as a runway. It was narrower than the standard width of a runway. And it was well known by Spitfire pilots that if left unchecked the machine would swing boisterously during the take-off run.

For reasons better known to Smithers he failed to check the swing. He careered off the runway going at full pelt with the roar of the Merlin stopping abruptly as it smashed into a stout defiant oak tree. The whole lot went up in flames.

Then late yesterday Chadwick force-landed at Biggin. There was a suggestion the engine of his machine would have to be changed.

Herby thought about the incidents as he put the Spitfire in a gentle dive to get under the base of the cloud where he found the visibility appalling. He crept along at five hundred feet, throttled back, and groped his way through the entrance to the Thames Estuary and followed its winding trace to Henley. He normally flew more southerly to take a peek at the roadhouse. But the weather ruled it out on this occasion.

He flew on, groping his way to Reading dodging around and sneaking between a train of hilly contours He was down to two hundred feet when he picked out the railway line which lead from Reading to Oxford. Ten minutes later, and by a fluke, he spotted the main gates to the country house. He selected the undercarriage down, slapped the prop lever into fine pitch and flew low over the house. He put on a bit of flap and followed the makeshift runway to its end then turned forty five degrees, held it for a spell then commenced a gentle turn back toward the runway. It seemed his wing tip was barely fifty feet from the ground when he banked. He flew the approach with a bit of sideslip so as to keep the runway in view. As he passed over the boundary hedgerows he kicked the machine straight with rudder and put it down, having to perform a bit of ballet dancing on the rudder pedals to keep straight on the narrow tarmac strip.

The engine lapsed into silence, the propeller ground to a halt, he slid the canopy back, and he unhooked his facemask, pushed his helmet back and sat for a time massaging his neck, and enjoying the silence. Two figures from Intelligence came and hushed the cameras away. The ground grew got busy refuelling, oiling, and changing the oxygen bottles. He got a message from the debriefing officer to report to the C.O.

"We've got a small problem." Carter-Hughes said. "Chadwick has got to have his engine changed, as you possibly know. Intelligence is screaming for his cameras because Bomber Command urgently wants to see Chadwick's film. The weather is too dicey to send someone over in my Maggie. And to crown it all we don't have any spare road transport." He paused. "I appreciate you have been up since the crack of dawn. But could I entice you to drive to Biggin to collect Chadwick and the film. I'll make certain you get an extra ration of petrol coupons."

He arrived at Biggin Hill just after teatime following a journey in torrential rain that frequently overpowered the windscreen wipers of his small car, and leaked through the canvas hood. He conferred with the mess duty officer, had a hot bath and changed into dry clothes he had wisely decided to bring, found Chadwick and shared a pot of tea with him. They agreed to stay overnight at Biggin and leave at first light. Then went their separate ways for the evening. Herby telephoned the roadhouse.

"Paul!" Melanie exclaimed softly. "Where are you?"

"I'm at Biggin for the night. I wondered if I might visit you."

He thought she might decline. Instead she said: "Of course. But use the rear entrance."

"I'll be there in within the hour. And I'm famished."

"Say no more. Leave it all to me."

The meal Melanie served to him at the roadhouse came as a feast considering he hadn't eaten anything substantial for twenty-four hours. It started with a bowl of game soup. To be followed by a medium-rare steak garnished with mushrooms, sliced tomato and his preference for raw chopped onion. The third course consisted of a sherry trifle. Pursued by biscuits and cheese. And she adamantly refused to let him foot the bill.

After checking the two local girls and her aunt could cope Melanie joined him in a back room. She removed her hat and apron and stood for a moment smiling that special smile, and looking very attractive in her black dress and stockings. She sat opposite him and he told her a little about the flying at his new posting and how he had come to end up at Biggin that day.

By return she told him the roadhouse business was picking up again after the changes at the surrounding aerodromes. And there were a lot of new faces amongst those who came from Biggin.

When a waitress came through from the restaurant to serve them coffee Melanie said: "That will be all Alice."

The girl went out smiling and closed the door.

Herby reached across the table and took Melanie's hand. "I've got to be honest and say I've missed you abominably, Melanie."

She made no attempt to withdraw her hand but an anxious expression swept into her face. "I'm worried, Paul. Worried I might hurt Robert. He is in the middle of a tour of operations with bomber command, and I'd feel very guilty if anything happened to him on my account."

He took her other hand. "Then I'll make certain nothing improper happens." he grinned assurance at her. "In other words I won't dash up to you on my brilliant white charger, and rush you off to my castle with amorous intentions." He paused. "I would only ask you to agree to write to me from time to time."

She sighed heavily and smiled her appreciation. "It's the very least I can do for you. And thank you for being so understanding."

He drove back to Biggin feeling happy and content. The mere sight of her, the sound of her voice and the touch of her warm soft hand had been enough; he could not have expected more in the circumstances. In the confines of the car he found himself whistling and composing a tune. He memorised the first line - created a second - a third - a fourth. Then he repeated the tune over and over again to commit it to his memory.

He derived the theme of the tune from an imaginary field of flowers in which a particular bloom stood out prominently from its companions. The long swaying stem supported a bright yellow cluster of petals. And when he stooped to view it from close quarters the petals unfolded and released a rich intoxicating perfume. Amongst it all he saw the radiance of Melanie's smile, and in her expression he saw a desire to be plucked.

Over the following weeks the memories of the detestable piano lessons, as a boy, came back to haunt him. He now had a great urge to master the art of music. He discovered an unused piano in the west wing of the country house along with some sheet music. Carter-Hughes gave him permission to use it and Herby did so after getting an airman from the photographic section, and who had been a piano tuner before the war, to tune it.

In every spare moment when he wasn't flying the pilot was at the keyboard initially refreshing his memory and practising the scales. Then he got down in earnest to sight-reading and keyboard practise. The need to play, and compose, consumed him. It came to him with huge waves of inspiration that drove him to transfer his thoughts and feelings to music. He did not have to think twice what it would mean to his long-suffering mother.

Marie Herby sat writing a letter to her husband when the notes of a piano began to float through the tranquillity of Hadley manor. She paused in her writing to listen. She smiled; it was no ordinary pianist she decided. Being a pianist herself she could feel the sensitivity in the touch of the keys - and the dedication. The music was alive, novel, and expressive and, for certain, she had not heard the melody before.

She abandoned the letter and made her way downstairs to trace the origins of the music. She trod quietly into the music room and was stopped dead in her tracks by the scene that greeted her. Paul sat there before her, engrossed, his body swaying, his eyes closed, as his fingers danced upon the ivory keys with the poise and elegance of a pianist in concert. She thought of the many times she had given up hope over the years and the times she had cried inwardly at his rejection of music.

The tears gathered in her eyes, she badly wanted to embrace him, to thank him to show him off to the world. Instead she walked slowly to stand behind him and rest her hands lightly on his shoulders. The music suddenly rose to a rousing and rapid conclusion.

He turned and grinned at her. "Did it meet with your approval, mother?"

She nodded and nudged the tears from her eyes with the knuckle of a finger. "Please play it again for me," she said hoarsely.

She drew a zest for living from the theme. There was a strong hint of romance about it. It was both gay and tinged with sadness. There was also a trace of intrigue and a wish for the world to know.

When he drew it to a close the next time she said: "Have you chosen a title?"

"But of course, mother." he said reaching for a pencil. And at the top of the music sheet he wrote in block capitals, MELANIE.

Much to her delight it was the first of many compositions, in the ensuing weeks, to spring from his musical skills and talents, during the gaps in his flying duties.

'Cottage on the Hill', 'Come - gather clover', 'You are my breath of Life', 'I am Waiting', 'Wings', 'The Hadley Theme', 'The Twilight Concerto were some of the titles his mother had printed privately and which she intended to publish after the war. Her ambitions for him to become a celebrated concert pianist who would tour the world capitals, after the war, became very real to her.

It was during this episode in his life that he had an unusual encounter with a Messerschmitt. He had come in over the coast in the area of the Wash, after a long jaunt to Berlin, when he happened to spot two aircraft several thousand feet below. At first he did not attach any significance to the two machines. But when he glanced down a second time he noticed smoke trailing from one of them. Conscious that he was low on fuel after his long flight something compelled him to dive down and investigate. The smoke he discovered was streaming from a twin-engine Blenheim. And out to the right curling around to come in for another attack was an olive coloured Messerschmitt boldly displaying black crosses on wings and fuselage. He dived upon the scene and flew a line that intercepted the German's attack. The German saw him approaching and broke away The Spitfire latched onto the Messerschmitt's tail and stayed there.

Much as he tried the German could not shake him off, and eventually lost face, put his nose down, and beat a hasty retreat back across the English channel.

Herby formated on the Blenheim and noticed the pilot had feathered the propeller of the damaged engine and doused the fire. He signalled all was well with a thumbs-up gesture and Herby continued on his way back to Oxford

Air Duel

The incident, as far as he was concerned, was all part of a day's work. He made no mention of it in his logbook and never bothered to report it in the debriefing at the end of the flight.

Three weeks later he was up before the solemn figure of Carter-Hughes. "It puzzles me deeply," he said. "Why one of my most experienced officers should suffer a lapse of memory."

"I'm afraid I don't follow you, sir."

Baker, the adjutant, said: "A Blenheim pilot has taken a lot of time and trouble to trace a pale blue Spitfire which rescued him from the clutches of a Messerschmitt. He was even more impressed to discover the Spitfire had no armament to fight the German. Yet, he says, the Spitfire pilot got stuck in and sent the enemy machine on its way. He is of the opinion the Spitfire pilot should be decorated for his courageous deed."

Herby did not comment.

Carter-Hughes said: "We have checked the date and time and, from your movements that day, we are confident you were the pilot of that Spitfire."

Herby said: "All I did was chase the Jerry away. It was all over in a matter of seconds."

"Be that as it may," Carter-Hughes beamed at him. "Those precious seconds undoubtedly saved a valuable aircraft and its crew. I'm putting you forward for a gong."

The pilot quickly pushed the matter into the background of his mind; he wasn't a great believer in medals. He liked nothing better than to get on and do his share of the flying from the unit and spend his leisure time practising on the piano and composing more music He took his turn to saw logs for the numerous fires in the country house. It reminded him of Canada and home, and the exercise kept him fit and helped to sustain him during the long flights in the cramped cockpit of the Spitfire

He thrived on his weekly letter from Melanie.

The winter deepened. Snow fell. Eyes and hearts turned toward the approaching festive season of Christmas. Off-duty personnel helped to hang the paper chains and select and dress a tree. Gramophones played records of carols. The feelings of goodwill intensified.

A week before Christmas day the pilot collected the mail from his pigeonhole in the mess and smiled at noticing Melanie's handwriting on one of the envelopes.

In the privacy of his living quarters he slit the envelope with a knife and withdrew a single sheet of writing paper. As he read a dark shadow swept across his face:

Air Duel

Dear Paul,

    As I sit here in my bedroom, alone with my thoughts, I try to think what I must say without hurting your feelings.

    You see Robert is due home in a few days and we are to get married. And as his wife I have a duty to be loyal to him and I think you would agree that our correspondence, although of a platonic nature, might be regarded as otherwise.

    I desperately hope you will agree and understand why we must stop corresponding with each other. And regard it as the right and proper thing to do in the circumstances.

    My sincere and very best wishes,

    Melanie

Air Duel

FOUR

Kruger, from Intelligence, jabbed a long wooden pointer at a red ribboned line that ran from the southern counties, in England, to Berlin, on a large wall map. "They fly high and fast and make their runs at first light or late afternoon. Your job, Staffel, is to harass and destroy them. Understood?"

Staffel nodded. A corporal crept into the room and deposited mugs of coffee on a small table to the rear of them.

"Be assured I do not relish this type of combat." Staffel said. "It stinks of unfairness. My fighting to date has comprised weapon against weapon. Not the shooting down of defenceless reconnaissance aircraft." He'd only been in the Netherlands for a week and the flat, monotonous terrain already depressed him.

"If I know anything of your past history, and a note on your records, I don't think you have much of a choice, Staffel. Come to my office and I'll acquaint you with the radio frequencies we use."

At an earlier briefing a poker-faced civilian had told Staffel he would be involved in a different type of flying. It was more disciplined - more controlled. He would be put in the air on the instructions of a strange breed of professors and staff officers operating sophisticated and classified equipment, which would guide pilots to, selected targets.

Staffel finished with Kruger at midday, had lunch, and went to his hutted accommodation that he had managed to set up as something resembling a home. With his own money he'd got hold of a heater for the advancing winter. Photographs and pictures of aeroplanes, in various modes of flight, sparked off the drab finish of the wooden walls. In the corner, on a shelf, he showed off his trophies, awarded in his school days, for sculling and shooting. A flimsy plywood wardrobe stored his clothes, and his ground crew had smuggled in, under the cover of darkness, a metal locker to store his flying garb.

Before a window a table was laid out with a writing tablet and blotter, an expensive pen as a gift from his parents, and a rare photograph of Ursula in the nude. She formed the hub of his life.

With her smiling out at him he settled down to familiarising himself more thoroughly with his new orders. He made several calculations in connection with the range and endurance figures of the Messerschmitt. He spent a considerable time studying a collection of aerial maps.

Boisterous knocking on the door interrupted, and heralded the appearance of Hultz, a pathetic figure badly burned about the upper torso and face, incurred, as it had been, during a bombing raid in Poland. The surgeons had made remarkable repairs to the scorched skin tissues, but poor old Hultz still looked a sorry sight. One eye appeared lower on the cheekbone than the other eye. His nose had a distinct twist to the right. And his shrivelled ears might have improved his looks had they not existed.

Staffel greatly admired him for his pluck to face the world with his hideous deformities, and did so with a great depth of humour. Rumour had it that Hultz had covered his head with a hood in order to get a girl to sleep with him. The hood evidently whipped up so much intrigue and excitement in the girl she had raped the delighted Hultz. He said he wished he had thought of the idea before his blazing hell in the Dornier.

He walked to the table. "I keep asking myself, Staffel, why an ace, such as yourself, is banished to the boredom and desolation of the Netherlands."

Staffel laughed. "I might ask the same question of you, Hultz."

Hultz's face twisted into a grin. "I would have thought it quite obvious. High Command claims their wives and mistresses are not safe in my company. You may observe irregularities above the waistline. But, below, the vital equipment is in good operative order."

Staffel got to his feet. "Hultz! You are a credit to the motherland. Shall we eat?"

Hultz bowed and motioned toward the door. "Lead on glamour boy."

Tauber made up the final member of the trio that had been hastily arranged and dispatched to the Netherlands to counter the threat of the reconnaissance flights from England. They joined him at the club for dinner, a serious, aloof, superior individual who enjoyed talking about highbrow music and classical history in which neither Staffel nor Hultz were well versed. He was tight-lipped about his family background. Hultz reckoned he was from the German aristocracy, had disgraced himself when it came to the business of flying, and his family and the hierarchy had decided to distance themselves from him by dumping him out of sight in the wilds of the Netherlands. Hultz had already warned Staffel that they might have to carry him.

Hultz said: "You realise you are on the o four hundred standby, tomorrow, Tauber?"

Tauber said: "It all depends on how I feel. And I'll have you know I can read." He resumed eating his meal and purposely tried to ignore them.

Staffel leaned across the table. "Be as snobbish as you like Tauber. But be assured that Hultz and I do not intend to carry you."

Tauber pushed his unfinished plate of food to one side and left the table.

Within a week he lived up to Hultz's prediction. He reported sick with a heavy cold and was barred from high altitude flying. Hultz said the cold was self-inflicted. The doctor grounded him for a fortnight.

Hultz downed his first Spitfire during this time. The Boffins, using their box of tricks, put him onto a target and he opened his throttle and went in pursuit. It all seemed so easy he thought a child could have done it.

But by the time he actually made contact, visually, with his prey his engine was gasping for air and his flying controls were flopping uselessly about all over the place. The Messerschmitt's ceiling at the very best was twenty eight thousand feet. The Spitfire he was after was flying well above thirty thousand.

Air Duel

It reached a point where the Messerschmitt ran out of speed and lost all inclination to climb. Above him the Spitfire sailed merrily on its way. Almost immediately an idea came to Hultz that had all the ingredients of a gamble. He put the nose of the Messerschmitt down at a moderate angle and put the throttle onto the front stop. He let the speed build up over the maximum permitted then eased the stick back and used the speed and momentum to carry him up toward the Spitfire. It came down slowly in the slant of the Messerschmitt's windscreen, trailing a steaming condensation trail. Hultz noted his diminishing speed, brought the belly of the Spitfire to the sight and thumbed the gun button.

At first he could not quite believe he saw bits falling away; he was more concerned with his rapidly dwindling speed. He eased the nose down to keep clear of a stall, and noticed the Spitfire was also slowing down and pouring out a mixture of black and white smoke. Suddenly it rolled over and spiralled earthwards. He followed it down, convinced the Britisher was up to a bit of trickery.

There was not, however, any aces up the sleeve of this unfortunate fellow. A mushroom of smoke marked his abrupt and fatal impact with the ground.

Hultz got a steer from base and headed for home, feeling ashamed rather than victorious. It hadn't been anything of a scrap, as Staffel had mentioned during a discussion on their style of operations.

The engineers and boffins celebrated the success of their new equipment that evening with a party at the club. He declined an invitation for him to attend. He spent the evening playing chess with Staffel and enjoying a good bottle of wine and an expensive cigar.

Staffel brought down a Spitfire the following week. He went down to the dispersal in the pale light of dawn, gave his machine a quick inspection, and went in search of the ground crew who, he found, in the hangar huddled around a heated stove like a gathering of cattle around a water trough. Muttered greetings were exchanged, a mug of coffee pushed into his hand, he nodded his thanks and they shuffled around to allow him to squeeze in and share the heat. His engine fitter went off to run and warm the engine of the Messerschmitt.

Some ten minutes later the shrill ring of a telephone scattered the gathering. The Boffins wanted Staffel in the air immediately. It actually took him three minutes to get airborne.

"Jagger niner, steer 278 for your intercept."

"278, Jagger niner."

Beneath the wings a pale white line stretching north and south showed him where the land ended and the sea began. Up and around him the retreating awning of the night was brushed golden by the sun rising up behind him.

"Jagger niner, steer 285 to maintain intercept."

He acknowledged and focused his attention on the thin trace of a condensation trail moving in high from the west. He tightened the seat harness, checked the flow of oxygen to his mask, and flicked the supercharger into top gear. It would be interesting to see how accurate the Boffins and their box of tricks was.

His track in relation to the approaching condensation trail began to diverge when: "Jagger niner, steer two nine five. You customer should be in your twelve o'clock position. Range 10 kilometres. Closing."

It became obvious as the range closed he wasn't going to be able to get up at the Spitfire. He cursed as the British machine passed overhead out of harm's way.

He dived back to the aerodrome, landed, and drew up in front of the hangar in a flurry of earth and grass. The engine died, the canopy hinged opened, and he leapt onto the wing, and onto the ground. "Get her refuelled immediately." he bawled to the waiting ground crew. "And fill her to the brim."

"What's all the excitement?" Kruger challenged him as he rushed into operations.

Staffel said: "Get your Boffins and their box of tricks to track the Spitfire they put me on to. I need to know when it is likely to get back here if, indeed, it intends to return to England on a reciprocal heading."

Kruger said: "What do you have in mind?

"Don't waste time, Kruger. Just do as I say."

Operations plotted the Spitfire's track across Holland into Germany. It made a number of sweeps over Dortmund and began its return on a reciprocal heading. Staffel arranged for the boffins to scramble him a little in advance of the Spitfire starting its journey across the north Sea.

From the time they alerted him he was airborne in record time. He climbed to an economic height, leaned the mixture as much as he dare, and stalked his target.

The white trail following the Spitfire thinned out as the machine sank into warmer air over the English coast. Staffel pulled the temporary power booster plug of the engine and closed in on the Spitfire. Over Harwich black puffs of shell bursts were sent up to warn the Britisher he had unwanted company. Staffel pounced when the Spitfire swung into the Thames estuary and momentarily presented itself almost in plan view through the gun sights. He let rip with a three second burst. He gave two more of similar duration and the contents of the glycol tank of the Spitfire burst into the slipstream like a stream of white blood. The British pilot abandoned the machine without waiting to incur further damage. The canopy went back, a figure slithered over the side of the cockpit and went over the wing trailing edge into space.

Staffel never waited to see if the parachute opened or where the Spitfire ended its flight; he was operating right on the limit where the range and endurance of the Messerschmitt was concerned. He crept back across the North Sea constantly playing with the mixture control, holding his breath, fingers crossed. The content gauges were on zero when he crossed over the Dutch coast. He tensed and prepared himself for the engine to fail at any moment. It held.

He put the wheels and flaps down and crossed over the boundary of the aerodrome, with a great sigh of relief, into a haven of welcoming green grass and his friends.

Air Duel

FIVE

Hadley Estate had undergone a number of changes over the years. The 140 acres it had once covered had dwindled to a mere 40. Lady Hadley had sold off land in order to remain solvent. Nevertheless she had made a point of retaining the trout streams, the picturesque walks through the woodland, the rides around Hadley hill, the church land and the cottages in the village.

She had sold the leases of the railway and the factory. The former, originally a small halt, was now a busy railway station. The factory had reverted back to the building of aircraft components. Between the wars it had concentrated on the production of automobiles.

She once had a total of 30 employees on the payroll. It now numbered 11. She had passed the farm and its land over to the farm hands, free of charge, but with the proviso they would supply her with a weekly supply of produce. She had long wanted to rid herself of the worry connected with the barley, wheat, vegetable and milk yields and the constant bartering for the sheep and cattle prices at market.

In 1937 she was on the verge of selling the remainder of the estate, lock, stock and barrel, and moving to a small thatched cottage beside a river, over at Bartley where she could happily spend her retirement years, painting, when the letter came from Timothy Herby asking her to accommodate Marie and their son, Paul, whilst he went off to join the air force.

Not many months later government officials visited the manor and said they would requisition the manor should the country go to war. She told them she had no objections providing they arranged some urgently needed renovation of the property, inside and outside. And that she and her guests, and a handful of staff could live in the west wing.

Renovation work started shortly after and she was told the manor would be used as a convalescing home for the war wounded.

A doctor and a token number of nurses were subsequently installed and she was given the task of recruiting local labour as kitchen staff and domestic cleaners.

The first patients to arrive at the manor were aircrew from the British Advanced Striking Force in France. There followed a steady trickle of wounded including bomber crews of mixed rank and from a variety of backgrounds.

Lady Hadley pottered happily in her own time speaking to the patients and staff, whilst Marie Herby supervised the kitchen and domestic staff.

As the weeks went by the war situation grew grave and uncertain. And Mr

Churchill broadcast a number of stirring speeches on the radio to rally the nation. The number of casualties arriving at the manor became a flood.

It reached a point where they ran out of bed space and someone came up with the idea of erecting a marquee in the grounds of the manor to accommodate the patients with less serious injuries.

Fortunately, for all concerned, the weather remained warm, dry and kind. But Marie had to take on more staff to cope with the swollen numbers.

Lady Hadley arranged various outings for the patients. Some were taken in wheel chairs to sit in the sun on the banks of the trout streams. Others were driven in a charabanc, in the evenings, out around Pritchards hill to watch the haymakers at work, and ended the short tour by visiting the PIGIT public house, a dark, dingy, grubby sort of place. But the patients loved it.

It could only hold 20 customers at a time and the landlord was far from the jolly character one would expect. Evidently this was all part of the charm of the place. Especially when the landlord started ranting and raving because the aircrews had drank his establishment dry.

No matter how he tried to adjust the quota of ale from the brewery he never got it right.

Lady Hadley also arranged entertainment at the manor in the evenings, which too had a certain novelty and a measure of amusement about it. The musicians she engaged had seen younger and better days and rarely played in tune. Nobody really cared. The old soldiers were a standing joke among the patients who respectfully never let it fester into a complaint. They were more intent on having fun as they lurched and staggered around the small dance floor on their sticks and crutches and were, more often than not, prevented from falling by their nurse dancing partners.

In the closing weeks of 1940 tragedy struck. Lady Hadley's daughter, Samantha, died in a flying accident. She'd been attached to the Air Transport Auxiliary as a pilot and as far as her mother knew Samantha, along with several other young women, ferried aircraft from the factory pools to the operational squadrons.

Throughout her life on the Hadley estate, and in the village she was known as the Herby girl. Which, in fact, was true. She had been conceived between Lady Hadley and Samuel Herby an employee of the estate: a union fully endorsed by the late Squire Hadley because of his inability to give his wife a child.

It had intended to be a personal and very discreet arrangement between the three people concerned but fate decided it would become public knowledge. Perhaps not in the nicest way. But as it so happened it didn't really matter because Samantha, as she matured, displayed the features and traits of both her parents. And her origins and parentage became quite obvious. She inherited her mother's shapely anatomy, long, fine fingers, shoulder-length golden hair and peach colour complexion. But she had much of the Herby about the eyes, the mouth and chin. And from a young age displayed their enthusiasm to take to the air.

She struck up a discreet correspondence with her father in Canada, care of the Calgary Flying Club, organised as it had been by her stepbrother Timothy when he returned to Canada after the First World War. In his letters her father told her about Grandfather Willy Herby's passion for flight. And then his own flying experiments with Timothy. He also sent her books on aerodynamics, and the principles of flight and aircraft construction. He was so very proud of her for

Air Duel

following the flying tradition of the family.

When it came to naming a present for her coming-of-age ball she said she wanted only financial assistance toward flying lessons. And her father provided the finance.

She soloed in a remarkably short time of four hours. And when she completed her tuition and got her ticket her mother presented her with her own private aeroplane, a DeHavilland Moth, which she kept in the paddock behind the Herby's old cottage on the hill and from which her father and step brother had made their pioneering flights.

Not only did she have a natural ability to fly but also, like her father, she had an inclination for the mechanics of her aeroplane. She amazed her mother by donning a pair of grubby overalls and lifting the engine covers of the Moth to change the sparking plugs, or clean the carburettor jets, or remove and clean the oil and the fuel filters. She was extremely fussy about the correct rigging of the wings.

In the early days she only flew around locally and many estate employees and quite a number of villagers owed it to her for their first taste of flight. Then she started flying further afield taking her mother to, and landing on, the estates of her mother's friends.

Then she began to spread her wings when she embarked on a long flight to Scotland. Which she followed with a flight over water to Ireland? She was one of the first three aviators to fly to the Channel Islands. And before long she ventured into the European continent.

In between her aerial gallivanting she helped her mother run the estate, and devoted some of her time to working for the Welfare Committee in the village. She was extremely popular with the villagers. Many of the older generation likened her to her cheerful, daring, adventurous father, Samuel Herby, and took delight in telling her about his spectacular pioneering flights from Hadley hill. And the kindnesses he paid to the needy folk in the village along with Mr and Mrs Sawyer.

Just how popular, loved and respected, she was, was demonstrated when her body was brought back to Hadley for burial, and the whole estate and village turned out. For her mother it was a very emotional event. Because not only was she overwhelmed by a deluge of floral tributes. But also the small courtesies and respect, which had faded with the diminishing status of the estate, and her position, were rekindled by the villagers as they gathered at the church gate after the service to pay their condolences to her. The women curtsied, the men bowed or touched their caps, and everyone addressed her by her title.

It later evolved, during a visit to the manor by an intelligence officer from the army and the air force, that Samantha had not met her death flying for the Air Transport Auxiliary. She had volunteered for special flying duties within the newly formed organisation. And she had been readily accepted because of her pre-war flying experience in Europe.

She was sent on a long flight to the border of Germany to dispatch two men by parachute and to combine it with a stint of photography using cameras fitted in her machine.

According to a message she sent in Morse code she picked up some AA fire and lost an engine. She was not however injured, the machine was under control, and she gave a new ETA for base.

What happened after that was a matter of conjecture? Very likely a German fighter got at her on the way home and seriously mauled her in the process. She was seriously injured and suffered a great loss of blood. But in spite of this she landed safely and brought back the cameras and film intact. She died before they could get her out of the aircraft on to a stretcher.

Lady Hadley was also told her daughter would be posthumously decorated. She would have much preferred to have her daughter still alive.

A week after the funeral Lady Hadley's adopted daughter, Mollie, and her husband Horace paid a visit to the manor from their farm in the West Country. Their absence at the funeral had been caused by a problem on the farm, the specifics of which Mollie had not disclosed when telephoning she would not be attending.

The moment Marie Herby saw Horace's car coming up the drive her stomach turned over. She had no real reason to feel threatened by Mollie. But she was. She had developed a complex at the end of the First World War when she came home to Hadley to learn Mollie had a child. And the gossip both on the estate and in the village claimed it was a Herby child - Timothy Herby's child.

She remembered her world falling apart when Lady Hadley confirmed that Mollie had confessed to Timothy being the father. Marie had used her qualities of dignity and restraint to pull her through that painful time. She remained calm and watchful and put on a brave face whilst Timothy prepared to take her to Canada with him. She could not escape Hadley fast enough.

Her new life in Canada served to free her of the unpleasant associations with Mollie. But just once in a while a letter from England would mention her name and Marie would relive the old prejudices.

What life had deprived Mollie of had more than compensated her with a powerful allure and, according to Lady Hadley, an ageless anatomy and countenance. At social functions men continued to flock to her like bees around a honey pot.

Marie did not despise her for this; it was the fact Mollie had wheedled herself into Timothy's intimate company whilst she, Marie, had been away helping in the war. She was equally aware that she, in part, had caused Mollie to get at Timothy. Had she gone to Canada when Timothy invited her by letter on numerous occasions they might very well have wed? By the same token had she waited for Timothy before she went off to war, that too may have thwarted the intimacy between Mollie and Timothy?

Apart from her pride being severely dented she never felt free of the humiliation that Molly caused her. She thought she made a good job of hiding it from the world, making herself appear dignified and composed. But Lady Hadley's power of discernment was to prove otherwise.

They were waiting at the top of the front steps of the manor waiting for the car to arrive. The two women had linked arms when Lady Hadley said: "I know you have good reasons to bear a grudge, Marie. But I do think it's time you forgave Mollie."

"Have I made it look that obvious?"

"You freeze each time her name is mentioned."

Marie checked to see they were not overheard. "It's not Mollie I actually despise. It's what she did."

"That's all the more reason for putting it all behind you. But for the grace of God you might very well be standing in those shoes that are about to step from the car."

"I don't understand." Marie frowned at her.

Air Duel

Lady Hadley said: "As far as I know you have led a sheltered and safe life in Canada. You never wanted for anything and you had your in-laws nearby as company during Timothy's long spells away from home. Alternatively fate might easily have put you in a certain place, at a certain time with a certain person and you might have fallen victim of the circumstances in which Mollie found herself."

The essence of what Lady Hadley said was to take a strange twist before the day was out.

The car drew to a halt at the bottom of the steps. It was one of the newer Austin saloons. And before Horace could get around to open the door for her Mollie was out and ascending the steps stylishly dressed in a pastel pink silk dress, black suede shoes, and a black pillar-box hat sporting a black feather traced with pink specks. She looked stunning and much younger than her years. She walked elegantly, negotiating the steps without the need to look down at her feet.

Greetings were exchanged. Then she led the way, linking arms with her foster mother and leaving Marie to accompany Horace as they passed through the entrance hall that thronged with the military guests. Horace had an arm around Marie's waist and just as they passed from sight of the guests and followed Mollie and Lady Hadley up the spiral staircase to the west wing Horace lowered his hand and gave her posterior a gentle squeeze.

Marie reacted by gripping his hand and returning it to her waist.

At dinner that evening in Lady Hadley's private quarters it became apparent that Mollie's visit was not really to pay her condolences regarding Samantha's death. Marie observed that she took little interest when Lady Hadley spoke of the moving tributes by the estate employees and the villagers.

They ate for a time in silence. Then Lady Hadley said: "How is Peter getting on in the air force?"

Marie winced; Peter was Mollie's son by Timothy Herby, Marie's husband. She couldn't help but feel the opening of an old, unhealed wound in her emotions.

"He's having a spot of bother."

" Really?

"I had a letter from him last week in which he said he is having great difficulty in landing an aircraft at night. And I don't think he is exaggerating."

"Could be he just needs a little more practise." Lady Hadley suggested.

Horace said: "I think Mollie is more concerned for when he ultimately gets on operations and is responsible for a crew."

If he should get that far, Marie thought. From what little she knew from Timothy, if a pilot didn't come up to scratch during training he would never qualify for operational flying.

Lady Hadley said: "How do you think we might help?"

"Well, his father - your husband, Marie - is serving as a wing commander, so Lady Hadley tells me. I don't think it would be too much to ask him to pull a few strings in order to help my son overcome his difficulties."

Lady Hadley looked across the table at Marie. "What do you think, Marie."

"Personally, I'd rather not get involved. Timothy is due for leave in a week's time. I can get him to contact you, Mollie, by telephone. Or you could arrange another visit."

Mollie didn't get a chance to agree. Lady Hadley said: "Right. That's settled. Let's repair to the drawing room for coffee."

Because of her duties in connection with the military guests Marie had to leave them at this point. She also explained she would be retiring to her bed thereafter on account she had to be up early. She bid them "Goodnight."

She had changed into her nightdress and was on the point of retiring to her bed when she heard tapping sounds on her bedroom door. She suspected it was one of the staff bringing her an urgent message. But she was shocked to discover it was Horace Chase who hastened her back into the room and shut the door. Suddenly she felt very vulnerable. He was only clad in a bathrobe, and she in a flimsy night dress.

"What are you doing here, Horace? It's absurd."

He moved towards her. She moved away from him. "This is all quite improper. What would Mollie say."

"She is too busy chatting to Claire. And they'll probably be there all night."

Marie was brought to halt as she backed into a wall of the room. Horace drew up before her and slid his fingers through her hair. "You look so delightfully wild with your hair let down, Marie. And you look as young as when I first moved into Hadley."

She took his hand. "It's a very nice compliment, Horace. But you know we mustn't."

His eyes bore into her. His other free hand smoothed her neck and slipped down over her shoulder and came to the point of caressing her breasts.

"No, Horace. Please." she pleaded, and knew immediately her voice was neither firm nor convincing.

He freed his other hand and embraced her. "I must have you, Marie. I've wanted you for so many years."

The grip of his arms seemed to squeeze the air from her lungs. He kissed her face - her neck - her bare shoulder. And after he ripped her nightdress away in one deft movement his mouth fell upon her breasts and suckled her with the appetite of a hungry infant.

He swung her around and toppled her onto the bed. And as he stood towering over her, removing his robe and exposing a very adequate specimen of his virility he said: "You have been neglected for too long, Marie. Your husband was rarely with you at home in Canada. And you can count on one hand the number of times he has visited you since you came back to this country." He wedged his legs between hers and parted them and slowly sank onto her and penetrated her cloisters with his long hard, hot stiffness. At first his actions hurt her. Then as he began to ride her, as might a vigorous man ride a horse, she succumbed and experienced a great explosion of physical joy that verged on insanity, and her thoughts burst into a world of divine oblivion, the likes of which she had not experienced for years…

How long she traversed this New World, she didn't know. She perhaps remembered somewhat regretfully leaving it and floating back to reality. At first grateful for the novelty and uniqueness of the experience. And then as Horace thanked and kissed her, farewell, she felt a measure of guilt steal up on her. She had broken her marriage vows. She had disgraced her husband. And more significantly she had enjoyed it.

She was debating how she would face her family and friends and how she might conceal her improper conduct from her husband when she became frantic with anxiety. She felt condemned. She had stained the untarnished reputation of her late parents. And as she plunged deeper into a whirlpool of despair she awoke from the nightmare.

Never had she been so consumed by such relief as that when she realised her intercourse with Horace had only been the contents of a dream. It suddenly came to her what Lady Hadley had said about fate and about being in a certain place, at a certain time with a certain person. It could quite easily have happened; Horace was in the house and had pinched her bottom not long after his arrival. Fate had decided she would escape. She was lucky.

She slept no more that night. She went and bathed, and dressed. She was about well in advance of the domestic staff who reported in the morning to prepare breakfast for the military patients. She supervised and worked alongside them pursued as she was by a mixture of emotions. A part of her still smarted from the impropriety of the dream whilst inwardly she felt stimulated and vibrant with energy.

She kept herself involved with her work for most of the day visiting Lady Hadley just after lunch to learn with great relief that Mollie and Horace had taken their leave shortly after breakfast.

Over a pot of tea Marie said: "Do you really think Molly's son, Peter, is as helpless as Mollie makes him out to be?"

Lady Hadley sipped at her tea and replaced the cup in the saucer. "Peter has inherited her looks and, I would say, many of her traits. He is tall and slim like her with fair skin and fine features, which make him, appear effeminate. And without being disrespectful he's not very quick on the up-take, academically, just as Mollie is prone to be.

Horace managed to get him into the local grammar school by bribing a school governor. He left school without any qualifications of merit. But he proved to be a good hands-on worker on the farm.

Mollie brought him here just over a year ago and I must give credit where credit is due. He speaks well and has impeccable manners."

Marie said: "It would appear he doesn't have much of the Herby family about him."

Lady Hadley smiled. "He's taken up flying, Marie. And that's in the Herby blood."

"But, as Mollie says, he is not coping."

"If I remember correctly it is only his night landings. If you cast your mind back Timothy, your husband, and his father had to deal with numerous problems during their pioneering flights from here all those years ago."

Marie did not pursue the subject further. She wasn't really interested. Peter was Molly's son. And Mollie was Mollie. She saw Lady Hadley off to her afternoon nap. And went to her own room, removed her shoes and dress and lay upon the bed to rest.

She awoke a little after four to discover her son, Paul, had popped home for a couple of days leave. His visits were a distinct joy to her. Particularly after he revealed his talents on the piano and her world ran riot with an immeasurable pride and happiness. For her his musical achievements were a dream fulfilled - a distant star that had come within reach.

When Paul was home the manor was rarely without the sound of his piano music. He practiced in the mornings. In the afternoons the French doors of the large lounge were opened to freshen the place and the music floated through the open doors and drifted toward the stable yard and the paddock and orchard beyond.

Air Duel

In the evenings Marie encouraged him to give concerts or provide an opportunity for the military guests and the nursing staff to let their hair down and get involved with a sing-along to all the old and modern popular songs played by Paul on the piano.

One evening amongst the audience were a number of guests invited by Lady Hadley from Oxford college to one of Paul's classical concerts during which he played several of his own compositions. For each and every piece he received a rapturous applause and a standing ovation. Marie cried an ocean of tears such was her pride and joy at her son's performance.

He was invited to give concerts on no less than six occasions before a celebrated audience up at the college all of which Marie attended and witnessed the adulation and salutations he received. She deeply regretted her mother and father were not alive to share her pride and depth of happiness at what Paul was achieving. They had both been competent pianists. And Marie herself had inherited their skills at the keyboard. Now - a grandson was entertaining the world. It was incredibly impressive and exciting. She wrote to her in-laws in Canada knowing grandfather Samuel would be more interested in how his grandson was coping with his flying. But Grandmother Rebecca would be delighted with the news of his musical successes and brag about it to her friends and neighbours.

When his father came on leave Marie could not wait to break the news and give him evidence of their son's capabilities. But first she told him of Mollie and her son's trouble with his night landings and he put in a phone call to Mollie to discuss the matter.

She mentioned Paul when they were in bed of a night. She told him how his musical talents had started and how it had escalated to the concerts at Oxford College. Lady Hadley claimed he would play to the world capitals after the war.

"But he mentions so little about what he is doing in the air force." Marie said.

"What has he told you?"

"That he is still flying a Spitfire. The flights are much longer. And he has more time to view the passing scenery."

"Then, he hasn't told you about his medal."

"What medal?"

"He was awarded a gong for rescuing a Blenheim and its crew from a marauding Messerschmitt. By all accounts Paul said he didn't know what all the fuss was about."

Marie said, "It might not mean much to him. But it is important to us as his parents. I shall have a word or two to say to him."

Timothy embraced her and kissed her on the forehead. "You must remember, my dear, the Herby family does not store much importance on the issue of medals. My father was decorated for his soldiering in the African skirmishes, but it meant more to my mother than it did to him. And on your side of the family you never found out about your father's medal until three years after his death. He could have given it to your mother. Instead he left it to his squadron as a tribute to his fellow airmen."

Marie said: "I still have the medal you received in the last war. And I treasure it. You should feel honoured and proud that your country saw fit to recognise what you did and what you sacrificed."

"I don't recall you getting a medal for administering and caring for our wounded and sick," he said

"Oh. That was quite different, Timothy. We were volunteers. And nurses don't expect accolades and praise. We were angels of mercy and proud of it."

He did not prolong the discussion on the subject. Unbeknown to her she had contradicted herself, and he grinned in the darkness. What was more her modesty about her part in the war was no less or no more than that of her late father, passed on, as it had been, through the genes.

Presently he aroused her and they made love. And when a Herby made love it was comprehensive. Within minutes Marie lay in the aftermath of the passion he had unleashed on her, drained and exhausted by his powerful virility and the potent response of her own body. She felt totally relaxed and at peace with the world. She drifted easily into sleep, cradled by his arms, and in total escape from her troubles of recent days, and the war.

Air Duel

SIX

The ground felt decidedly hard beneath his heavy step and he exhaled small clouds of condensation as he walked in the icy air under a starlit sky. It was a little after 0400 hours. And in spite of wearing boots and gloves the frost succeeded a little in nipping at the tip of toe and finger.

Trees and bushes passed by on either side gripped by a ghostly white, strange and fascinating, in the total silence of the early hours.

He skirted a small lake, sheeted by ice, and he thought of the fish trapped in the air pockets. It made him reflect on the warm, comfortable sanctuary of his bed that his flying duties had forced him to vacate. He walked for a half mile between an avenue of elm trees. Then a little further on he came to a clearing before a blister hangar in which his Spitfire sheltered, its engine shrouded in a heated curtain. He walked in past a succession of wooden offices to one at the end, which served as the flight office and in which an airman had lighted a small coke stove. It managed to fight off the harsh winter cold. But only just.

A tired, unwashed face appeared in the doorway of the office holding a steaming enamel mug of hot sweet tea. "Ready for your cuppa, sir?"

The pilot nodded and thanked him with a smile. And the fitter said, "Do you want the engine run yet?"

"Wait until the intelligence officer puts in an appearance. Then give the canopy a final polish before you run the engine."

"Rightee o, sir."

The pilot was always conscious of wasting fuel on long engine runs, on the ground. Fuel that might be needed for a diversion caused by bad weather. Or needed to out-run or outwit an enemy machine during an unexpected encounter.

He was standing before a large wall map, hazarding a guess at where the morning's flying would take him when Bradley, from intelligence, arrived.

"Morning, Paul." he said cheerily, and immediately got down to business by unrolling a map on a nearby table, and putting a met forecast, in teleprinter form, on an adjacent chair. "I'm afraid it might be bit of a bore. But it's Bremen again. Bomber Command are eager to know how they scored in their thrash last night."

The pilot looked at the red line drawn on the map by Bradley and who had also entered track angles and distances on a small flight log. The Bremen run was not unknown to the pilot. Though he did not take it for granted that it would be a trouble-free flight. Unpredictable weather conditions and enemy fighter activity could be disruptive.

He settled down to computing true airspeeds and heights, courses and groundspeeds, and range and endurance figures, during which voices echoed in the hangar and his Spitfire was pushed out. Presently its engine roared into life and settled down to warming-up revs.

The pilot double-checked all of his figures, used the toilet, and donned his Mae West life jacket, and crouched into the harness of his parachute.

The PR Spitfire differed from the type he had flown from Biggin. Painted in an overall duck egg blue it looked less aggressive and much sleeker. It carried cameras in the place of armament. Its up-rated engine with a twin gear supercharger gave it a superior ceiling so that the unarmed machine could fly free of any pursuing enemy by climbing out of range. A modification to the engine exhaust manifold served to muffle the roaring crescendo of noise and this made it more comfortable for the pilots on the long jaunts they were making.

Jones, the fitter, signalled he was ready. And in the icy slipstream from the propeller he and the pilot changed places in the cockpit. The pilot took his time settling comfortably in the seat, securing the harness, connecting the radio and oxygen leads, strapping the flight log to a thigh and arranging his map.

Some pilots complained of the cramped cockpit. Whereas he liked it, the snug fit made him feel part of the aeroplane. Not a single movement in flight went unnoticed and, equally, the tight fit gave him an instant indication of any irregular beat in the engine. The slightest vibration and rough running of the engine was conveyed to him instantly through the airframe to his hands and feet upon the controls.

He waved the chocks clear and got under way with a touch of throttle, giving Jones a customary salute as he did so. The mischievous grin of the airman reminded the pilot of the chat he'd had with his father prior to going on operational flying from Biggin. His father had told him to never underestimate the value of his ground crew who he claimed would contribute at least eighty percent to his chances of survival, and his success as a fighter pilot. A word of praise for them from time to time and a packet of cigarettes or a round of drinks for them at their local would never go amiss, his father said. Evidently a practise he had followed with his ground crew in the First World War.

He smiled as he taxied past a pastoral scene of trees and hedgerows on the private estate, and rabbits scurried for cover as the growling Spitfire approached. Up through the windscreen the stars were dulling and there was a hint of light to the east. He brought the machine to a halt and made his take-off checks and satisfied himself with the instrument readings.

He turned onto the tarmacadam drive of the estate, lining the nose up with a distant fir tree and eased the throttle up to full power. Initially it was necessary to perform something of a ballet on the rudder pedals to keep the Spitfire straight and to correct the swing to the right as the tail came up. But once it got into its stride its obedience was total and immediate. It accelerated keenly and a touch of backward pressure on the stick sprang it into the air. The earth fell away quickly and the strip of light on the far horizon became a band. He retracted the undercarriage, adjusted the boost and revs, and trimmed the machine for climbing flight.

By the time they reached the East Coast they were soaring up through twenty thousand feet. Mid way of the North Sea they reached the Spitfire's ceiling and levelled off, blazing a dense condensation trail. Spokes of sunshine radiated up from the horizon delicately lighting the blueness of the wings and the many rows of flush rivets. Ahead and on each side of the engine covers the protruding exhaust ports shook almost imperceptibly.

He never failed to enjoy the loneliness, the freedom, the commanding view, the intoxication, dampened as it was by the need to remain alert to the fitness of the Spitfire, the life-sustaining flow of the oxygen supply, the unpredictable traits of the weather, and the sudden appearance of unwanted company.

He thought he saw one of the latter as they passed over the Dutch coast: a small German aircraft shape several thousand feet below behaving like a frustrated fly trying to get out from under a sheet of glass. He gave the Spitfire a temporary burst of throttle and the shape lagged behind.

He made Bremen in just over an hour, completed six sweeps in the unheard whirl of the cameras, and set course for home.

By now the sun was riding high behind him. He remained vigilant for unwanted company. Very distant he thought he saw the silver glimmer of the sea. He consulted his navigation log for a spell, made a couple of mental calculations, and relaxed a little. The weather ahead looked reasonable. The golden cascading sunlight made him think of Melanie. Young, in her prime, he likened her to a flower in full bloom, the stem of her body swaying to the motion of her step, her smiling mouth and eyes shining bright as a sunflower: all of which continued to haunt him and dominate his thoughts. Her letter had done nothing to alter his rampant feelings for her.

A division of land and sea slid beneath the shimmering wings. And as he rolled to the inverted to check for enemy activity he again saw the fly trying to escape from under the imaginary glass plate. He was in no doubt that it was a German aircraft, which he noticed, began to follow his route across the desolate expanse of the North Sea.

As he approached the East Coast of England he put the Spitfire in a gentle dive in preparation for fixing his position on the Thames Estuary and then heading for Bentley. He took care to make it look casual to the pursuing German.

If there should be a scrap the German would have to make haste if he was to get back across the sea to his base with sufficient fuel. He had a feeling it was the same one that attacked Peterson and made him take to his brolly and suffer a chilly ducking in the Thames.

Suddenly a flurry of shell bursts scarred the air behind him giving an indication of the enemy's presence. He quickly scanned the earth below for an open area to get down in, since his planned destiny for the German would involve him and the Spitfire in something of a gamble.

As he suspected the German chose the blind spot of the Spitfire to make his attack. A combination of stick and rudder rolled the Spitfire neatly out of the line of fire and he looked down through the canopy at the Messerschmitt breaking off its attack. Herby drew the stick back and went in pursuit. But as he got astern, the German pulled off an Immelman roll and came roaring down at him, all guns blazing. He spoilt the German's aim by flying a series of alternating sideslips. Then as the Messerschmitt flew under his nose he hauled the Spitfire up into a stall turn. And as he came out of it he put on full power and went in pursuit. The first part of his plan worked; he herded the German further back in over the coast. A move that cost the German precious fuel and further eroded his chances of making it back to his base across the North Sea.

Herby got on to the tail of the Messerschmitt and the scrap became a battle of wits and stamina. The German tried for a time to shake him off by cavorting through a series of dodges. Having failed he settled for a steep turn hoping he would tighten it enough to get on the Spitfire's tail. The more he tried Herby pulled tighter. A heavy force piled up on the head, shoulders and limbs. Rivets strained under the load. The engines roared their might as each machine fought for supremacy.

On the ground the ack-ack guns had fallen silent and the crews looked up in eager anticipation as the two machines pursued each other in an ever-decreasing circle.

"Why don't that Spit hose him down and have done with it?" a gunner remarked.

"Might 'av run out of ammo." another suggested.

A sergeant said: "For your information, laddie, those blue Spits don't carry guns. They're photo-recce Spits according to our aircraft recognition posters. They only carry cameras."

"Cor blimey." a voice exclaimed. "That Spit is chancing it a bit. He's nearly got his nose up the arse-end of old Fritz."

With the increasing force of the turn pressing his head onto his chest and impairing his sight Herby looked with some difficulty at the nose of the Spitfire drawing closer to the braced tail of the Messerschmitt. He could just see the German pilot hunched over his controls. He pulled the stick back a fraction more and the tail slid from view beneath the nose of the Spitfire. He tensed and eased the power of the engine. And for a brief moment the nose dropped and the propeller churned through the tail unit of the Messerschmitt with a grinding wrenching sound that filled the air with a debris of wood, metal and fabric. Herby gambled on the German momentarily continuing his turn to port. He reversed bank and turned away to starboard easing the power of the engine that was vibrating madly in its attempt to drive a mortally damaged propeller.

The gunners cheered loudly when the Messerschmitt fell tail-less out of the turn and immediately began to spin helplessly to earth.

"Come on you bastard Kraut. See if you can get out of that one!" a gunner shouted triumphantly.

A strange silence filled the air. The gunners watched with morbid curiosity as the German pilot spun to his death on the other side of the marshes.

"Come on you lot!" the sergeant shouted. "Get those bloody guns cleaned and reloaded. Don't you know there's a war on."

Herby managed to get the stricken Spitfire down in the sports field of a school, which, mercifully, was empty at the time. And for his exemplary airmanship and unorthodox manner for disposing of an enemy aircraft he received a bar to his DFC.

The medals were of no importance to him. But Melanie was. Not a day passed without something reminding him of her - a colour - a sound - an overheard comment - a certain time of day - a date: all had him recalling his brief moments with her.

He had curtailed his visits to the manor after he received the letter from her. His zest for music had died overnight and he found it impossible to explain his lapses to his mother. And neither did he think she would be impressed if he told her Melanie was spoken for when he met her. And had since married an officer in Bomber Command. He told her the work was piling up at the unit and leave was being cancelled for all. Which to some extent was true. Bomber Command was attacking numerous targets each night with heavy bombers whilst medium bombers stabbed at key installations by day. And as a result the PR units were constantly in demand for photographic evidence of the successes of the raids.

To some extent he found it easier to cope with the loss of contact with Melanie in the quiet comfortable dignity of Bentley manor and its acres of surrounding countryside in which there were some good walks. More often than not, however, he felt more relaxed when he was flying. It got him up and away from the niggling disappointment and the daily confrontations with his feelings, and his yearning to see Melanie again and knowing it was out of the question.

On the wing his bottled up feelings and emotion seemed to float away and dissolve allowing him to look at his life more rationally and in a different perspective. The crisp untouched blue sky and the pure whiteness of the heaped clouds brought to him a greater clarity of thought and a dominant feeling of well being. The earth, many thousands of feet below, could not see the scene as he saw it. Nor appreciate the powerful steady growl of the engine as he heard it. He felt safe and well treated up here.

He noticed the fog rolling across the southern counties as he let down on the approach to the East Coast and from his lofty viewpoint he could see it spreading towards Oxford. He rolled to the inverted to check for any cunning Jerry then set about making a decision in view of the fog threatening to disrupt his landing back at Bentley.

Within minutes he was touching down at Biggin Hill, throttling back to spluttering revs and tap-dancing on the rudder pedals to keep the Spitfire running straight on its narrow undercarriage and jockeying, lightly-loaded tail wheel. As he did so the fog came rolling over a distant boundary of the aerodrome.

He parked the Spitfire between the black sinister shapes of a single engine Defiant and a twin engine Beaufighter: members of night fighter squadrons currently operating from Biggin, he later learned. He stopped the engine, slid the canopy back, removed his helmet, and was sat massaging his face when a voice said: "Hullo there, sir."

He turned his head to find his engine fitter, of late, standing at the wing root behind the trailing edge. He clambered from the cockpit and shook his oil-stained hand in greeting.

"It's grand to see you again sir. Care to join us for a mug of tea after you have reported in. The lads will be so pleased to see you."

"Most certainly, Mr Simkins. Be with you in about ten minutes. And by the way do you still have my mug?"

"Kept in a place of honour in our crew room, sir. It's not been used since you left."

After reporting the reasons for his unannounced arrival to Biggin control, he put in a telephone call to Bentley and learnt that his decision to land away from his base had been a prudent one. They had a real pea souper and couldn't see a single tree on the estate from the mess.

He arranged for a guard to be put on the Spitfire and its cameras and vital films and joined up with his old ground crew. They greeted him enthusiastically and proudly served him tea in the blue and white enamel mug they had presented him with back in the hectic days of the Biggin battles, and on which someone had painted 12 swastikas and his squadron number. The drab decor of their crew room was livened by a great number of pictures featuring voluptuous ladies in various stages of nudity. They reminisced for a time about the old days. Then they told him about their current life with the night fighters which wasn't half as exciting.

They told him they had heard Sergeant Kent was doing hit and run raids across the Channel, from Tangmere. And they'd heard tell that flight sergeant Ross had been posted overseas to Malta.

The two NCO pilots had formed the other elements of his flight at Biggin. The general rule was that they should protect his tail, the flight leader, when doing battle thereby allowing him to concentrate on shooting enemy machines down. But from the outset of them joining the flight under his leadership he told them it was every man for himself and that they were entitled to make as many individual kills as they liked.

Naturally, if they could help each other out in a tight spot, all well and good. But on no account were they to concentrate on his safety at the expense of putting their own in jeopardy. During their time with him Kent had disposed of seven AE, and Ross, five. Added to Herby's score this meant the flight had knocked down a grand total of 24 German aircraft.

What was more the flight had not lost a single aeroplane in combat and none of them had been grounded for technical reasons.

The ground crew thought it a fantastic record and felt justly proud at being a part of it. And evidently were regularly telling the rest of the air force about it.

In parting company with them he thanked them for the tea and their hospitality, and shook them by hand in farewell. Sergeant Dexter accompanied him out of the hangar and when they were alone he said: "Don't think I'm meddling in your affairs, sir. But I think it might be an idea for you to visit the roadhouse you officers used when you were here."

The pilot was not aware his ground crew knew of his visits to the roadhouse; he'd always been discreet, or, so he thought.

"They've had a rough time of it in one way and another." sergeant Dexter said. " A stray Jerry bomb hit the place one night and killed the old girl who owned it. Volunteers were called for by the CO and I took the lads to the place to tidy it up and get it back open for business by putting a tarpaulin over the roof and re-building one of the walls.

Then to pile on the agony a month after the young niece buried her aunt she received, news that her own husband was missing, presumed killed on operations. He'd been on a trip to Essen."

"But what has all this got to do with me?" the pilot pleaded innocence.

"When we were working there we happened to mention your name She didn't say a lot. But it certainly bucked her up. I'm certain a visit from you would not go amiss. Here - take the keys of my car. It's parked behind the hangar."

The pilot went to the mess and from a Batman he got a clean shirt and a razor to freshen himself up. And what was normally a twenty-minute journey to the roadhouse took him nigh on an hour. The dense fog rarely allowed him to get above third gear or travel in excess of 20 miles per hour. The little Austin 7 got him there just on teatime. He did not dare think how he would get back to Biggin in the hours of darkness and the fog. He felt relieved and privileged to have got there in the first place.

He made his way in feeling uncertain and unsure of himself; the tone of her letter was still fresh on his mind. She might take exception to his visit and regard it as taking advantage of her in her time of grief. He found himself trying to concoct what he should say to her as an excuse for his visit. He chose his normal chair by a window. Ahead and to the left a log fire cast shadowy reflections on the walls and ceiling and glinted on the brass wall lamps. In a far corner he could just see the dark forms of a man and woman conversing in low tones at a table. It appeared the fog had deterred any other customers.

Behind him a door swung open and a waitress came and took his order for two poached eggs on toast and a pot of tea. On inquiring about Melanie's whereabouts he was told she was resting.

Throughout the snack he wrestled with how he should make the approach to Melanie. He eventually decided to forget it and leave. Perhaps it would better to write her a letter in the circumstances.

He was certain it was the best way to tackle it, and was paying the bill when the waitress said she had passed his comments to Melanie. And Melanie would like to know his name. He told her and the girl smiled and walked away, leaving him in a quandary as to whether he should depart or not.

Presently the girl appeared in the doorway and beckoned to him, and then directed him to the entrance of the lounge. He thanked her and walked in to be halted by what he saw. Melanie sat with her feet up on a couch and in sharp contrast to the blossoming flower, he had known previously, she drooped and wilted under a dark, heavy cloud. Her face lit up, however, on seeing him. She rose slowly and greeted him quietly. Unthinkingly he embraced her, and rather than objecting she cuddled up to him and looked up at him with her large eyes, her long copper hair surrounding her girlish face and tumbling down upon her shoulders, her full blooded lips, tempting, inviting.

"I did not come with the intention of causing you any embarrassment," he said. "But the weather forced me down at Biggin. And sergeant Dexter told me you've had a hard time of it lately."

"I don't suppose I'm much worse off than a lot of others in the chaos of this war." she sighed. "But try as I might to work up some enthusiasm I feel so empty, so tired."

He said considerately, "That's quite natural after what you've been through. You should get away from here for a spell and take a holiday."

The hint of a smile crept onto her lips and traces of colour seeped into her pale cheeks. "Are you suggesting I should dash away with that gallant knight, on his white charger, to his castle?"

It pleased him to know she had not forgotten their conversations of the past. Although he was eager she did not draw the wrong conclusions about his visit. He looked fondly down at her. "Not that exactly. But I must confess you are still very important to me."

Her smile brightened. "Really!" she exclaimed. "And there was me thinking you only came here for the steaks and raw onion."

He embraced her more tightly, kissed her respectfully on the forehead and said, "You were my star during that hectic time at Biggin, Melanie. I hung everything on you. I flew and fought with one objective in mind: to protect my hide and get back down in one piece in order to see you again." He paused. "And now if I have said too much or offended you, you can ask me to leave."

He thought she would remind him of the last letter she sent him and possibly point out she was a widow in mourning.

She did neither. She placed a hand on each side of his face and regarded him with a hint of moisture in her eyes. "It was very considerate of you to come, Paul," she said huskily. "And I am very glad that you did."

What struck Melanie the most when the train pulled out of Hadley station and she waited outside for transport were the silence and a great sense of peace? The brilliance of the sun faded the blueness of the sky. A small, solitary white cloud drifted aimlessly overhead. Somewhere, not far away, a lark got up and started its gay overture of song to a hushed audience.

So enchanted by the atmosphere she was quite carried away and didn't notice Paul arrive with the car until he was by her side, relieving her of her small case. He was dressed in air force trousers, held up by braces, and an air force shirt in the collar of which he wore a white silk muffler. He asked her about the journey and she told him the train was very crowded to Oxford, but she managed to find a seat on the connecting train to Hadley. He saw her into the car, put her case in the small space behind the seats, and slid in beside her.

"All set?" he smiled at her.

She acknowledged with a return smile and said, "And is my Sir Galahad dashing me off to his castle in his motorised steed?"

He lifted her hand and kissed the back of it. "I'll let you be the judge of that m'lady."

He set the car in motion and soon she felt the wind upon her face and through her hair as the open top sports car with its stiff suspension got up to speed. Hadley Hill came up on the right side looming steeply to its 800-foot summit. Behind gaps in the hedgerows to their left Melanie spotted a river snaking through the countryside reflecting the blue of the sky and splinters of sunlight. Further beyond she spotted a large white impressive building. Then the car was slowing up in response to the sudden appearance of a string of horses and their riders around a bend in the road.

Directly the horses were behind them Paul moved back up through the gears and they moved on. The playful air around the windscreen tempted her eyes to shed tears. They passed through an avenue of trees. Then they were running alongside a meadow which gave way to an orchard of mixed fruit and over which a kestrel hovered. There was something different about this place. And then it came to her. The whole scenery, the whole atmosphere, exuded an air of antiquity and a magnificence that appeared to embrace her. She felt it as the wind plucked playfully at her hair and streamed it behind her. Light, feathery fingers of air touched her bare knees and crept under the hem of her dress. The sun poured its warmth on her upturned face, and caressed the long slenderness of her neck.

The tragedies in her life, of recent months, began to distance themselves from her. A New World beckoned. She had no idea what Paul had in store for her at Hadley; he had invited her to stay for a week. She not only felt vulnerable to his emotions but also her own. Each time she caught him glancing down at her bare legs, his attention caused her a quiver of excitement.

He turned the car off the main road and began to follow a winding track up Hadley hill. "If you look up and a little to your right you will spot my humble castle, m'lady. Our abode for the next week."

Melanie saw a cottage perched on the brow of the hill. It was the sort of enchanting scene depicted on a picture post card. Her feelings began to gather pace in anticipation of what lay ahead of her. She took one of his hands from the steering wheel and kissed the palm. "Be gentle with me, your Grace. Be gentle," she said.

SEVEN

Staffel arrived at the tenement building in Essen after flying part of the way in a Junkers 52 and travelling the rest of the way by train. He'd left the Netherlands in the grip of ice and snow. His only regret was that he had left Hultz to do all the work; Taube was missing, presumed dead. He had been scrambled to intercept an intruding Spitfire and that was the last anyone had seen or heard of him. Hultz had heard a whisper that the Boffins had made a blunder with their box of tricks and given Taube a false steer, and he had run out of fuel and perished somewhere in the expanse of the North Sea.

Staffel looked up at a blacked-out window on the fourth floor, feeling a gathering of warmth in anticipation of the welcome that awaited him in the apartment. He stepped eagerly up several flights of stairs and pressed the button of the doorbell. The tall, slim figure of Ursula came to view dressed in a black chiffon dress, with her long silky blonde hair falling loose about her shoulders.

"Staffel!" she exclaimed. "You've made it!" she pulled him in, closed the door and embraced him tightly. "It's been a long time," she said. "I've missed you badly."

He held her face and kissed her boldly. "You don't change, you gorgeous creature."

She eased him away and inspected him from head to toe. "You've lost weight, Staffel."

"Worrying about you." he suggested with a grin.

She took his bag, overcoat and cap, pushed him into a chair and relieved him of his boots. She poured, and handed him a glass of cognac. "Take a drink whilst I prepare you a bath."

In her absence he looked around in the dim lighting of the room. Soft music played in the background. Vapours of her perfume traced the air. He closed his eyes and revelled in the luxuries, which rarely came his way these days. He also thought himself very fortunate to have Ursula as his friend and lover and he was in no doubt that his life would have little meaning and purpose without her.

Later as he lay in the warm scented water and her hands moved over him she said, " I overheard you were lucky not to have been sent to the Russian front."

"I'm not surprised," he said. "After my skirmish with the SS in France."

A hand squeezed his left shoulder and he felt a stiffness that had not existed before. It slowly disappeared at the will of her massaging hands.

He said; "Do you really know what happened in France?"

She said considerately, "I don't wish to know. I like to think you acted in the way we were taught in the youth movement."

She urged him to roll over and her hands began to play along his back. He said: "The SS made up for their suspicion. I am presently employed to shoot down unarmed reconnaissance aircraft."

"So I am told. And added more enemy aircraft to your score. Who knows, you might be decorated, Staffel."

"Decorated for what?" he said irritably. "Decorated for killing defenceless airmen. It's in very poor taste."

"From what I hear it's better than flying on the Russian front."

He looked over a shoulder at her. "Since you refer to it so often, how is our progress in the Russian campaign?"

She raised his left leg and drew his attention to a creaking sound when she pivoted his foot. He admitted he suffered at times with stiffness in the foot. She manipulated the joint with a thumb and index finger and the stiffness mysteriously disappeared.

She said: "Between you and me I hear the severity of the Russian winter is bogging our troops down. High Command has suggested that I might go with others in a concert party in an attempt to raise the spirits of our fighting men."

He rolled onto his back. He would much prefer she did not go; since the war started they had spent less and less time together. If she went east he probably wouldn't see her for six months or more. But he knew as well as she did, from their indoctrination in the youth movement, the Fatherland came first in such decisions.

In a surge of determination he rose up, dripping, from the water, asked her to pass a towel and said: "I suggest we forget the war, for the moment, and live for ourselves. Let's eat; I'm famished."

They dined quietly and drank a lot of wine. Afterwards they sat for a time listening to the music. Then touched by the nostalgia of the moments they had shared at the rallies and parties and summer camps in the youth movement they danced on the carpet of the room with their shoes removed.

"You always recharge me when you hold me like this, Staffel." she whispered.

"Is that all? You make me feel on top of the world."

"Like flying?

"Not quite. But you are getting better."

She pressed hard against him, stirring up a multitude of desires that were numbed pleasantly by the wine. She regarded him with glistening, desirous eyes, and he took it as a signal to guide her to the bedroom. She removed his shirt. He slid her dress down over her shoulders and the momentum carried it to her feet. She loosened the belt of his trousers. He removed her underwear and caressed her warm, smooth, subtle body. She stroked him about the loins and sighed loudly with the urgency of what she wanted from him. She fell backwards onto the bed, pulling him on top of her. He probed her to a tempo dictated by the drumming of her fingers on his hindquarters and which increased to a frantic pace where they lost all sense of time and place. They were only aware of surging along on a blissful wave of ecstasy that seemed to sap their strength and blot out all the unhappiness of the world.

"How do you see us when we win the war?" Ursula said later as they lay recovering in the aftermath of the intercourse. She nestled her head on his chest. And he absently played with her hair.

"I see you as a national celebrity in show business with your voice." he said. "And me as a married man with lots of children and very little money."

She rolled on top of him. "Not if I have anything to do with it, Staffel."

"You are too important to High Command to end up as an ordinary common housewife," he said.

She dabbed at his nose with a finger. "You forget the Fuhrer is eager to produce a dominant race. What better than you and I to be part of that programme."

"Me!" he laughed. "You forget I am from a farming background. I am given to understand the experts say they want couples from the intelligentsia."

"Then I shall advise them that a mix with farming stock would be more suitable." She rose up, slid down on him, and commenced to bring pleasure to him yet again with the seductive rise and fall of her thighs.

Hultz was preparing to make a pass at the Spitfire when it rolled out of sight. In the next instant it was glued to his tail. He pulled into a loop to find the Spitfire still in pursuit when he recovered. He threw the Messerschmitt into a roll. The Spitfire mirrored him with a precision that only came from a seasoned fighter pilot.

He banked into a steep turn and tightened it. The Spitfire clung to him like a leech. He was growing rather desperate as to how he would escape when he noticed the Spitfire had left his tail and disappeared. He checked, and double-checked it was not hiding in his blind spot. He scanned the whole sky and eventually deducted the Spitfire had made its escape into a plain of cloud below. He was certain the British airman was the one that Staffel had warned him about. Nerves of steel and in total control of his machine.

Partly out of amusement and partly out of frustration at failing to bring the Spitfire down, and losing it, he rolled the Messerschmitt onto its back and held it there. He had trained as a bomber pilot; he'd had the briefest of conversion training to fighters. Inverted as he was, he tested his nerve by easing the throttle back and watching the airspeed fall away. At the same time he tried to keep the nose up by pressing the stick forward.

The machine became motionless. He drew a tense breath. An uneasy silence provided him with a sensation on being poised on the edge of a cliff top. Vestiges of grit fell into his face from the upturned cockpit floor. Nothing was happening. Suddenly his rump left the seat and the safety harness bit into his shoulders. What was it Staffel said if you stalled inverted? Centralise the controls. For several moments he put the stick in what he thought to be central position. But nothing happened. He'd never felt so helpless in his life.

He never did really determine what really caused it. Without warning the nose dropped away and the Messerschmitt descended for him to bring it back on an even keel. He breathed a huge sigh of relief, glanced toward the Heavens, got a bearing from the Boffins and headed for base.

He found his mind drifting back to his days in the glider corps. Days when he was catapulted from a hillside to test his gliding skills and do battle with thermals in a search for lift. Hot, sunny days when the spiralling, rising heat currents tossed him about like a feather and flexed the wings of his flimsy glider.

Flights in the evening were less battering, less exhausting, but demanded a keener vigilance to find the existence of the lift. Competition with the elements, and the other pilots, was strong. However, his determination brought him out on top.

He moved on to train with the Luftwaffe, flying powered aircraft. So proud was he to fly he did not question the decision of his superiors to dispatch him to bomber operations which began with the offensive against Poland.

He had done about a dozen raids and thought he was getting into the swing of things when he brutally learnt there was another side to the war. It started with a stunning explosion followed by an intense heat and smoke that tried to suffocate him. He smelt the nauseating stench of scorched flesh. A voice shouted desperately amongst the confusion. He couldn't see. A strong hand dragged him from the seat of the Dornier. The hatch appeared to small for him to go through. He wasn't given a choice. The heavy sole of a boot firmly pushed him out into a world of cool, clear air. Something struck him with a heavy thudding blow and he passed out

He remembered nothing more until he was aware of vague white figures moving quietly about him, talking in soft, gentle tones, and encouraging him to lie still. He forgot what it was like to be hungry; he'd lost his taste; he could smell nothing but burnt flesh. He often thought he was destined to smell nothing else.

He spent six months undergoing intensive treatment to his severe burns, with his life alternating between oblivion and drowsy reflections that were often wracked by pain.

A mixture of his youthful arrogance and determination helped him fight back to the surface of life and to hit back at his hideous deformities. He may have lost a lot to the explosion in the Dornier. But above all else he had retained the most precious gift to mankind - his life.

Inspired by a thought to celebrate his good fortune he put the Messerschmitt in a dive to gain speed. Then he eased back on the stick, pushed the throttle fully open. The earth slipped down behind him. Nothing but blue sky filled the windscreen. Up…up…up keep a steady pressure on the stick. He has still not got quite the hang of it; the wings were not level as he reached the inverted and went over the top arc of the loop. And he thought the stick was shaking in the light grip of his hand unnecessarily. He did remember however to reduce the power as the opposite horizon came into view and he dived to complete the final part of the loop.

He tried an Immelman roll. He used too little forward stick on completing the half roll and ended up roaring vertically earthwards. He reduced power pulled out of the dive - paused - took a breath - and tried another.

The sea and sky revolved around the wings and nose. As he approached the inverted position he slackened off the top rudder, and moved the stick slowly forward. On reaching the inverted he halted the roll and the rudder stirrups tugged at his boots and the seat harness took his weight. He pushed more boldly on the stick. That's much better; no screaming dive this time; the nose is above the horizon. As the airspeed falls away draw the stick back and down they go curving gently back into level flight. At last he was getting to know the machine better. A few more discussions with the experienced Staffel and he might feel worthy of being called a fighter pilot.

The aerodrome came to view. He let down, joined the circuit, slapped on full flap as he made the final approach, increased the power marginally and, after adjusting the tail trim, flew slightly nose high over the shoreline - over the high netted barbed-wire fence. Down…down…down…move the stick to check the speed. Floating. Gently close the throttle. Juggle with the stick to keep the nose poised and the wings level. He holds his breath. The ground starts to rise. He drew the stick right back - and they fell to earth in a perfect three-point landing. Most satisfying! Perhaps he would do it every time like Staffel, after a bit more practise.

"I'll try and get one for you this afternoon." he told the waiting ground crew.

"Why not this morning?" corporal Keisel ribbed him.

"Because my dear Keisel he was smarter than me

He was sat in the crew room that afternoon, smoking a cigar, and pleasantly dwelling on a forthcoming date with a nurse, that evening, when the boffins came on the line and ordered him into the air.

"Go get 'em, Hultz !" the ground crew chorused as they ran after him to the Messerschmitt.

He threw the cigar over his shoulder to them. "Put that in your pipe and smoke it," he laughed. In two great leaps he was up on the wing and up and over into the cockpit. He prided himself on getting airborne within three minutes of being summoned by the telephone. Twenty-five seconds - his parachute and seat harness were secure. Prime the engine, set the controls, alert the ground crew and hey presto! The Daimler Benz awoke with a roar. Another twenty seconds to satisfy himself the instruments and controls were functioning correctly. Then it was a short burst of power to check the magnetos. Wave the chocks clear and get under way with a blast of throttle. He did the take-off checks as he taxied out across the field.

He swung into wind, lined the nose up with the hangar, and unleashed the full power of the engine. He'd got used to the swing. In anticipation of it he toed on a bit of rudder as he eased the stick forward to raise the tail. The Messerschmitt no longer tried to evade him like an unschooled horse.

The moment the wheels started to skip over the grass he assisted it with back pressure on the stick. The machine left the ground; he snapped the undercarriage lever up flew the machine level and aimed the nose at the figures of the ground crew, by the hangar, already making rude gestures at him in farewell. He shaved the top of their heads and pulled the Messerschmitt into a battle climb. The pointers of the altimeter spun like the berserk hands of a clock. The controller told him his prey was almost directly over the aerodrome. Hultz told him to give him a steer that would him range him up behind the enemy machine. A layer of cloud fell on him at great speed. The Messerschmitt bladed through it and he was back in the clear before he had a chance to think about it. He switched the supercharger to high gear.

Why the pale blue Spitfire deviated from its normal lofty altitude nobody ever found out. It was flying a couple hundred feet above the cloud blanket, Hultz discovered. He stalked it under the guidance of the ground controller. He got into its blind spot and patiently and carefully, brought it to the sight and at four hundred yards thumbed the gun button. The Spitfire immediately started to jink about and dodge in and out of the rings of the sight. Hultz ruddered viciously to get it back in the sight. He clung to it releasing short bursts from his guns to keep the Britisher on edge.

His perseverance paid off. The Spitfire stopped jinking and pulled into a loop. Hultz followed and pulled tighter. The image of the Spitfire came slowly down to the pip of the gun sight. The Messerschmitt shook vigorously to the chattering sound of its guns. Small bits flew away from the Spitfire, followed by larger pieces. A flicker of flame - a tongue of flame - the spectacle loomed large in the windscreen of the Messerschmitt threatening a collision. Hultz stall-turned his machine to avoid it.

Shortly after he saw the Spitfire gyrating helplessly to earth trailing a corkscrew of smoke. It came down a quarter mile from the aerodrome killing its pilot.

The ground crew welcomed him back with rousing cheers and hearty congratulations, and a number of Boffins came out of their magic black boxes bringing with them a bottle of champagne to toast his success - his second success.

Keisel painted a second small red, white and blue roundel on the fuselage of the Messerschmitt, just below the cockpit coaming. Hultz acted out his appreciation to both the Boffins and his ground crew but inwardly he felt a measure of guilt at taking the life of the Spitfire pilot. And when it went down in flames the roasting death of his victim brought back vivid memories of the devastating fire in the Dornier. Staffel was quite right: it was all a rather unfair and merciless way of conducting aerial combat.

Sleeping with Elsa, the nurse, that night, he decided was more his scene and he totally lost himself in his and her erotic excesses.

Staffel came back two days later.

"Hultz! As the British would say, How the jolly well are you?"

Hultz sat on the steps to his hut, wearing sunglasses for protection from the bright reflection of sunlight on the surrounding snow, got up and greeted him with a handshake. "I'm jolly good, old bean." he laughed. "Absolutely spiffy."

They sat together on the steps and smoked a cigar.

Staffel said: "I trust all is well."

Hultz nodded. "I brought another Spitfire down a couple of days ago and regrettably the Britisher was killed." He paused. "On the brighter side of the coin I'm getting to know the Messerschmitt better. Thanks to your advice my Immelmans are coming together. But I can't get used to the inverted when I fall into the straps and my boots strain at the rudder stirrups."

"Try tightening your harness. And always remember that if by some strange fluke you did fall out you've got your brolly. What about your landings?"

"The last four - every one a three pointer. Anyway that's enough about me. How did your leave go."

"Marvellous time. Plenty of food, wine and you-know-what. But I hear our troops are having a rough time on the Russian front."

Hultz said: "I don't wonder at it. In my opinion they chose the wrong time of year for the assault."

Staffel said: "It's so bad they are sending Ursula with a concert party to cheer our lads up."

"Sending women, are they?" mused Hultz. Then more brightly, "Make her wear a big chastity belt, Staffel. The Ruskies are like bears, they say."

Staffel laughed with him. "Something tells me you have been indulging, Hultz."

Hultz drew jubilantly on his cigar. "Mustn't let it get rusty, old boy."

Staffel was pleased for him. "And who is the lucky girl?"

"Fraulein Hiener."

"The nurse!"

Hultz nodded and his eyes grinned from the mask of his plastic surgery.

"She's ravishing." Staffel said.

"I take it you approve?"

"Indeed I do."

Hultz looked at his chronometer. "It's ten and I'm famished. Care for a late breakfast at the club."

"Lead on glamour boy. Nurse Hiener indeed!"

By late afternoon Staffel was back in harness. Hultz and Kruger had briefed him on the actions in his absence, and brought him right up to date with the overall situation. He finished the day by going to the hangar and presenting his ground crew with cigars and wine he'd brought back from Essen.

In return they led him inside the hangar to his machine which gleamed from the spit and polish they had lavished on it in his absence. On each side of the fuselage to the rear of the engine bulkhead Fritz Walters, the armament fitter had written in red paint, Der Vogel.

Staffel stood admiring it for a time; he felt it gave him a form of individuality - a status of sorts. He turned and beamed at the ground crew in appreciation and boldly announced, "Gentlemen! I am ready for battle to commence."

AIR DUEL

EIGHT

After surviving the explosion in the Stirling and falling 19,000 feet to earth with a burning parachute. And after several weeks in hiding with a German aristocratic family, he was spirited to France. Where he spent several months on the run with the underground resistance, barely keeping one step ahead of the Gestapo, before he made a perilous journey across the English channel in a small open boat. Thus it was in such a manner flight lieutenant Carter turned up from the dead stunning his air force superiors. It was six months since he'd been shot down, and three months since he had been officially listed as being killed on operations

The experience had made inroads on his health. The ferocious blast in the Stirling had robbed him of his hearing in the right ear and he was prone to bouts of ill temper and impatience. He was sent to a quiet, secluded cottage hospital to recover. But soon enough he was making a nuisance of himself by demanding he should be sent home to recover or be put back on flying. There was nothing wrong with him, so he claimed.

His medical records indicated he was mentally disturbed. He refused all medication and treatment and eventually the authorities gave in to his demands and sent him home, grateful and relieved to be rid of him.

His mother became the next victim of his tetchy and volatile moods, which at times threatened to reach the heights of intolerance.

"Did I? Or did I not? Have a wife before I was shot down, mother." he demanded of an evening as they sat listening to the radio.

"Yes, Robert."

"Yes, what?"

"Yes - you do have a wife."

A foolish grin masked his face. "And would you say she is conspicuous by her absence?"

She nodded.

He rose from his chair, tensed, and clenching his fists. "Then, where in hell, is she!"

"Sit down, Robert." she pleaded. "I have tried to explain several times. And you persist in changing the subject." She drew a deep breath. "Losing you was bad enough for Melanie. Then a stray bomb landed on the roadhouse..."

"By golly," he interrupted with a guffaw of laughter. "I bet those fighter boys must have shot out of there quicker than a squadron scramble."

"It was nothing to laugh about, Robert. There were a lot of casualties and Melanie's aunt was killed."

"And how was Melanie when you last saw or heard from her."

"Bearing up remarkably well under the circumstances. Why don't you telephone her at the roadhouse and find out for yourself."

He strode out of the room to the telephone in the hall.

"I want to speak to Melanie Carter." he demanded.

"She's not here at the moment." a girlish voice informed him.

"When is she expected back?"

"Monday or Tuesday."

"Where is she?"

In the absence of an answer he shouted: "Where is she!"

"Staying with friends in Oxford, I think."

"What do you mean, I think. Don't you know?" he said irritably.

"Well - I mean, she's been there quite a lot lately. That's all I know."

He drummed his fingers impatiently on the small telephone table. "Are you in charge when she is away?"

"Yes."

"What's your name?"

" Maggie Taggart."

"Right then, Maggie. When next you see Melanie, will you make certain she is told her husband, Robert, is back from the dead and urgently wants to speak to her."

"Did you say her husband?"

"That's right. You seem surprised."

"No. I just thought she," she stopped abruptly.

"You thought what?"

"It's nothing really. I must go. I've got a lot of customers to attend to."

"Very well. But make certain you give Melanie my message. Tell her to telephone me at my mother's house. She has the number."

After a hurried assurance that she would do as he asked, she closed the line.

The pilot noticed the change the moment Melanie received him at the door of the cottage. Her response to his embrace lacked warmth and affection. She tried to avoid his eyes; she faked a smile, quickly took his coat and bag and sent him off to the sitting room whilst she prepared tea.

He stretched out uneasily before the flickering hearth fire, and rose and fell upon waves of fatigue; the air force was working him harder than ever before. The Bentley operation had lost several machines and pilots. At one stage recently he'd been the only available pilot. He'd flown two, sometimes three, sorties a day.

For the last week he had been showing sergeant Headland and pilot officer Forbes the ropes. The prospect of 48 hours leave with Melanie came as a bonus for his long stint of flying. Now, he was not so sure.

Melanie came quietly into the room and put a tray bearing a pot of tea, milk jug, sugar bowl and a plate of biscuits on a table next to his chair. She normally sat on the arm of his chair. Today she went and sat in a chair on the other side of the hearth; hands clasped, and stared into the flames of the fire, motionless and seemingly very troubled.

He said gently, "What's ailing you, Melanie?"

She lifted her head to look at him, her eyes on the verge of spilling tears, her lips quivering. "It's Robert." she croaked. "He's turned up. Evidently he survived the explosion in the Stirling and has spent most of the time on the run with the French underground resistance."

"Have you been in contact with him?"

"I had to, Paul." she cried. "He wouldn't stop pestering the staff at the roadhouse. They were telling lies to cover for me."

"Do I take it you intend to return to him?"

Tears welled in her eyes. "Please don't make it more difficult for me, Paul. I am only doing what I think is right. After all I never had my marriage to Robert annulled after I was told he was dead. So I am still legally his wife."

"Have you considered how he might react to news about the baby? It might be better for you to write to him and prepare him with the news."

She passed the suggestion off by saying she would not write and that she'd have to cross the hurdle, of confronting Robert with her pregnancy, when she got to it.

From that moment on the relationship floundered. Day by day, hour by hour, they drifted further apart, divided by an impenetrable emotional barrier that contained in it a growing, unbearable tension. Dialogue between them became a painful experience.

In line with her wishes he drove her to the station. He took her case to the platform and they waited for the train, chilled, muted, and isolated as total strangers. When the train arrived he placed her case in the carriage. And Melanie swept herself into a corner seat as if to escape the embarrassment of his presence.

He remained on the platform till the train left. He hoped he might catch a glimpse of her face at the carriage window and a wave of her hand in farewell. He saw nothing; the train puffed and clanked away from the station and disappeared round a bend in the track.

That evening down at Hadley manor as the daylight faded the air grew alive to the musical strains of a pianist in concert. The notes, some light and airy, others, heavy and sombre appeared to penetrate every wall in the building. There was no mistaking that each piece the pianist played was traced with a grievous sense of loss.

Rachmaninov, Mozart, Grieg, Chopin raised their noble heads in turn to his interpretation of their compositions. To be followed by his own works, 'Cottage on the Hill', Come gather clover', 'Melanie'...

"There is no doubt he will be playing to the world capitals after we win the war." Lady Hadley said to Marie as they sat listening in an adjoining room and sipped at glasses of sherry.

"I wished I shared your optimism, Claire." Marie said. "The truth is that Paul only produces his best performances following a happy event or a crisis in his life."

"And you think Melanie's sudden departure, without bidding us farewell, is behind his present supreme concert."

"Without a doubt."

Claire moved to the drink cabinet and refilled their glasses. "Have you managed to find out why she left so secretly?"

"All Paul would tell me was that she had some staff problems at the roadhouse. Other than that he didn't want to talk about it."

Claire handed her the refilled glass. "All rather odd is it not. I thought we went out of our way to make her feel welcome."

Marie said: "I can't help feeling for both of them. It hurts to hear the pain and anguish in my son's music. And yet I have Melanie to thank for inspiring him to get at the keys, after all these years, and achieving the success that he has."

In the next room the music rose to a crescendo and then ended abruptly. Followed immediately by thunderous applause that went on and on, as did the cries of 'Encore! Encore! Encore!"

Marie nudged a tear from each of her eyes in turn. She sipped at her sherry in an attempt to control the growing lump in her throat and an ache in her bosom both of which conveyed to her the distressing lament in her son's music.

Melanie reached Tetley four hours after leaving Oxford, having changed trains twice and suffered the overcrowded conditions of the wartime railways. Her unfastened cloak hung back from the protrusion of her pregnancy, her hat was about to slip from her head. She trudged into the station yard, grimly struggling with her suitcase.

Mrs Carter didn't recognise her at first. It annoyed her to think the wretch approaching the car was the type to request transport as suggested by the wartime posters. And when she did realise it was Melanie she was appalled at how her daughter-in-law had let herself go downhill.

They greeted each other cordially and after Mrs Carter had placed the case in the boot she explained that Robert had stayed at home because he was feeling unwell. "I must also warn you Melanie that Robert is far from the person we once knew." she said and started the engine of the car.

The reunion with Robert went badly from the start. The instant he saw her portly form he put two and two together and formed an ugly conclusion. When he spoke he snapped at her. At other times he lapsed into stony silences and ignored her. Within days the situation deteriorated, the tension in the house reached breaking point, and snapped in the early hours of a morning drawing Mrs Carter from her sleep.

"You either get rid of the brat. Or we don't have a marriage." his voice bawled from the bedroom from across the landing

Melanie shouted more rationally, "Blame me if you must Robert. But don't condemn the child."

"Then give me one plausible reason why I should accept the brat."

"Because I came back to you as a dutiful wife."

"Dutiful wife!" he scorned. "You sleep with another man, then dare to claim to be a dutiful wife. You don't know the meaning of the word madam."

Melanie said defiantly, "Dougie Hill and his crew said your aircraft got a direct hit, and none of you had a chance. And the air force eventually officially confirmed, in writing to me, that you were listed as killed in action."

"That being so it didn't take you long to jump in bed with another man, did it. I thought respectful widows wore black and mourned for a year."

"That's unfair, Robert."

"Unfair, perhaps. But true all the same."

"Has it ever occurred to you how I felt after losing you, and then my aunt to the bomb at the roadhouse. I can assure you I was in no fit state to get into mischief."

He laughed hysterically, "Then tell me how that baby got in your belly. A stork brought it in the middle of the night?"

"Please, Robert." Melanie pleaded "I'll do anything for you in exchange for your acceptance of the child. Be patient and in time we can have children of our own."

A long silence followed. Mrs Carter wished earnestly that her son would change his mind and goodwill would sprout from it.

"No! It's not on." he insisted. "I don't want the brat. As far as I am concerned you can live here till its born. Then I suggest you go and live elsewhere. In the meantime I shall sleep in the spare room and badger the air staff to get me back on ops,"

"That's one for Hultz." Staffel shouted triumphantly as the pale blue Spitfire rolled and spun to earth minus a wing that his well-aimed cannon had severed. He dived low amongst the batteries of AA guns, pretending to surrender by lowering his undercarriage and pumping the engine throttle. The guns fell silent. He whipped the undercarriage up, opened the throttle, dived on a conveniently near gun emplacement and mutilated the entire gun crew with a mixture of his ammunition.

It all added up to cost him time and fuel. Fuel he could ill-afford. Three miles from the Dutch coast his engine died from fuel starvation. The Messerschmitt lost all ambition to fly when the propeller ground to a halt and only remained in his control by descending at speed. It was a long time since he'd practised a forced-landing. He misjudged the wind, overestimated his height, and found himself dragging the machine onto the aerodrome by the skin of its wing and not without losing the undercarriage to the boundary fences in the process.

The undignified landing would have hurt his pride some weeks back. Now, he didn't really care what happened to him or on whose toes he trod. His national and personal pride had dissipated into thin air the moment he read the newspaper that reported the death of Ursula and the concert party near the Russian front when the Junkers in which they were travelling iced up and plunged to earth.

It would be at least a week before the ground crew could make his aeroplane flyable. And as he was the only surviving airman, and there were no other aircraft available, the unit was non-operational. Kruger and the Boffins sat twiddling their thumbs whilst he went off to find Schelling, the evasive area commander.

After a lot of fuss and bother from the commander's henchmen who tried to stop him from troubling Schelling, Staffel ran him down in a Dutch night spot, hiding in an alcove that had a prime view of a small stage on which a sensuous blond-haired female vocalist swayed before a microphone and sang to the accompaniment of a four piece band.

Uninvited Staffel joined him at the table and immediately got down to business. "I need replacements for Tauber and Hultz, Feldmarschall. Also we must have more modern fighters if we are to reach these Spitfires flying at anything up to forty thousand feet."

"But of course, Staffel." Schelling said casually, his attention drawn to the figure on stage who pouted her lips and winked at him from time to time.

Staffel waited a short time before he demanded his attention with a cough and a nudge.

Schelling turned to him. "Have no fear, Staffel. I'll make sure you get the replacements." As quickly he turned away and raised his glass to the stage."

Staffel said: "With respect, Feldmarschall, I would like to select the replacement pilots. The Netherlands and the type of flying is not everybody's cup of coffee."

Schelling retained his sight on the stage. "Who do you have in mind, Staffel?"

Staffel said: "An ober leutnant Unter. And a feldwebel Pragda."

"And where are they stationed?" Schelling raised his glass again to the figure swaying before the microphone.

"The last I heard, Unter was attached to a bomber wing in Russia. And I left Pragda in Cherbourg about a year ago."

"I see." The music trailed down to the conclusion of the act and Schelling started to chafe at the bit in an attempt to get away from him.

The singer bowed and made her exit from the stage. "Very well, Staffel. Leave it to me. Now you must excuse me." Schelling made to slide from his chair but Staffel grip him by an arm; it was not uncommon for high-ranking officers to deny everything they said on the morning after the night before. And Schelling was already trembling at the knees where the blonde beauty was concerned.

"I trust you will not forget the promises you made this evening, Feld Marshall."

Schelling released the grip of his hand. "I'll have you know, Staffel, I am a man of my word. Now, I insist you excuse me."

Staffel watched with amusement as Schelling bounded away like a dog freed from its lead.

But Schelling was as good as his word. Three Messerschmitts with improved engine performance arrived three weeks later. Staffel took one on an air test to discover it could get up to thirty eight thousand feet. It struggled a bit during the last couple of thousand and the controls got decidedly sloppy. But he was careful not to mention it when he telephoned his thanks to Schelling.

Schelling said: "I upset a lot of people by letting you have priority, Staffel. So make certain you look after them."

"Indeed I will Feld Marschall. By the way, did you do any night flying with that delicious blonde from the night club?"

There was a long silence before Schelling said: "If I did it's no business of my subordinates. Now get off the line you impertinent scoundrel."

Staffel thanked him and closed the line.

Unter and Pragda arrived a week later both rather perplexed at being sent to such a desolate place in the Netherlands, until they saw their old friend Staffel and learnt he had requested them. He gave them a day to settle in their quarters, another day to meet the other personnel of the unit and a further day pottering around their aeroplane. Pragda had been flying Messerschmitts in the desert backing up Rommel's army in the North Africa campaign and he had notched up a considerable score of enemy aircraft destroyed. 19 in fact consisting of a mixed bag of Hurricanes, Spitfires and Tomahawks.

Unter had been flying the twin engine Dornier on raids against the Russians, machines he personally referred to as 'Donkey Droppers'. His conversion back to fighters did not go easily. His first attempts at landing were of a tongue-in-cheek nature with Staffel looking on with clenched fists and pounding heart as Unter's Messerschmitt ballooned and returned to earth like a bouncing tennis ball.

After some twenty attempts he began to get to grips with it. And Staffel went on to brief him and Pragda on the nature of the interceptions and how the

Boffins and their big black boxes of tricks played a major part.

He also warned them of a particular Spitfire pilot who was not only a master in the art of flying but also had nerves of steel.

Pragda said: "You've mentioned these Spitfires have no specific markings. How then do we tell this Spit from the others?"

"Point one: he's got no armament but he'll challenge you regardless of the odds; if he gets on your tail you'll have your work cut out to get him off."

Unter rubbed his hands. "I like do-or-die merchants." he said. "Give them enough rope and they'll hang themselves."

Staffel said, "Don't underestimate this one, Unter. Or he'll hang you with the rope."

Pragda said, "I can't see how he can be much of a threat if he hasn't any guns or ammo."

Staffel laughed, "Oh, he's a threat alright. According to one of our agents working in London he was awarded a medal for slicing the tail off one of our machines with his propeller. And it's been suggested that poor old Hultz went the same way. And I can assure you that Hultz was no fool in the fighting game."

"Perhaps Hultz should have left the nurse alone." Unter made to inject humour into the conversation. "From what I've seen of her she could snap a man's back, and sap his strength, at the height of an amorous combat. Wouldn't get you the Iron Cross, of course. But what a divine way to go."

Staffel ignored it and set upon acquainting them with the duty roster. He would accompany them on the interceptions for the first week. After that they'd be on their own.

The spell in bombers had dulled Unter's senses and slowed his reflexes. An eager Spitfire was after him and it meant business. The Boffins had got him into the air a bit later than they should have done. To intercept it he had to chase it across the North Sea. He caught up with it near the English coast and it started its descent. It had rolled onto its back a number of times during the crossing and he thought it was indulging in some aerobatics to break the monotony of the flight.

It half rolled and swooped down under his nose and to the rear of him and, by the time he had decided what he should be about, the Spitfire got on to his tail. It clung to him like glue. He cranked into a steep tight turn his vision blurring as the forces of acceleration piled up against him dragging at his face and a heavy hand threatened to crush his rib cage and force his head into his shoulders. He rather hoped he'd turn tighter and get on the Spitfire's tail. Instead he started to black out. He released the pressure on the stick and rolled out of the turn. He pushed the nose down and opened the throttle wide. A glance over a shoulder and the Spitfire was pursuing him like a whippet after a hare. He pulled the nose vertical, let the speed fall away, kicked on rudder and as the nose fell away he drew the throttle back. The stall-turn took him racing back in over the English countryside where the ground gunners started to take pot shots at him. They so distracted him he realised his error too late.

Staffel had repeatedly warned him and Pragda to watch their fuel gauges if a fight took them to the English coast. He told them to make one attack only, climb as high as they could, lean out the mixture as much as possible, pray to old Nick for fair and fine weather and with a bit of luck they'd get home with dry feet.

He cursed more than ever the time he had spent in bombers. Not only was it a job for old lags, it turned young men like him into one. He was too slow and unfit to deal with the rigours of aerial dogfights. The ground guns fell silent. Staffel had told him this meant the Spitfire was in the near vicinity. He opened the throttle, lowered the nose to gain speed and threw the Messerschmitt into an Immelman turn in the hope of catching the Spitfire lurking in his blind spot. He came out of the turn firing his guns at an empty sky.

Suddenly a shape appeared from nowhere passing from his left to the right. He gave it a frantic burst of cannon. Too late! It escaped unscathed due to his slow reflexes. The Immelman turn had taken him back out over the sea. The erratic fuel gauges registered something or nothing. Most certainly the prospect of ending up floating about in a rubber boat did not appeal to him. Over his right shoulder he spotted the Spitfire closing in on him, its long snout and searing disc of a propeller creeping toward the tail unit of the Messerschmitt

The tale of what happened to Hultz and the other fellow loomed large in his imagination. Well - he was not going to sit back and let it happen to him, he decided with a surge of determination. He would show the British glamour boy he was made of stouter stuff. He flung the Messerschmitt around to confront the Spitfire and let rip with his guns and cannon. The Spitfire broke away. He chased after it and got on its tail. That was the easy part. The difficult part was getting the image of the Spitfire to the gunsight and holding it there. The Spitfire skidded, pitched, rolled and looped, never in the sight long enough for Unter to get a bead on it.

The continuous jinking, ducking and diving made Unter feel sick and disorientated. His clothing clung to him with a profusion of sweat. It was quite obvious the pilot of the Spitfire was the professional Staffel had talked about to him and Pragda.

The Spitfire pulled a very sudden tight turn and came roaring back towards him, involving him in a game of roulette. He fired his guns to deter it. But the duelist in the Spitfire had nerves of steel. The propeller spinner, the swept back engine exhaust stubs, the wings and fuselage loomed in the slant of the windscreen. Unter cringed as it passed so close overhead the swiftness of its flight tossed him about in the cockpit like a cork in an ocean.

He heaved a sigh of relief when the engine of the Messerschmitt faltered, tried desperately to recover, and spluttered into silence. Instinctively he lowered the nose to maintain flying speed. A quick check on the whereabouts of the Spitfire showed it to be slinking away in a westerly direction, it too obviously short of fuel.

He tried to relax and admit he didn't care anymore. He'd lost a duel to an unarmed adversary. That was quite unforgivable. And to add to his shame and humiliation he was about to surrender on the enemy's own soil. Total disgrace!

Petty officer Hooper, on brief shore leave, was out walking with his wife and their pet mongrel when the descending Messerschmitt passed overhead.

"Blimey," he said grabbing his wife and heading her for the limited protection of a roadside ditch. "It's a bloody Jerry."

"Don't be daft, Harry." she protested. "It's only coming down slow and gentle like."

"Of course he's coming down you fool. They do it over the ships. They pretend to be in trouble. Then when you stick your neck out they blow your bloody head off."

His wife refused to go down in the ditch. She said it would mess her shoes and stockings. She crouched below a hedgerow and looked over the top. "He's turning. And coming back this way, Harry."

Air Duel

"Get your head down, woman. I don't want the job of taking it home in a bucket if he shoots it off."

She ignored him. She moved stealthily to a five-barred gate not far along the way, trailing the dog behind her. Harry joined her in time to see the Messerschmitt float down over an avenue of elms, slink over a line of hedgerows, and slump with a hollow metallic thud on to ploughed land. It slithered across the furrows for a distance before it veered suddenly to the right and was fetched to an abrupt halt by a stout, solitary oak tree. A pause. A puff of smoke. A tongue of flame. A sheet of flame, the olive green aeroplane exploded and quickly became a raging inferno.

Air Duel

NINE

Climbing up through the first few thousand feet was like travelling in a dark tube dimly lit by the luminous glow of the instrument faces. Climb a little higher and one got the impression of flying out to meet the stars. A magic that was short-lived because as he climbed higher a chink of light appeared on the eastern horizon and progressively widened to a strip and grew into a band of pale yellow. At thirty thousand feet it seemed as if he was peering over the edge of the world. Cones of sunlight reached up for him lighting the wings and clearly showing the rows of flush rivets. The propeller spun a few feet in front him as a golden disc, powered by the growl of the engine.

He inhaled deeply from his oxygen mask. He had seen it several times before, of course, but he never failed to feel privileged at witnessing the splendour of the dawn from such a lofty vantage point. What was more he had escaped the petty irritations of the earth and the recent developments in his life? He spotted a Stirling bomber several thousand feet beneath him limping home with smoke trailing one of its engines. He offered up a silent prayer for the crew and watched the bomber pass to the rear of him strangely reminiscent of a large black bird thrashing and clawing at the air in the absence of vital plumage.

Amongst his periodic checks on the oxygen and fuel and for ice accretion, and the appearance of unwanted company, the Spitfire carried him effortlessly into the growing daylight. The coast of Holland came and went. In just over an hour he was well and truly over enemy territory. But up where he was there were no signs of the war. He and the Spitfire were gloriously free. Free of the daily carnage reported in the newspapers or on the radio. Of a land battle that incurred many casualties, of a ship lost with all hands, of British bombers missing from a previous night's raid. Of disputes between military leaders and the clamour of dissatisfied politicians and of friends lost in battle. And of thwarted romances…

Now it was all far below buried by a white shroud of mist whilst he hung suspended in a pure blue sky whose grandeur was accentuated by golden rays of sunshine. Given the choice he would be quite content to fly on…and on…and on.

Within a further forty-five minutes he'd identified the grid references, rolled the film over four sweeps, turned his back on the sun and settled down for the jaunt home. For what?

There was nothing really for him to go back home for. The whole world down there was in turmoil, as was his personal life.

Staffel and Pragda slept in the crew room for the night, stretched out as best they could in easy chairs, Kruger and the Boffins having briefed them the previous evening of their intention to get them airborne at first light.

Corporal Kessel roused them at half four and greeted them with mugs of coffee. He poked the stove back into life, banked it up, and told them the weather looked promising for flight. Staffel gave him a cigarette. "Have you looked the machines over?"

"Yes. Everything is in order. I'll get the engines run and warmed after my cigarette."

Staffel moved away from him and joined Pragda outside the hut where he was taking a look at the weather.

"I've got a hunch the British ace is going to be up there this morning, Pragda. I want you to leave him exclusively to me."

"And if you run into trouble, am I expected to turn a blind eye?"

"That's right."

Pragda turned to him. "I don't understand, Staffel."

"The point is: I want this duel with the ace alone. You may chase off any others who may try to interfere. Or, if need be, drop down and harass the ground gunners if they make a nuisance of themselves. This is a personal fight in which I intend to show the Britisher I can match his stamina and courage."

The idea of them hunting as a pair had been introduced by Staffel after poor old Unter was killed. He felt it made it a bit safer. And he was reluctant to tell Schelling, the area commander that he'd already lost one of the new pilots and machines.

Operating as a pair had brought results; they'd brought down two more Spitfires during the fortnight after Unter's death. Kruger, from intelligence, claimed they were on the verge of annihilating an entire PR unit in Britain. "To our knowledge they've only got one machine left." he'd told them the previous evening. "Get this one and you two could be in for an Iron Cross apiece."

The interception took place over English soil, the Boffins planning it that way. It made for an element of surprise and at the same time had the potential of humiliating the enemy by witnessing the destruction of one of their own aircraft over their own territory. Staffel and Pragda were waiting in the area of the Wash on the East Coast when the Spitfire came floating down on its approach to Bentley.

After reminding Pragda to stay out of the fight Staffel flew headlong at the Spitfire. And the fight, as it developed, was the strangest Pragda had ever seen. More so it resembled a duel in which the duellists thrust and parried each other. One moment the Spitfire had the advantage. In the next instant the Messerschmitt. For certain Pragda had never witnessed such superb flying by duelists who, it seemed, were of equal capability and skill.

At first the machines fought for the supremacy of latching onto the other's tail and staying there. Then they began diving at each other.

Pragda began to grow concerned; Staffel made no attempt to use his guns. The duel was going on too long; fuel drained away fast under the boisterous use of throttle, and they were a long way from home. And finally, the machines were barely leaving a margin for error when they flew at each other.

In the mind's eye Pragda saw an area of heath land at the break of day.

Air Duel

Ribbons of mist rise and fall and swirl almost imperceptibly. The air is cold, damp and traced with foreboding.

Two horse-drawn coaches appear on the heath. A figure emerges from each carriage, both dressed in black tailcoats and tall black hats, and walk to a point midway between the two carriages ceremoniously bearing pistol cases, and stand side by side.

Next came the duellists in tight black trousers, buckled shoes and white silk shirt followed, as they were, by their aides attired entirely in black. The mist floats about them like lingering mournful shrouds waiting for death to provide them with a victim or victims.

The duelists arrive at the midway point, bow courteously to each other but say nothing. To the side of them a voice announces: "You will stand back to back. And when I give the order, "March" you will walk fifteen paces, turn, and discharge your ball in your own time. Is that understood."

The duellists nodded solemnly.

"Go to it, gentlemen, and chose your weapons."

A pistol in their hand they are ordered to stand back to back.

"Are you quite ready gentlemen?"

"We are." they chorused.

The referee, his assistant, and the two aides retreat a safe distance.

After a tense pause, "March!"

The referee counts the paces aloud as the duellists walk.

They walk with slow, measured paces, one hand behind their back the other hanging by their side gripping the butt of the pistol. The aides hold their breath and offer up a prayer for their respective charges.

"Fifteen!"

The duellists stop walking - turn about - cock and raise the long barreled pistols with great coolness and courage. Speed there must be in sighting but not with such haste that the ball misses its target. The eye lines up with the outstretched arm and the small sights forward most on the small barrel of the pistol.

Crack! Crack! Barely a fraction of a second separates the two discharges from the pistols. The two balls sear unseen through the morning mist perhaps vapourising a little. Momentarily the duellists remained poised with their weapons, dignified in their moment of peril, their neat white silk shirts bright against the deteriorating greyness of the mist.

The victim of a streaking ball reels from a thud - a jolt - a fleeting burning sensation as the ball pierces the skin - a poker tip of intense pain as the skin tissues alert the nerve ends. The victim lurches, staggers, and loses balance. The buckling legs offer no more support. The eyes lose their sight. The world spins into a whirlpool of confusion. The journey is ever downward - the last breath - nothing but an unending black emptiness…

Pragda is shocked to see that neither of the duelists have survived. Both bodies lay prone upon the heath, separated by thirty paces, one face down, the other on his back, arms outstretched, looking up with blank, staring eyes, and blood oozing from a hole in the middle of the forehead…

He could not decide who struck the first blow between Staffel and the Britisher. But touch they did, pausing in mid air for a glancing moment, before the two machines broke away from each other.

The Spitfire made the next move. It swung carefully toward the

Air Duel

Messerschmitt and crept up on it from the rear.

"Your tail, Staffel!" Pragda shouted over the radio. "Watch your tail!"

Staffel threw his machine into a half roll. The Spitfire mirrored him. And as they nosed down from the roll the Spitfire pounced. It nicked the right elevator of the Messerschmitt before Staffel wheeled out of the way. Then it pulled back a bit as if assessing the damage, having probably picked up some vibration from its damaged propeller. Poor old Staffel limped on, and Pragda discovered his thoughts were torn. Torn between going down and luring the Spitfire away from his friend, or whether he should beetle off back to Holland before he used up any more precious fuel. A glance at the fuel contents and his chronometer told him his situation was more critical than he thought. He quickly came to the conclusion that his prospects looked better in a POW camp than ditching in the middle of the North Sea with no one to attend his funeral. The Spitfire slinked again beneath Staffel's tail. Pragda shouted a warning. Staffel put on throttle and moved out of the way. The Spitfire continued to stalk him. Quite suddenly Staffel pushed the nose of the Messerschmitt over into a vertical dive. Pragda froze. For a terrifying moment he thought the nick in the elevator had developed into something more calamitous. But a few thousand feet down the Messerschmitt recovered.

He lost sight of the Spitfire for a time. Then he spotted it careering down the sky to meet Staffel head on. "Use your guns, Staffel!" he shouted.

Staffel ignored him. At the very last moment the machines veered away from each other. They came around again and approached head-on to break away only just in time. They did this twice more. Then on the third time Pragda looked on in horror as the two machines collided. He heard nothing of the collision but in his mind he heard the pistol shots of the duelists. He clearly saw a cloud of smoke, a wing falling away, a flap rolling in the air; the air is littered with debris. To his left a lone aileron and cockpit canopy deserts the carnage. An engine ripped from its mountings, and minus its cowlings, floats earthwards. Amongst the smoke an explosion, a mixture of red and orange flame, that hangs like a giant wounding against the sky for a time before gravity dominates its downward trajectory.

Long after the wreckage had rained to earth the spectacle of the moment of impact is engraved on Pragda's memory. He set the Messerschmitt down on an unploughed field with the fuel tanks empty according to the gauges. It was bit of a tight squeeze to get into the field; he ended up about 3 metres from a hedgerow. He raised the canopy, tore off his mask and inhaled deeply. Never had the air tasted so sweet, so fragrant. Never had he felt so grateful to be alive.

He watched three figures advance cautiously towards the Messerschmitt, odd figures of farming stock, carrying weapons equally odd in appearance. They split up as they drew near and surrounded the machine. He chose to remain seated in the cockpit thinking that to do otherwise might panic them.

"Stick your hands up Boche!" one ordered from before the leading edge of a wing, brandishing what looked like a pitchfork.

Pragda was not conversant with the language but the stern command and the irate expression gave a good indication of what was expected of him.

As he hauled himself up from the cockpit and placed a leg out onto a wing a voice from behind said, "Try anything funny and I'll blow your brains out!"

With both feet on the wing he turned, hands raised, and looked down at an old man wearing a tin helmet and brandishing a firearm that was reminiscent of a museum piece.

AIR DUEL

What happened after Pragda jumped from the wing to the ground will remain a mystery. One witness suggested he tried to overpower the old man with the blunderbuss, whilst another witness claimed Pragda had merely pushed the gun away from his face whilst two others searched him for weapons.

One point is certain. Another young German airman met with a hasty, violent death that morning on farmland in the southern counties.

AIR DUEL

TEN

The leaves were changing colour. The green hills meadows and pastures wore a jaded expression. Ponds and rivers mirrored the cold, blue of the autumn sky. The air had a crisp bite about it. Marie Herby sat before the window of the room her son had used at the manor when he came home on leave. In recent weeks it had become her bolt hole, a refuge, a sanctuary, following the delivery of the small yellow telegram bearing the news of Paul's death on flying operations.

At first she could not believe it. Then she felt numb to everything going on about her, a numbness that gave way to a painful anguish. Why him! Why my son? A cry put up by several hundred other mothers that day. It was if she had been reconnected to the umbilical cord and was embroiled in a powerful conflict between the heavy labour of bringing him into the world - and a desperate fight to stop death leading him away.

After weeks of tear-stained handkerchiefs and pillowcases she went through another of phase of disbelieving. She looked through the window of the room expecting to see his small sports car come up the drive at any minute. He always parked in the same spot. In winter he wore a white roll neck sweater, and his flying jacket over his uniform. And if he'd come straight from flying he wore his flying boots. If he mocked any of the air force regulations it was the way he wore his cap rakishly on his head.

In the summertime the canvas hood of his car was folded down and he came in air force trousers with braces. He detached the collar of his shirt and wore in its place a white silk scarf. Marie had only heard recently that his grandfather had given him the scarf as part of a farewell present when they left Canada. Samuel Herby had worn the scarf on all of his pioneering flights from Hadley.

She looked through the window at the distant slope of Hadley hill and at its feet the meandering trout streams, the village church and the cottage lodge in which she had grown up with her gentlemanly father and gracious mother. They had enjoyed a comfortable and happy life.

The friendship with the Herby family flourished and was made memorable by their success at achieving manned, powered flight. She never forgot the two occasions she went aloft with Timothy who was only a year her senior.

She missed him terribly when he was taken, at short notice, to live on the other side of the vast Atlantic Ocean. They corresponded with long letters and though the years came and went she was certain they would eventually get married.

Air Duel

The First World War led to her marriage but not before she made a number of sacrifices. Her father was killed in the war whilst serving as an observer with the Royal flying Corps, and it struck her hard. She joined the VADs as a diversion to her grief and, in part, it did something to avenge his death.

For the first time in her life she ventured well beyond the village boundaries meeting people from a variety of backgrounds and who behaved quite contrary to anything she had ever known. She never did get accustomed to sharing sleeping quarters, latrines and ablutions with other women. She accepted it with a quiet tolerance in the same way she thought her parents did when dealing with difficult situations on the estate or in the village. At all times, in all situations, they remained unruffled and in complete control of their emotions. She'd had the good fortune to inherit their dignity through the genes, a quality that helped her to cope, over the war years, with great many personal and public problems.

Her next trial came when Timothy confessed to his indiscretion with a French lady and her claim she was carrying his child. She passed that off as being part of her fault for not waiting for him when he wrote of his intentions to come to Britain and join the RFC. Had she waited they might have married on his arrival.

But her pride, and her affection for him was sorely tested at the end of the war when she returned home to Hadley to learn, during a confidential conversation with Claire Hadley, that Mollie Langdon's son was sired by Timothy. And, from a source Claire was not prepared to divulge, Timothy had also bedded a nurse in France who carried his child and who, because of her misconduct, was discharged in disgrace from the nursing service.

Marie had never felt so humiliated, so hurt. The spark for Timothy was reduced to a spluttering flame. But she accepted his proposal of marriage because when he returned to Canada he would be taking her with him, taking her well away from all the reminders of his waywardness and relieving her of all the pressing public humiliation.

The big open spaces of Canada, the new complexion of life it offered, were just the tonic she needed. At 33 years of age she lost her virginity and celebrated true womanhood by becoming pregnant and giving birth to a baby boy: an event that did not pass without a great deal of pain and discomfort for her. But which she quickly forgot when he was delivered safely to the world, and lay peacefully up against her breasts.

She paused in her reflections to watch a string of horses and their riders set out from the manor. Riding was used as a therapy to help some of the wounded aircrew get back to full health. She spotted sheep grazing on the lower slopes of Hadley Hill. She could just see children mingling in the playground of the village school.

It took her mind back to a small boy in short trousers, dark, wavy hair, dancing eyes and a cheeky smile. He had inherited traits from both sides of the family: determination, at times, defiance, versatility and unpredictability. He spent many an hour tinkering with an old automobile engine with grandfather Herby. Just as frequently they hiked in the forest together.

At eight years of age his father bought him a pony and taught him to ride. For the same birthday the grandparents presented him with a Labrador pup.

In the hope of furthering his academic pursuits Marie purchased a piano for him, hoping he would follow her and her parents' interest in music.

Much to her great disappointment he rebelled; he wanted no part in it. She tried to negotiate with him by suggesting he have a private tutor if he preferred she didn't teach him. He was adamant that music did not interest him; it held no adventure. His idea of fun was riding his pony in nearby woodland with Conko, the Labrador, as his other companion.

Like all caring mothers she wanted only the best for him. He finished his schooling with low grades in every subject and added to her anxiety by admitting he had no idea what he wanted to do to earn a living. He declined his father's invitation to take up flying. Grandfather Herby suggested he might like a career in the mounted police. He rejected that on the grounds that law had too many restraints. Grandmother Herby tried to steer him toward the diplomatic service. He thanked her for her interest but said it was not for him.

Six weeks after leaving school at dinner one evening, with the grandparents in attendance, he announced it was his intention to ride off into the wilds for six weeks to consider his future

"Alone?" grandmother Rebecca said in amazement.

"Yes. Apart from my mount, a pack horse and Conko, grandmother."

"It's ridiculous. How do you propose to guard yourself against grouchy bears, packs of wolves and unsavoury criminals? A very risky adventure if I may say so."

Paul eyed her steadily a smile playing at his lips. "With respect, grandma, did you have any idea what it would be like before grandpa brought you to Canada."

"I was a lot older than you." she made a blustery attempt to thwart his argument.

He reached across the table and held her hand. "No. Tell me the truth. Did you really know what you were letting yourself in for?"

Rebecca, renowned for her indomitable spirit and determination to win an argument on her terms, melted under the charm of her grandson.

"Do you really think he is serious?" she said after he left the room.

"As serious as you, Rebecca." grandfather Herby laughed.

"What do you mean by that, Samuel?"

"Like you, if he sets his mind on something, he does it."

Rebecca rose from her chair. "Come Marie. Let us go and wash the dishes. I suspect we are to be dealt a flurry of flattery in order these men may win the argument for Paul."

Samuel leant back in his chair and lighted his pipe. Timothy put a match to a small cigar, and reached across and refilled his and his father's glass with port.

Rebecca, leading Marie from the room, said: "I still maintain he is too young and inexperienced for such an adventure."

The men ignored her protest, as did Paul. He left three days later and the six weeks he intended to be away turned into a two-year exploration of the northern territories. He sent news of his whereabouts by telegraph, by letter or by word of mouth by travellers he met and who were heading for Calgary. Marie missed him badly but at the same time she admired him.

According to one of his letters he spent a year way up north living with Wolf McTay. The scenery was magnificent. Animal and bird life was in abundance. They ate lots of fish. Their nearest neighbours lived 400 miles away. Wolf taught him to how to adapt the available resources to the essential needs of food, clothing and shelter, and not to treat it as a fight to survive but rather a way of life to be enjoyed.

The following year Marie received a letter saying he was sojourning with Indians on one of the reservations.

AIR DUEL

He arrived back home unexpectedly just before Christmas.

Marie happened to look through a back window and saw a figure on horseback, trailing a pack mule, moving up the long winding track to the property. She suspected it was one of the many travellers to call and ask for directions or for food and drink. She always obliged but always kept two dogs in attendance.

Normally the visitors had the grace to tether their mounts by the main entrance and walk to the house. Not so this bold individual. He came through the gate, admittedly had the good manners to close it behind him, and came right up to the front porch and dismounted. He was heavily dressed in buckskin trousers, a long hide coat with fur collar and a beaver fur hat.

Marie went out of a side door, sending the dogs ahead of her and expecting them to break out in frantic barking and snarling. There was total silence. She reached the corner by the verandah and turned. At first she only saw the head of the horse and the mule. Then as she moved closer she saw the visitor, bent down, stroking the dogs who reciprocated his greeting by wagging their tails excitedly.

The man looked up at her grinning boyishly. She fought hard to hold back the tears. But failed. He stood up and she hurried to him, arms outstretched, and embraced him. She buried her face in the thick collar of his coat and wept with all the force and joy she had used on the occasion of his birth.

He gradually eased her away from him and held her hands in his. "You haven't been worrying about me, have you mother?" he laughed.

She looked up at him with tear-swept eyes. "No." she sobbed. "But we have all missed you terribly. You're not going away again, are you?"

He looked at her with the impish smile that had accompanied him from the cradle. "I don't have any plans at the moment, if that answers your question."

She made to lead him indoors but he checked her. "I must get the mounts fed and rested, mother. They've been on the move for twelve hours."

She went inside and announced his homecoming to his grandparents by telephone, and to request hay and feed.

When he came in and before he could undress she hurried to him and held his mittened hands. "I can't tell you what it is like to have you back home, my son."

He grinned at her. "I may not do everything to your liking or in line with your wishes, mother. But you are very special to me."

She patted his gloves nervously. "I know - I know." she said quietly and hurried to the other room before he could detect her tumbling emotions.

For Marie it was one of the best Christmases of her life. They ate and drank lavishly and made merry at the slightest excuse. She got them round the piano and they sang all the traditional carols. Grandfather Herby told amusing stories: incidents drawn from life, exaggerated and heavily traced with humour. It was generally accepted in local social circles that, "None could tell 'em like Sam Herby"

At 70 years of age his frame had shrunk and he slouched a little. He continued to play an active part in the Calgary flying club where his lack of formal flying qualifications was totally overlooked. As an instructor he had turned out a steady stream of good pilots over the years which had contributed to enhancing the image of the club.

There had been talk recently of the government's intention to land a major training contract with the club. The only problem was they couldn't give a date. Bill Cornell was instructed to get fully prepared, and during this process he told his partner, Sam Herby, to expect to get busy back in the cockpit.

The whole family went to the flying club for the New Year's party following that

Christmas. They went in a horse-drawn sleigh, as did the majority of guests on account of a heavy fall of snow. A number braved it with automobiles. And wished they hadn't. Their horse-drawn counterparts overtook them with ease, sleigh bells tinkling clearly in the cold night air, and the runners gushing effortlessly through the snow.

From where Marie sat in the rear seat next to her husband, and opposite her in-laws with a rug thrown over their legs she could watch Paul at the reins, occasionally giving words of encouragement when the mount faltered or stumbled. She thought of all the many happy things that had happened in recent weeks and in the privacy of the darkness she offered up a short prayer of thanksgiving.

The party developed into a riot of music, song and laughter. Paul, Marie noticed, chose to stay out on the fringes and politely declined to drink alcohol: a trait of her late father. And it amused her during a dance with Paul a younger woman came and took him from her during a Ladies' excuse me melody. And at the end of the dance the young woman tried to entice him to join her circle of friends. An invitation he refused as a matter of courtesy to his family who he had not seen for two years.

The woman, rather the worse for drink, raised her voice and tugged at his arm in protest. A male companion at her table joined in with a mouthful of abuse forming a joint effort to embarrass Paul.

Marie stood to go and protect her son when Timothy held her back. "Don't interfere, Marie. He's quite capable of sorting it out."

Paul walked to the bar, held a brief exchange with a barman, during which money changed hands. Moments later a tray of drinks went to the table of the offended woman. The crisis passed.

The evening moved to its inevitable conclusion ending at midnight with Auld Lang Syne and the National Anthem as a tradition of the flying club. As the family congregated at the sleigh the shouting, laughter and song of other families surrounded them. The stars mounted the sky as clear as crystal and the northerly wind had a wanton bite about it. A number of horses snorted their disapproval at the intoxicated incompetence of their driver. Paul quietly broke the sleigh out and they were soon mushing through the snow, the horse maintaining a steady trot, the bells tingling merrily, and grandfather Herby humming a tune that none of them recognised.

The warm comfort of a bed could not come quick enough for Marie but on reaching the homestead the women prepared a night cap whilst the men unhitched the sleigh removed the harness and fed and stabled the horse. She eventually went to bed with Timothy; Rebecca went to the guestroom, leaving grandfather and grandson talking by the hearth.

Marie snuggled into the crook of Timothy's shoulder warm and content. For a time they talked about the evening then Timothy said: "How would you like to go back to England for a spell?"

It spiked her out of the stupour into which she was lapsing.

"Are you serious, Timothy?"

"Yes."

"Is my decision important?"

"Your feelings are most important. Because if you are not happy with the idea of going back there is no point in discussing the matter further."

She raised herself onto an elbow and looked down at him in the darkness. "I've often thought it would be nice to go back for a holiday. I'd rather like to see my mother's grave, and father's name on the tablet in the church." She paused. "How long would we stay? And would Paul go with us?"

"The duration of our stay would depend on a number of factors. And, of course, Paul is welcome to accompany us if he so wishes."

Marie said: "You know my reasons for wanting to go back. What are yours, Timothy?"

He said: "There are some nasty rumours circulating from Britain that Germany is spoiling for another war. By all accounts gangs of undisciplined individuals are roving around causing mischief with the Jewry. And the country is arming itself to the teeth with tanks, ships and aeroplanes."

Marie kissed him lightly on the face. "And how do you think you might help, dear husband?"

"I'd like to be in Britain if she was invaded."

"Doing what?"

" I'm thinking of rejoining the air force."

She kissed him again. "I thought you said your fighting ended at the end of the last war."

He pinched her nose. "Your memory never fails you. Yes, it's true. I did. But there's something in me that says I have a duty to go back and do my bit for the old country in her hour of need. Don't ask me what it is because I don't know. My father claims it is just good, old British patriotism exerting itself."

On the 1st of March 1938 they gathered on the dockside prior to embarking on SS Britannica for the 10-day voyage to Britain. There were sniffles, a lump in many a throat; nervous coughing and the inevitable tears were shed. Grandmother Rebecca, normally unemotional, held a small handkerchief which she frequently dabbed at her eyes, whilst she fussed around her grandson straightening his collar, fingering his hair and giving him advice that she had given him since he was in short trousers. Paul, tolerant and charming as ever, agreed to abide by everything she said. He held her to him for a time, smoothing her silver-grey hair. Then she moved away from him and turned her back on him to hide the tears cascading down her face.

Grandfather Samuel, after some parting remarks to his son, moved to Marie and took her hands. "My young and gracious Marie. What would we have done without you." the warmth in his voice and the sincerity in his eyes moved her deeply. He had compensated much for the premature death of her father in the last war. "It goes without saying that we will miss having you around. But I am grateful to know that these boys of mine could not have a better woman to look after them. And to keep them in order." He exerted a momentary pressure in the grip on her hand. "I am relying on you to make certain we get regular news of you all."

She reached up and sealed a kiss on his cheek. "I promise, father. I promise with all my heart."

He thanked her with a long, generous hug. And moved on to confront Paul. He placed a hand on each of Paul's shoulders and said, "One of the great honours in my life, my boy, is having such a fine young man as my grandson. You are a credit to us all."

For a moment or two the impish smile left Paul's face. He stood there facing his grandfather, humbled, and filled with respect.

"I am not your keeper," grandfather continued. "And therefore I do not intend to ask what you intend to do when you arrive in England. I would only invite you to remember that you represent not only the Herby family but also the Sawyer family."

Nobody was quite sure what Grandfather Herby meant by his final remark, except Paul. They stood there looking at each other sharing a secret that was strictly confidential and confined to them alone.

Air Duel

It may have had something to do with Paul's decision to join the Royal Air Force not long after the family arrived in Britain. And his subsequent desire to learn to play the piano, which he did, in a remarkably short time. Of course there may have been no connection at all.

All the same grandfather Herby received the news of his grandson's decision to take to the wing as one of the best moments in his life. Some sources said he celebrated so hard he wasn't sober for a week.

Marie gave Melanie the full credit for igniting her son's musical talents. For her, personally, Melanie had inspired him to the pinnacle of success that Marie had always wanted for him. It also cured an ache that had long been in her breasts, and fulfilled a desire that had haunted her since his birth.

Never would Marie forget how his music brought so much life and colour to the manor. And the rapturous applause he received at the number of concerts he was invited to give up at the old university and which she attended.

He looked incredibly handsome in evening dress behind the footlights, bowing courteously, somewhat shyly. Then he took to the piano stool, flicking the tail of his coat rearwards, seating himself and launching into a lively introduction that invariably drew the audiences to the edge of their seats.

And how could she ever forget the finale of the concerts when everybody were on their feet about her, clapping wildly and shouting, Encore! Encore! Bravo! Bravo!

It was one of the most exciting and rewarding times in her life. Her only regret was that her parents were not alive to witness the talents that had originated on their side of the family.

Then everything began to change. The passion in the friendship between Paul and Melanie seemed to die overnight. Next an uneasy disclosure that Melanie was pregnant. They might have celebrated it, Marie was delighted, but they didn't. The couple became very remote, distant, and Paul cocooned himself in silence.

Marie tried to reach out for them yearning for them to confide in her so that she could offer help. But, regrettably, her silent pleas went unheeded, veiled as their crisis was in a cloak of secrecy. Melanie's sudden, mysterious departure was painful in itself.

Then, for Marie, further devastation. Paul was snatched abruptly from life in the course of his flying duties. Such news being conveyed to her on a small piece of yellow paper…REGRET YOUR SON FLG. OFF. TIMOTHY HERBY KILLED ON FLYING OPERATIONS…

Words that went over again and again in her mind, making her feel numb and desolate. She badly wanted to escape. She didn't want to believe it.

She walked along the drive of the manor praying it was all a bad dream. And that, at any moment, his little sports car would turn into the drive and she would see him grinning boyishly at her, his cap set jauntily on his head and the white muffler tied at the neck.

The silence in the room was interrupted by the clatter of hooves down on the cobbled yard beneath the window; the hack she had watched setting out hours earlier was returning

By the time the mounts were removed of their tack, rubbed down and turned out, and the bantering riders had retired to the manor the light was fading and she imagined the air to be growing chilly. By rights she should have been downstairs helping the staff prepare tea for the air force guests. But she could not bring herself to leave the room. The room allocated to him by Lady Hadley and which he used in between Melanie's visits. It soothed Marie to be amongst the memories of his life: his bed, his wardrobe, his small writing desk and chair, his clothes and the file containing his musical compositions. It did a little to help her come to terms with her grief.

A telephone began to ring somewhere in the manor. She ignored it; the apparatus rarely brought good news in time of war. Then tapping sounds summoned her to the door of the room where a girl member of staff said: "Telephone call for you in the hall, Mrs Herby,"

Marie thanked her and hesitated for a moment. She felt unsteady on her legs, her hands were trembling and her heart was beating uncontrollably. She was filled with a sense of dread - of foreboding. She turned back into the room for a moment in an attempt to pull herself together. And that's when she saw Paul standing by the bed smiling reassuringly at her. She stood there looking and smiling back at him. But when she tried to touch him he disappeared leaving her outstretched hand pointing at the wall behind his bed.

The ache in her breast had gone. A warmth began to replace the cold, hollow emptiness of her body. A new hope embraced her thoughts. She was so pleased that he had not gone without saying, goodbye. Pleased that he had not looked injured or in pain. And there was something in the way he looked at her that urged her to answer the telephone.

"May I speak to Paul Herby." the plea was strained, distressed.

"I'm sorry I can't hear you very well." Marie said. "Could you possibly speak up."

It turned out to be Melanie. Paul's Melanie

Marie said, "I regret it's not possible, Melanie. He lost his life on flying operations not long after you left Hadley." She thought she heard a gasp at the other end of the line. Then it went very quiet.

"Are you still there, Melanie?"

"Yes, Mrs Herby. I'm sorry, I don't really know what to say. The point is I am in rather a lot of trouble…"

"Then come back to Hadley, Melanie. You'd be most welcome." She had visions of the forthcoming grandchild that, in her mind, would compensate, in part, for the loss of Paul. "You may stay as long as you like. And you and I can decorate a room as a nursery."

Melanie did not answer.

Marie said, "Would you like that?"

"Yes. Thank you. I'm very grateful to you…." the pips sounded and petered out to an abrupt click as the line went dead.

"The chaos and futility of war." Marie murmured and slowly replaced the receiver in its cradle.

****